MURDER
at
Maddleskirk
Abbey

By the same author

MURDER
at
Maddleskirk
Abbey

Nicholas Rhea

ROBERT HALE · LONDON

© Nicholas Rhea 2013
First published in Great Britain 2013

ISBN 978-0-7198-1168-5

Robert Hale Limited
Clerkenwell House
Clerkenwell Green
London EC1R 0HT

www.halebooks.com

A catalogue record for this book is available from the British Library

2 4 6 8 10 9 7 5 3 1

Typeset in 11/14.5pt Palatino
Printed in the UK by the Berforts Group

CHAPTER 1

WHEN I ANSWERED the phone during breakfast on Monday morning, a rather breathless voice gasped, 'Nick, can you come quickly? To meet me at the crypt?'

'It's the prior, isn't it?' Despite the anxiety in his voice, I recognized his distinctive accent. It was a delightful combination of his native Irish and the lilt of Northumberland.

'Yes it is. Can you come straight away?'

'Is there a problem?' I'm always cautious about reacting to events rather too swiftly, as I like to know what I'm letting myself in for.

'We've found a body. We don't know who it is. It's all very peculiar. I'd appreciate your advice.'

'A body? Peculiar, you say?'

'A man, he's dead. Lying in a coffin in the crypt. A huge stone coffin. We're not sure what to do next.'

'It's not an ancient burial, is it? You've not discovered a medieval grave with its occupant?'

'No. The coffin might be from a bygone age, but the body's not. He's as modern as we are.'

'Have you told the county police? Or a doctor?'

'A doctor, yes. Then I thought I'd contact you, you'll know what to do.'

'Don't touch or move anything I'll be there in a couple of minutes.'

It was a few minutes past eight on a bright sunny morning in early summer, a complete contrast to the previous night's damaging gales and torrential downpours. Things were calm now but the radio had said there were reports of damage throughout the region with some roads blocked and buildings damaged by falling trees. There were also reports of floods, along with damage and the ruination of crops. Although we had experienced the storm in and around Maddleskirk, the village and its environs, including the abbey, seemed to have escaped lightly despite being surrounded by deciduous woods. But storm or no storm, life, death and work had to continue.

It was Monday and a new working week was underway for the staff and monks of Maddleskirk Abbey. Gulping down the last of my coffee, I told Mary I had to rush off because a body had been found at the abbey. She groaned, and muttered something about me no longer being a police officer, adding her strong opinion that the discovery had absolutely nothing to do with me. She remarked that such things were the responsibility of the local police and not of a retired inspector.

I reminded her that having helped very recently to create the abbey's brand new private police force I held one of their warrant cards and had been sworn in by a magistrate so I was officially a police officer and furthermore I was paid a useful retainer for my services. It meant I had some responsibility for actions by its members, all of whom were very inexperienced in police work when it came to serious crime. Dealing with a dead body was not part of their daily monastic routine either, but the prior's call hinted at something mysterious – peculiar, as he had said. The overall role of the monk-constables was keeping the peace and supervising the security of the vast abbey campus.

Putting my empty mug on the draining board, I told Mary that both she and I had additional new responsibilities with my unexpected inheritance of several acres of woodland adjoining the southern boundary of Maddleskirk Abbey estate. It included an old building known as Ashwell Barns and even a holy well, both part of the ancient but ruined Ashwell Priory. I had heard about my good fortune less than a week before and had not told anyone except Mary, nor had I signed any papers, so neither the Abbey Trustees nor the abbot knew of my inheritance. That alone gave me an added interest in anything connected with Maddleskirk Abbey – now we were close neighbours. But that was a secret I did not want revealed.

There had been no suggestion the body might be lying on my land, but that was not impossible – the old priory had been buried for centuries. Not surprisingly I was keen to learn more about my inheritance but not just yet. I explained to Mary that I had no idea how long I would be away; it might be just a few minutes – if the fellow had suffered a heart attack or something similar, it would not be a matter for the police and I could advise them accordingly, then come home. Maddleskirk Abbey was only a couple of minutes away by car and there was ample parking with a space directly outside the crypt entrance.

During the short drive, I acknowledged there were bound to be instances when the brand new monk-constables sought advice. The monkstables – as everyone was already calling them – were private police officers whose duty was to supervise and deal with all aspects of security in and around the Abbey complex. That included Maddleskirk College, a private school that currently accepted boys only, though the admission of girls was likely within a year or so. The abbey estate had its own working farm along with a host of other facilities, indoors and out, all adding up to an establishment as busy and populous as a large village or small market town. It had its own theatre, cinema, sports centre, swimming pool, two infirmaries (one for monks and the other for students), two libraries (one in the monastery and the other in the College), a visitor centre, an ambulance, a fire brigade, post office and shop. There were also accommodation blocks for the pupils and domestic staff, and rows of houses for the teachers and other workers.

When on police duty, the monkstables wore black police uniforms, white helmets and clerical collars, reverting to their black habits during normal priestly activities. They were sometimes called Black Friars or Black Monks and formed the first

7

private police force in Britain to consist entirely of monks, and the abbey's own fire brigade comprised monks trained by the county fire service. The monkstables were recruited from Maddleskirk Abbey's resident Benedictine community. York Minster, Salisbury Cathedral and Cambridge University all made use of private, non-clerical police officers for their internal security.

In the case of Maddleskirk, I had been fortunate to have the help of retired Sergeant Blaketon and ex-PC Ventress from Ashfordly Police. Together we had trained the force of nine recruits in police law and procedure to a standard that would enable them to deal with fairly routine duties in and around the abbey and college. Further afield, their responsibilities included churches, chapels, parishes and other properties owned by Maddleskirk Abbey. From time to time, one or two monkstables would patrol them and deal with minor security matters.

Prior Gabriel Tuck, head of the eight-strong police unit, was also deputy to the abbot and he was clearly worried about the discovery of a man's body. The fact he had called me suggested this was not a normal death – on occasions, visitors had collapsed and died within the complex and, in most cases, the deaths had been dealt with by the abbey's own infirmary and medical staff. At least two of the monks were qualified doctors, one also being a surgeon. However, Prior Tuck had come from a different background: he was a former police officer.

The prior was a jolly, rounded individual with a mischievous sense of humour and a yearning to organize a slap-up feast to celebrate almost anything that deserved praise. He was also very partial to Mars Bars and carried a supply in a pocket hidden somewhere within his habit. His few years of police service had been in Northumbria, so it was not surprising he had been invited by the abbot to lead the tiny in-house police force. Among the Maddleskirk community several monks had names that reminded the prior of Robin Hood and his Merry Men. Indeed, the abbot was called Merryman and many of the students referred to the prior as Friar Tuck. He and his monkstables lived up to Robin Hood's reputation by suggesting to offenders they might care to donate something to charity as penance for a minor transgression. These were likely to be litter-droppers, noisy youngsters, careless car-parkers or inquisitive women wandering "accidentally" into the monastic corridors. Most offenders responded to an invitation to donate funds to charity. Major crime was rarely within the scope of the monkstables and if something serious happened, the county constabulary would be called in.

That was why Prior Tuck had rung me. As I drove the short distance, I recalled that Abbot Merryman was the equivalent of a managing director or chairman of a multi-million pound corporation, but in his case much of that work was conducted in addition to his demanding monastic duties. The sheer scale and complexity of the abbey's numerous functions never failed to impress me. In addition to its college campus, it was surrounded by constant activity, much of it involving hundreds of building workers engaged on a massive expansion programme that included new buildings and the upgrading of older ones. The abbey was being bullied into acknowledging the twenty-first century.

As if that wasn't enough, a small archaeological excavation was underway under a marquee in a corner of one of the cricket fields. It lay beside the internal road I was now using. Known as George's Field, it had been created from a patch of rough ground to become a splendid cricket pitch that was maintained in prime condition. This year it was 'resting' to allow its several worn pitches and outfield to recover from constant use. As I drove past slowly, I saw the sides of the marquee had been raised to allow in light and fresh air, and I could see six or seven people at work. Parked nearby on the field were a white camper-van and a six-seater people carrier. I had been told that this excavation resulted from an aerial photograph that had indicated the outlines of what might be medieval or even Roman buildings underground.

Certainly there had been a Roman settlement in the dale and to the trained eye, the routes of some Roman roads were still visible on the surrounding hills. The presence of the archaeologists had sparked off a good deal of speculation both in the village and the abbey campus and we had been told they were expecting to confirm either a Roman settlement or a medieval structure. I drove past without stopping and followed several builders' vehicles and private cars which were also making their way into the grounds. It was a form of rural rush hour in this normally peaceful setting. In addition to those going to work, I encountered several who were leaving the abbey and college and travelling home in the opposite direction. A cyclist with his helmeted head down was pedalling against the flow of traffic and dodging fallen branches and twigs. There was a hiker who had perhaps spent the night in guest accommodation, and several young women who worked short early shifts, perhaps cleaners, kitchen workers or waitresses. Pupils and monks had early breakfasts in separate dining areas, whilst guests on retreats were fed in the Retreat Centre. Occasionally after breakfast, guests walked against the flow of traffic into Maddleskirk village to buy a newspaper or obtain something else from the shop which opened at seven. So, the hours between seven and nine in the morning were very busy for the abbey and college whilst within it all the community of monks would be quietly undertaking their own specialist work with prayers. In the abbey church, matins would be over with lauds just finishing. Clearly the prior had been summoned from lauds to deal with the body.

Hoping to find a parking place I wondered if last night's storms had damaged any of the buildings currently under construction, or indeed the woodland and buildings on the patch of land I had inherited. I would check before I went home.

As I drove towards the abbey church I wondered where exactly to find the coffin. The crypt, sometimes known as the undercroft, was a massive underground area containing the meagre remains of yet another medieval abbey. It had once been known as Ashlea Abbey. I wondered if this former abbey had been associated with the old Ashwell Priory that I had inherited. A priory was a monastic establishment that was governed by its parent abbey, although some priories were known as cells.

The modern abbey church of Maddleskirk had been constructed around 1950, directly above the Ashlea ruins as a result of which the ancient stones and pillars had become the modern crypt. Due to a lack of windows, poor lighting and the ever-present uncertainty about safety of its old stonework, which did not bear the weight of the new church above, access to crypt was not actively encouraged but neither was it forbidden. Mass was celebrated daily in one or other of its thirty-six chapels. Guided tours were possible with a monk to oversee the conduct and safety of the visitors, particularly the infirm or schoolchildren.

There were three entrances, one of which was to the south; that door was close to the long flight of steps that led into the modern church via its own door which was the one I would now use. I parked and locked the car but there was no sign of Prior Tuck. I guessed he would be inside. I opened the heavy wooden door and could see the eerie crypt illuminated by dim lights so I left the door open to benefit from daylight. I was familiar with the place having often attended mass or other functions in the chapels, and knew about the legend of vast treasure supposedly hidden in an underground tunnel guarded by a giant raven. The modern church had been built into the heavily wooded hillside to make its crypt like a gigantic dark cellar smelling of age and dampness.

Architects had claimed the crypt was quite safe because it bore none of the enormous weight and strains from above; in effect, the church straddled the old and protected it like a mother hen caring for her chick. As I entered the vast dark interior, the clock was striking quarter past eight and I saw a large man in black clothes to my right, a few yards away but close to the Lady Chapel. I thought it was a monk in his habit, but, as I walked past, I saw he was working at a bench with the aid of strong lights. He was noisily sorting through a mass of tools spread about his bench and was quite unaware of me. I realized it was a sculptor. Some weeks ago I'd been told he was working on a triptych featuring three scenes from the Crucifixion. The commission was a gift from a benefactor and when finished, it would be inset within a wall of the Lady Chapel. I shouted 'Good morning' but received no reply. The noise of his activity drowned my voice and such was his concentration that he seemed unaware of what was happening around him.

I noticed on the proof of one section, a scene where the spear is plunged into Christ's side to determine whether he was alive or dead, another where he hangs alongside two criminals and the final one where he is shown being nursed in death by his distraught mother, the Virgin Mary. I had never met this sculptor and did not know his name, nor had I ever seen any of his previous work although I'd heard he disliked observers whilst working and would walk away if people were too inquisitive or getting too close.

I wondered if he was aware of the dead man only yards away. The area contained lots of walled-off sections and alcoves as well as a number of small chapels so it was quite possible he had no idea what might be lying in the gloom not far away. Anxious not to disturb him, I moved steadily into the darkness and then heard the prior call, 'Over here Nick.'

There was a beckoning flash of torchlight that illuminated my way across the uneven stone floor and I saw Father Prior standing in front of a heavy black curtain hanging from the ceiling and concealing the space behind. It appeared to be of very thick material, perhaps velvet, and I was not sure of its purpose.

Father Prior was waiting to unveil its secret.

CHAPTER 2

On previous visits I had noticed the curtain but had never been sufficiently curious to push it aside to see what it concealed. There were no prohibition notices to excite curiosity and I would imagine few visitors would venture behind it, probably assuming it was a store for old furniture, or somewhere to preserve ancient stones from the original building.

'Sorry to interrupt whatever you were doing,' apologized Prior Tuck. Normally there was a smile on his face but not now.

'Just trying to get myself properly awake!' I smiled.

'Anyway, thanks for your quick response. This is something beyond the scope of our monk-constables. It's a man's body, Nick. Behind this curtain. Now I know you are aware of my brief police experience, but it was very brief and never included a dead body, nor even a routine sudden death enquiry. I'm quite ignorant of modern procedures although I know that unexplained deaths require great care and special attention to preserving evidence. I've never forgotten that which is why I need your advice. I don't want our inexperienced policemen making a mess of this incident.'

'You did the right thing.' I noted he had inadvertently slipped into police jargon by referring to the body as an 'incident' but I needed a more information before I ventured behind that curtain. 'Are you saying it's murder, Father Prior?'

'Quite honestly I don't know, but I thought it best to leave him alone.'

'Good. The less interference, the better. So, how do you know he's dead? Perhaps he's asleep.'

'No, he's dead, Nick. I had him examined by Father Robin Bowman, he's a qualified doctor as you know, and one of our monkstables. He confirmed the man is dead, but couldn't, or wouldn't, express an opinion about the cause or time of death.'

'So what else has been done?'

'Nothing. His was a very short examination. I called you immediately.'

'What about the sculptor who's working in the Lady Chapel? Is he or anyone else aware of the body?'

'I doubt it. I haven't informed anyone yet, not even the abbot. The sculptor – Harvey – arrived about half an hour ago, he leaves his tools on his workbench or in a cupboard near the Lady Chapel and does some of his work here and more in his studio, wherever that is. He's never told anyone where it is. In fact, I don't think many of us know his full name or anything else about him. He comes and goes as he pleases without reference to anyone, sometimes arriving very early.'

'Has he a key to the crypt?'

'No, it's opened at five each morning by the duty monk. We get up to be ready for matins at six in the church. There are three doors – north, south and one that leads from reception. The crypt is open until eleven in the evening which is when the duty monk locks the north and south doors. The internal door in reception is locked by the evening receptionist, usually around eleven.'

'So anyone can enter at other times?'

'I suppose they can. Usually, visitors use the south door when they're touring the whole site. The other doors are generally used by monks and staff. We'd never allow a drunk or a known troublemaker to enter unsupervised – that's when we ask the monkstables to deal with them.'

'There is some form of regulation then?'

'Not overbearing, Nick. We're very tolerant. To be honest, apart from people attending mass, few visitors venture into this rather creepy crypt.'

'Who's on duty at reception after normal working hours?'

'We have civilian staff between eight in the morning and eleven at night, but if they are ill or something prevents them, then one of the monks – or a monkstable – takes over.'

'It does leave the crypt rather vulnerable, Prior Tuck. Even when it's closed anyone with access to the key in reception could enter.'

'I suppose that's possible. Perhaps we should tighten our procedures, but I must say there's never been any difficulty until now.'

'Well, I can't see the sculptor's presence is a problem because we don't know if this death is suspicious. But let's hope the crypt doesn't become a crime scene! So how long do you think the dead man has been lying behind this curtain?'

'That's something else I can't tell you – I don't know.'

'All right. My next question: Who is he?'

'Sorry, Nick, I don't know that either. I'm not being very helpful, am I? This sort of response is not good enough in a police enquiry, but the truth is I've never seen this man before and neither has Father Robin. We thought it wise not to mention it to anyone at this stage. He might be a visitor who has collapsed and died here.'

'You did all the right things, but I must say this gets more intriguing by the second. Maybe he just went to sleep and didn't wake up? It happens! Or a heart attack, or some obscure illness. So, Father Prior, before I have a look, tell me who found him. And how or why did the witness come to peep behind this rather forbidding curtain at such an early hour of the day?'

'We call it the Coffin Curtain, Nick.'

'Coffin Curtain? Why?'

'Because it hides a coffin and nothing else. The dead man is lying in it. It's carved in stone. A massive hollowed-out body shape in a huge lump of solid stone on top of a plinth cut from rock. All carved from a single piece.'

'This isn't some kind of bizarre suicide or even a joke, is it?'

'I can't rule anything out, Nick.'

'So if anyone looked behind the curtain out of curiosity before this man arrived on the scene, they'd see nothing but an unoccupied stone coffin? The room is otherwise empty, isn't it? And thieves would not be able to steal the coffin on its plinth because it's far too heavy for anyone to move. Am I right?'

'Yes, spot on. It's far too heavy to manhandle. In fact there's a tradition that it must never be moved. That dates to medieval times, but we think the coffin is much older, possibly dating to the Roman era before Christianity arrived in these islands.'

'So, as far as you know, it has never been anywhere else? Not in another abbey? A Roman graveyard?'

'We can't be sure, but this community respects that ancient wish – we have never tried to move it. If we allowed visitors to enter unaccompanied, you can be sure they'd throw sandwich wrappers or other litter into it. You know what the Great British Public is like, they drop litter anywhere except in the bins – so because successive abbots have always wanted the coffin to be accorded respect, that heavy curtain is very effective in shielding it from unwelcome attention by casual passers-by – not that many casual passers-by come here. The usual reason is to visit the chapels and perhaps to spend a few quiet moments in one of them.'

'It would be interesting to establish the coffin's age and history.'

'I'm sure there's something about it in the monastery library and even on the Internet. It's a well known artefact. We believe it pre-dates the earliest days of the old monastery and that it was possibly destined to be the final resting place of a very senior person, not necessarily a priest or abbot.'

'I have seen similar huge coffins overseas,' I added.

'Quite likely. This might have been copied from an overseas example for a manorial lord or even a royal personage. A Roman leader of some kind? Its sheer size suggests that; it was not built to be moved anywhere.'

'And now it contains a dead body! Not it's first, I suspect. Who found the body?'

'That's debatable.'

'Debatable? How can it be debatable? Was it you?'

'I didn't discover it. A note was left at our abbey police office, the cop shop. It had been pushed through the letter box. It just said 'Look behind the curtain in the crypt.' No name on it. Nothing to suggest who sent it, or when it arrived. So I went for a look, found the body then called you.'

'So where is that note now?'

'At our cop shop. It's quite safe, I've made sure of that.'

'Good, we must keep it. This is all a bit weird. All right, Father Prior, show me, but remember we must be careful what we touch and where we put our feet. If this is a crime scene we don't want to contaminate it.'

'I understand.'

He moved the right-hand side of the curtain far enough towards its centre for me to enter ahead of him and he followed, each of us realizing this might indeed be a crime scene. Once inside, he allowed the curtain to fall back into its closed position and then switched on a light. A solitary bulb in the ceiling came to life and its dim glow was brightened by his torchlight. I was surprised that an electric light had been installed here, but, after all, this was a modern monastic establishment even if the coffin and crypt were from ages past.

We were now standing in a bare room that reminded me of a featureless police cell, except it had no feeding hatch, no lavatory and no window, barred or otherwise. With rough stone floor and walls, it was about four metres wide, four metres long and four metres high with a stone roof and a stone floor. It was like a large hollow stone cube, albeit with the curtain forming one side.

There was nothing inside apart from the huge stone coffin on its knee-high plinth. It lay in the centre of the room with the head facing west and its foot towards the curtained entrance at the east. Inside the coffin there lay what appeared to be a middle-aged man dressed in hiking gear with his hands crossed over his chest. If he had been carved from stone and adorned with colourful medieval clothing or armour he would have looked absolutely right in his surroundings – but this fellow was a modern man, not a statue or stone replica. And his clothing told me he was not a mummified survivor from former times.

Prior Tuck handed me his torch in case I wished to inspect anything more closely but I did not touch anything. I merely stood and shone the torch as I tried to absorb the key elements of the scene with Prior Tuck at my side. He appeared to be standing in an attitude of prayer with his head bowed and his hands clasped beneath his chin. For several minutes, we stood in absolute silence with not a sound anywhere near us in this dark, remote and eerie place. The beam of my torch scanned the entire floor, walls and roof but it revealed nothing, I couldn't even hear the sculptor at work. We were standing in the midst of history in a dark and cold room that must have witnessed thousands of events over the centuries.

I reasoned that because there was such a huge heavy coffin here, the room itself might have once been a large tomb. Perhaps it was part of a former mausoleum or underground burial chamber of that ancient abbey church. Or had there been a pagan Roman graveyard here? Did the coffin pre-date Christianity? Certainly it would have been difficult if not impossible to move the coffin so it might have been carved *in situ*. But right now it was inside a windowless, stone walled room below a modern church and it contained the corpse of a recently deceased man. And the corpse also presented a mystery.

Because a doctor's initial examination had confirmed the death and because we were refraining from walking unnecessarily around the coffin, I continued my silent observations aided by the torch. I had no means of accurately measuring the height of the dead man, but, because he fitted into the coffin, I reckoned he was quite small in stature. Such ancient coffins were not generally carved for large occupants. His clothing was typical of a modern hiker – a colourful woolly hat of patchy red with a symmetrical white and blue pattern, with a pompom on the top. The hat came down over his ears but the loose knitting style allowed some of his greyish/brown hair to poke through. His eyes were closed and I noted he did not wear spectacles. He had rather pale skin, a moustache and short beard the colours of which matched the straggles of hair poking through his cap.

The body had a thick, plain white sweater, a coloured shirt beneath it with its collar showing, and sturdy plus-four style corduroy trousers fastened with Velcro below the knee just above long thick red socks. On his feet were a pair of well-used hiking boots of soft tan-coloured waterproof material, not leather. If this death was not natural there would need to be a forensic examination of the earth and other materials clinging to his boots and clothing. That might tell us where he had come from. In his pockets there could be documents to provide his identification, home address or a contact point, but due to the need to preserve the scene, I did not search him or his pockets.

Without disturbing his clothing, I could not see whether his body bore tattoos or other marks, there was no hiker's stick beside him or haversack or back-pack of any kind. There were no binoculars and no map hanging around his neck in its waterproof covering. I estimated his age at around fifty but his hat prevented me from seeing whether he had a bald patch.

'I'm going to touch him,' I told Father Prior. 'I know he's been examined by Father Bowman but I need to be sure in my own mind that he's dead, not merely faking death or lying unconscious. Mistakes can be made.'

Maybe I was arrogant in doubting Father Bowman's diagnosis but I needed to be sure, so I moved closer to the coffin and touched the man's cheek and then tested his pulses on both wrists. He wore a cheap wrist watch that showed the correct time and there were no rings on his fingers.

'Stone cold and no pulse,' I commented. 'But that's not surprising in here. So, yes, I'm sure he's dead, Father Prior but I can't guess the time of death. *Rigor mortis* is present but that is never an accurate guide especially in a cold place like this. Father Bowman was correct but we do need to have him examined more thoroughly.'

In the brief silence that followed, I could hear the choir of monks in the church directly above us. They were rehearsing a Gregorian chant, *Veni Creator Spiritus*, a tenth-century hymn to the Holy Spirit. It produced a highly emotive moment. I took a deep breath and moved closer to the body shining the torch into the coffin to see whether any of his belongings had fallen down the sides. I could not see anything but the corpse and, as I looked at the head area, I realized why his hat bore a strange red design: it was soaked with blood.

CHAPTER 3

NEITHER OF US spoke for a few moments, not really compre-
hending what we were looking at, then I said somewhat
inanely, 'This is just what we didn't want, Father Prior.' I indicated the bloodstained hat and the pool of thick blood in the
head-well. The blood had apparently oozed from beneath the
recumbent head. 'We are probably looking at a murder victim.'

He peered into the coffin and said, 'He couldn't have clambered up here and tripped, could he? Fallen in, banged his
head in the process?'

'And then lain down to fold his arms neatly across his chest?'
I issued a long and heavy sigh. 'No, Father, I'm afraid we have
a suspicious death on our hands. This looks like a very serious
head wound and there are no weapons here to suggest it was
self-inflicted. Didn't Father Bowman notice the blood?'

'No, he can't have done, otherwise he'd have told me. It was
a very cursory examination, Nick, merely to determine
whether he was alive or dead. A trained police doctor wouldn't
have missed something as obvious as that.'

'Probably not, but I must say doctors have been known to
miss such things. I recall one who failed to spot that a man had
been shot in the back! It was pure chance I spotted this. A self-
inflicted fatal wound at the back of the head would be
impossible to achieve, except perhaps with a pistol shot. If that
had happened, the weapon would be here. With a blunt instrument I doubt if you could kill yourself with a blow like this –
and there's no weapon. It's clearly a vicious attack – in other

words, it's murder. We must close the crypt and call in the CID. This is now a crime scene.'

As we were walking from the coffin, ensuring the curtain was closed behind us, the prior sounding worried, said, 'It's a good thing you came here, Nick. This is dreadful. It shows how inexperienced we are.'

'It's all part of the learning process, Father Prior. Everyone makes mistakes, that's how we learn. Every police officer has to start somewhere.'

'Well, this is going to be a new experience. Does it mean the abbey will be crawling with detectives, journalists and morbid sightseers? It will surely disrupt our routine....'

'That's bound to happen, but any disruption will be kept to a minimum, especially where the monks' divine office and the college routines are concerned, it means it's in our interest to control events. Anyway I must now call the local CID to get things moving. We've no time to waste.'

'Shall I inform the abbot and headmaster now?' he asked.

'Yes, that's important. Then we need to ask that sculptor to keep away until the initial investigation is over and the body has been removed. He'll be able to return once examination of the crime scene is complete, but I'm afraid we can't let him remove any of his tools.'

'You're saying they could be murder weapons?'

'There are some useful-looking hammers and chisels among them, but I'm not suggesting Harvey used one of them! But someone else could have done. We need to secure the entire crypt immediately, but before we leave we must search it in case the killer is still hiding here, or there are more bodies. Or a murder weapon that has been thrown into a dark corner.'

'Is that likely?' He sounded even more worried at the thought.

'It's not impossible,' was my response.

We carried out the search, working together for safety reasons as we examined every possible hiding place for people and weapons, checking all the chapels, cupboards and dark spaces. It took half-an-hour but we were both satisfied that the killer was not concealed within the crypt and that no more bodies awaited discovery. Similarly, we did not find anything cast away that might have been the murder weapon, but a more thorough search would have to be undertaken by the police, perhaps with dogs. Our tour of the crypt led us back to Harvey's work bench, now deserted with its tools scattered haphazardly about it. Not far from the coffin curtain, we stood briefly to admire his unfinished work. When finished, it would be fitted into a wall of the Lady Chapel; its measurements had been determined and the abbey's estate workers had created a space by removing several courses of stones to create an upright trough which would house this beautiful work.

'He works in wood and stone,' Prior Tuck told me. 'His work appears in several churches and cathedrals. Apart from creating works of art he carries out repairs to damaged statues. I don't know how he'll react to this disruption, though, he's very touchy. He's left already.'

'I'm sure the detectives will do their best to let him continue working,' I assured the prior. 'All I can say is that if the killer is quickly identified and caught, normal services will be restored as soon as possible.'

'Now I must break the bad news to the abbot and head-master, and I'd better include the procurator. They might want a chat with you, Nick, to outline exactly what we might expect.'

'I'll be happy to do that.'

'The actual murder enquiry – if it turns out to be murder – won't really involve us, will it? By us, I mean the monkstables, as I'm beginning to call them!'

'We might be allocated some modest local enquiries, Father Prior, bearing in mind that we have been sworn-in as local constables and we know a lot about the establishment, its routine, personnel and so forth.'

'It would be fascinating to be involved….'

'It would, but a lot depends upon who's in charge of the investigation. Now we must leave and lock the crypt. While you inform the abbot and the others, I'll call the CID. I'll use phone in the cop shop.'

'I hope the sculptor doesn't return – he won't be able to get in.'

'Then that's one security problem solved! Next we need to know the sculptor's full name, Father Prior. The murder team will definitely want to interview him, if only for elimination purposes.'

'I know him as Harvey, but don't know his other name or where he comes from. The procurator should know. I understand his work is being paid for by a wealthy benefactor, so both his name and that of the sculptor will surely be on some sort of contract.'

'Good. So we've already made a start to our own investigation. I see no reason why we can't carry out our own enquiries quite independently of the police, especially if the CID doesn't want us to join them. But there's another matter to think about. The detectives will require secure accommodation they can use as their murder room – it'll need desks, a blackboard, computer terminals, telephones, seating, space for refreshment breaks and probably more besides. They'll provide all their own equipment. A lecture theatre or conference room would be ideal – there'll be regular conferences of detectives throughout the enquiry when lots of tea and coffee will be consumed. And it will need to be made secure when they're not using it. This enquiry could last for several days, or be over in just one.'

'That won't be a problem, we've plenty of suitable venues. Leave it with me, Nick, I'll check after I've locked the crypt. Where shall we rendezvous?'

'How about the cop shop?' It was called that because it had previously been the school tuck shop – some said it was named in honour of Prior Tuck, not only because of his name but also because he had been a frequent customer to buy Mars Bars. 'I'll wait there for you, then I can brief the monk constable on duty. He's going to be very busy.'

'It'll take a few minutes to explain things to the abbot and others. Will you be remaining? Perhaps working with us?'

'I don't think the detectives will want me, a retired police officer, hanging around, but with our combined and specialized knowledge, the murder team might find the monkstables useful for local enquiries. I'll be happy for us to help. It's a case of waiting to see what the CID need. I'm not going home just yet.'

I called Mary on my mobile to say I would not be home for some time and would probably have lunch in one of the refectories. Father Prior and I went our separate ways as I headed for the cop shop. Its normal times of opening were listed outside the door. When the duty monkstable was not in the police office, he would be patrolling the grounds and buildings in uniform to deal with whatever occurred – litter dropping, foul language, lost and found property, trespassing in secure areas, inconsiderate car-parking, noisy motor bikes roaring past the abbey during mass, or any other nuisance or problem. There was a POLICE sign complete with an illuminated blue lamp above the doorway and, as I arrived to make my call, a woman rushed to the counter. I stood back to allow her to complete her business for I had no wish to have my call overheard at this stage. I recognized the woman as Miss Dawson, one of the teaching staff.

It was already approaching nine o'clock and the enquiry desk was staffed by Constable Will Stutely – Father Will Stutely – whose shoulder number was 14. At Maddleskirk, each of the constables' shoulder numbers began with figure 1 because they were the first of Britain's monastic constables. As duty officer, Monkstable Stutely would spend his scheduled time behind the desk dealing with queries and problems and, in between times, he would patrol the buildings and grounds.

'Good morning, Miss Dawson,' he greeted his visitor.

'I never know whether to address you as Father or Constable....' she began.

'As part monk and part constable, I answer to anything, but

a lot of people call us monkstables. You could always call me One-Four. That's how they used to address police constables. Numbers instead of names. Anyway, how can I help?'

She told the boyish-looking fair-haired monk about the non-appearance at class this morning of one of her pupils, Simon Houghton, and expressed her concern. None of his classmates had seen him and none knew of any reason for his absence.

'You'd better hear this, Nick,' suggested Father Stutely, beckoning me forward. I realized he must be aware of the mystery in the crypt – the note had been pushed through the cop shop letter box and he would have read it before contacting Prior Tuck. 'Miss Dawson, this is former police inspector Nicholas Rhea, he's the adviser to our monk-constables. He may be able to help organize a search for the boy around the campus by using our officers.'

'Thank you. That would be a big help. I do hope he is not in any danger.'

'So what can you tell us about him?' asked Constable Stutely. 'We'll deal with his absence as low-key at this stage. Certainly it's not yet within the realms of a missing person. He's just one teenage lad who hasn't turned up for lessons.'

'I hope it's nothing more than that. I've allowed him time to get here – quarter of an hour – but with him not appearing and no word, I'm concerned.'

'Has he done this before?' I asked.

'No, never. It is most unlike him. He's never late, not like some boys, and always turns up even when he's not feeling well. If there is a problem, he sends a message.'

'You're sure there's been no word from him? Could he have asked one of his pals to tell you?'

'I'm sure. I've asked around. Usually if Houghton can't turn up for any reason, he lets his tutor know. But I haven't checked his room....'

'Leave that to me,' Father Stutely assured her. 'I'll go and check and if it's locked, or if there's no sign of him around the college, I'll contact his housemaster. We'll find him. He can't be far away.'

'Thank you, that's a relief.'

'I'll let you know the outcome as soon as I have news. He's probably got his head stuck into a book in the library and forgotten the time. You go and deal with your class.'

'Thanks. I'd better get back before they wreck the place.'

When she was out of hearing, he smiled his understanding and said, 'I'll set things in motion, Nick. He's probably crashed out in his bed, fast asleep in the land of Nod after a hectic weekend. Boys do that sort of thing. Oversleeping on a Monday morning isn't exactly a matter of great urgency. Now it's your turn, so what can I do for you?'

'I'd like to make a phone call to police headquarters, Father Will. But first, I need a word. I believe you received a curious note this morning?'

'Yes, it had been pushed through the letter box before I opened up. It was on the floor. I've kept it—'

'You must keep it very safe, Father,' I said.

Taking it from a drawer, he handed it to me. On a piece of lined writing paper, I read the handwritten words in black ball-point: *Look behind big curtin in cript*. I noted the mis-spellings and passed it back to him.

'Can you make sure no one else handles it? Keep it secure as the CID will want to examine it. Do you know who sent it?'

'No idea, sorry. I can't tell you exactly when it was delivered, but it was here when I opened up at eight this morning, but it wasn't here when we closed the office last night at eleven.'

'The paper looks rather like the sort you'd find in a cheap writing pad or notebook of some kind.'

'It does; you can see where it was torn from its spiral binding. There are some small jotting pads like this in the school shop. Here's a ruler, Nick, you might want to measure it.'

It was 125 mm x 100 mm (5" x 4"), the sort of small notebook that a schoolboy or even a hiker might carry in a pocket or handbag.

'Thanks, Father. This could be an important piece of evidence....'

'Evidence? You mentioned the CID just now. What's happened?'

'Father Prior obeyed the instructions in that note and looked behind the curtain in the crypt. He found a dead man lying in that stone coffin.'

'Dead?'

'Yes, with a head wound. Almost certainly it's murder,' I said. 'I'm going to call the CID and Prior Tuck is notifying the abbot, the headmaster and the procurator. As it's murder, Father Will, things are soon going to get very hectic.'

'So what can I do?' The shock was evident on his face.

'You need to remain here until further notice to deal with calls and visitors. We'll need you to act as our focal point.'

'I understand. You'll keep me informed? Help me to deal with things?'

'Of course. Ask if you need help.'

He didn't speak for a moment or two, and then said, 'A missing boy, and now this. Are they connected? Murder investigations are out of our league, aren't they?'

'They are, but our services might be called upon, Father Will. At the moment, the crypt is locked because it's a crime scene. Father Prior has the keys. The sculptor will not be allowed access and neither will anyone else. I know you keep a crypt key here that you share with reception but don't let anyone have it whatever reason they give. Perhaps notices on all three doors until the police give the all-clear?'

'We've got some "No Entry" signs, I'll use those. One of the estate workers can place them.'

'That sounds sensible. Now I'll call the CID but they'll also want to find that missing boy ... in their books, he'll be either a suspect or another victim.'

'Dear God, this gets worse.'

I telephoned the CID and asked to speak to Detective Chief Superintendent Napier whose name I knew from his regular appearances in newspapers and TV broadcasts. I had never met him – I retired before he transferred from the Northumbria Constabulary to the North Yorkshire Police. I must admit I was surprised when I found myself speaking directly to him as I had expected an introductory conversation with a secretary or his deputy.

'Napier,' a strong voice answered.

'My name is Rhea,' I responded. 'Former Inspector Nicholas Rhea, I used to be the press officer for North Yorkshire Police. I'm retired now.'

'Right, Mr Rhea. I've come across your name in our files; so what can I do for you? I hope you don't want me to speak to a group of sleepy pensioners?'

'No,' I assured him. 'I have a murder – or at least a suspected murder – to report.'

'Have you, by jove! Tell me what's happened but keep it brief.'

'I'm ringing from Maddleskirk Abbey and College. There's a male body lying in an ancient stone coffin in the undercroft beneath the abbey church—'

'You're making this up! Is it a modern male body?'

'Yes, he's not just a pile of old bones, nor is he made of stone. I know it sounds like a crime novel, but it's true. It looks as if he has a head wound, and furthermore, we don't know who he is.'

'Been confirmed dead, has he?'

'Yes, by a doctor.'

'Is the killer still around?'

'I don't think so, we searched the crypt—'

'The what?' he interrupted.

'The crypt, it's under the abbey church. A very old place. That's where he was found. Some call it the undercroft. There's more.'

'You're not going to tell me a monk has seen the Virgin Mary, are you?'

'No, but I am going to tell you that I've just learned that a schoolboy is also missing from the college, it adjoins the abbey, We're just about to begin a search for him in the grounds and buildings.'

'Are you saying he's a suspect?'

'I'm just saying he's missing, Mr Napier.'

'Another victim then?'

'Clearly we can't rule it out.'

'You said "we" are going to begin a search for the lad. Who are "we"?

'The abbey has its own private police force. They know their way around the place; they'll be conducting the search.'

'Well, that'll keep your own cops busy, but make sure they keep away from the murder scene. I don't have to tell you why. Right, I'm not one for believing in coincidences so leave the suspected murder to me. Don't foul up the murder scene. I'll get my DS from Scarborough to come along and make a preliminary investigation but before I do that, can I ask what all this has got to do with you, a retired copper?'

'I helped to create and train Maddleskirk Abbey's private police force of monks – monkstables, we call them. The prior called me when the body was found as they didn't know what to do about it. They had no idea it was a murder. I learned of the schoolboy's absence when I arrived.'

'You have been busy, haven't you? Right, well, I hope you and your pious police haven't messed up any of the evidence at the scene.'

'We haven't, apart from being there when we examined the body. I've sealed the crypt, Mr Napier. It's locked and the keys will be at reception or at the cop shop.'

'Cop shop?'

'The abbey's own police office, it was a tuck shop before its current use.'

'Good for you. My sergeant will be with you in a few minutes, he's just been to a burglary not far from Ashfordly and is on his way back to his station. I'll divert him directly to you. His name is Sullivan, Jim Sullivan. A useful chap.'

'Thanks. Ask him to report to the police office in the reception area of the abbey. I'll be there. Is there anything I can be doing in the meantime?'

'I suppose you and your pals could be asking around to see who the victim is, that would be a good start. There'll have to be a thorough search of the entire campus to see if the villain is hiding anywhere or has topped himself, so if you're looking for that missing lad, you and your monkstables can carry out a dual search.'

'I'll inform the prior.'

'I'm not used to working with monks and priests but you could also ask whether anyone has recently noticed anything out of the ordinary. In a quiet place like your abbey, I would imagine someone must have seen the killer moving around.'

'It's not a quiet place, believe me. But I'll get them started straight away.'

'That's what I like to hear. I think your constables could prove very useful but don't let them get into a dangerous situation. Hunting murderers can be dangerous. And we need to know where that schoolboy has got to and whether he's responsible. Or whether he's another victim. We'll need a suitable room we can use as a murder room – maybe you can find one for us? You know the drill. It means your officers are going to be very busy, Mr Rhea. I'll join you as soon as I get a situation report from my DS.'

As I settled on a bench in reception to await the return of Prior Tuck, probably accompanied by the abbot and other officials, I realized it would be a good idea to summon all the monkstables to a meeting to explain what was going to happen, and to encourage their co-operation. I had no doubt they would be an asset to both investigations and so asked Father Stutely if he would contact them. I suggested they assembled in the Postgate Conference Room (named in honour of a local martyr) where I could address them pending the arrival of Detective Sergeant Sullivan. I had used that room during their training and it was ideal for such a meeting. Then I must get them to search the entire campus as soon as possible. Having got things moving I settled down to await Abbot Merryman. He soon arrived together with Prior Tuck, Father Bede Templeton, the headmaster, and Father Sixtus Gold, the procurator, an ancient name for the financial director.

'I've called on the monkstables to assemble in the Postgate Room,' I advised them. 'They're all expected anytime now.'

'Then let's join them as this affects us all.' Business-like and brisk, Abbot Merryman set off at a fast walk with the rest of us trying to keep pace. I asked Father Stutely to inform the detective sergeant of my whereabouts when he arrived. The monkstables responded very quickly, all dressed in their uniforms and within twenty minutes everyone was seated. The room was quietly located in the basement below the main entrance to the abbey church but it was too small to serve as the police murder room.

The abbot said, 'Prior Tuck, you're in charge of our police officers, perhaps you can tell us what's going on?'

'Thank you, Father Abbot.'

Prior Tuck provided a brief but lucid account of the discovery of the man's body and the action we had already taken, and then asked me to inform the group about events since that time. I told them about the missing Simon Houghton, adding that his housemaster was arranging a search of his room and other likely places, and if the boy was not quickly found, the monkstables would be required to search the entire abbey and college campus. I ended by saying I had called the county CID, adding that a detective sergeant would arrive at any moment and that our part in searching for Simon had been welcomed by the detective chief superintendent.

Detective Sergeant Sullivan arrived during my address, accompanied by Father Stutely who introduced him. For the sergeant's benefit, I was asked to outline events, but before inviting the sergeant to visit the crypt, I took the opportunity to ask Father Stutely whether there was any news about Simon Houghton.

'Nothing.' He gestured with his hands to illustrate his words. 'His room has not been used overnight, his bed is made, he did not attend breakfast this morning and it seems he was away from here all day yesterday in that terrible storm. We're continuing to search for him, but I fear it is more than just a boy missing a lesson. Once the monkstables have finished here, perhaps they could join me in the cop shop and we can issue plans and maps for them to broaden their searches.'

'Consider it done,' said Father Prior.

'Thank you,' said the abbot. 'And now, Sergeant Sullivan, you will want to hear our story?'

'Can I do that in the crypt together with the monk who found the body, and also ex-Inspector Rhea? My boss mentioned a head wound. It will help if I am looking at the scene as the story unfolds.'

'I'm sure it will,' I added my own opinion.

The abbot said, 'Whilst you are doing that essential task, Sergeant, I will return to my office. No doubt Mr Rhea will keep me and my colleagues informed.'

'Of course,' I agreed, and so the headmaster and procurator followed him out.

'One thing before you go, Father Abbot,' said Sullivan. 'Is this missing lad causing great concern or is such an event rather normal here?'

'At this stage, it seems to be nothing more than a pupil skipping Monday morning lessons. It happens all the time, except that this pupil isn't the sort to dodge lessons. We've no reports of anyone else missing.'

'Well, like most detectives, I don't believe in coincidences. I think we should treat his absence with genuine concern.'

'We'll do all in our power to help,' smiled the Abbot but I detected just a hint of a frown on his face.

Whilst the prior and I accompanied Detective Sergeant Sullivan to the crypt, I suggested that Father Bowman should be in temporary charge of the monkstables as a search plan was organized. He agreed. As Father Prior led the way to the internal entrance from the reception area, collecting the key *en route*, Abbot Merryman hailed me.

'The minute you've finished with that policeman, Nick, I need an urgent and very confidential word with you. In my office. It's about Simon Houghton. It's vital we speak at the earliest opportunity.'

CHAPTER 4

ONCE INSIDE THE crypt, I walked behind Detective Sergeant Sullivan as Prior Tuck led the way and switched on the dim lights. He had also brought his torch. There was no one else with us and no one spoke as the detective looked around. I found myself wondering if I had encountered Sullivan during my service but decided I hadn't. He struck me as very business-like, smartly dressed in a well-cut sports jacket which was predominantly green, along with chinos, a pale-cream shirt, green tie and brown shoes. He reminded me of some estate owners I knew and I wondered if he was from that kind of rural background. Not particularly tall, and certainly not overweight, he had a good head of fair hair, was clean-shaven and did not wear spectacles. He carried a brown leather briefcase and I thought he looked like a rural general practitioner, racehorse owner or perhaps a vet.

'This is like descending into the Black Hole of Calcutta,' he commented. 'What happens down here? Is this supposed to represent Hell?'

'No,' I told him. 'Hell is the staff car park at going-home time!'

Prior Tuck, who was leading the way, responded, 'This is what's left of an old abbey that used to occupy the site,' he explained. 'Our abbey church has been constructed over the top of it, a form of protection I suppose, but we make use of the crypt for occasional masses – there are thirty-six chapels, some with national associations and others dedicated to certain saints.

We use them for baptisms and weddings and such. Also, at the moment, we have a sculptor working down here in the Lady Chapel. I'll show you.'

'He's not still there, is he?' Sullivan sounded shocked.

'No, he's been and gone. He has a studio somewhere,' said Prior Tuck. 'I locked all the doors after searching the place for the villain or other victims.'

'That's a good start. Now head wounds are rarely if ever deliberately self-inflicted except by firearms. And if it is murder, your sculptor will be in the frame as a suspect. Meanwhile he'll have to find somewhere else to work. Does he work in stone, or wood? Or metal?'

'Wood and stone, I understand.'

'So he'll have plenty of hammers and other tools that could inflict a nasty wound on someone's skull. We need to talk to him – and seize his tools for forensic analysis. Unless he's taken any with him. Or thrown them away. Now show me the body and be careful where you put your feet. Use the approach route that you did when you found him. It was you who found him, wasn't it, Prior Tuck?'

'I was advised where to look,' affirmed the prior as he led us on the approach to the coffin curtain. In the near darkness, Prior Tuck told him about the curious note that had been left in the police office. 'Because of it, I came and found the body.'

'Well, you seem to have done all the right things....'

'I used to be a police officer,' Prior Tuck told him. 'I didn't last long as it didn't take me many months to realize police work wasn't for me, so I left.'

'And became a monk?'

'Yes.'

'Well, that's an unusual career change! A lot of our senior officers should do the same, preferably joining a silent order. Which force were you in?'

'Northumbria.'

'Same as my boss. He was a DS in Northumbria and then transferred down here to the DI's job.'

'I might know him.'

'You can't miss him! He's been with us in North Yorkshire ever since and was eventually promoted to the top CID job.'

'What's his name?'

'Napier. Detective Chief Superintendent Roderick Napier, a big man in all respects, loud and forceful. He has the biggest feet in Christendom, I reckon. His shoes and boots have to be specially made. Size 16 or something like that.'

'Now I do remember him,' smiled Prior Tuck. 'When I was a probationer constable at Hexham, I think he was DS in Whitley Bay. Our paths never crossed, but I remember the lads talking about the size of his feet.'

'The whole force talks about the size of his feet – in fact, so did the whole of the Northumbrian population! Some of his regular customers called him Bigfoot or the Abominable Yeti. We just called him Large Sarge. Now he's Super Large.'

'Well, here we are,' announced the prior as he approached the curtain. 'We call this the Coffin Curtain because there's a stone coffin on the plinth behind it. That curtain is always closed, as it is now. During the period of this abbey, I don't think the room has ever been used for any other purpose although we've never locked it against visitors. If they look behind, they'll see only an empty stone coffin on a stone block. There's no chance of it being stolen.'

'Except that now it's occupied? Show me and mind where you put your feet.'

The prior drew aside the heavy curtain to reveal the coffin with its occupant lying there peacefully. From this angle, there was no sign of his injury. Detective Sergeant Sullivan stood silently with his chin cupped in his right hand as he studied the scene before him. He spent some time observing but not taking notes. No one interrupted; no one moved. Then he stepped forward carefully, peered into the head section of the coffin, and retreated.

'There's a fair bit of congealed blood about so I think you're right about the head wound. And he didn't get into that coffin by himself, did he? Somebody must have put him there. But doesn't he look peaceful? That's the influence of this place.... So where does that sculptor operate?'

He turned to leave and Prior Tuck allowed the curtain to fall back into its normal position. We led him towards Harvey's work area near the Lady Chapel, and showed him the images that would eventually form the triptych.

'What's this chap's name?' he asked.

'We don't know, except that he calls himself Harvey.'

'Harvey what?'

'Sorry, I don't know. Nobody knows.'

'I've heard our boss tell tales about a villain called Harvey. I wonder if it's the same chap? Anyway, he's got a nice looking face for the Virgin Mary,' commented Sullivan. 'And I see he leaves some tools on the bench, so where does he keep the others?'

'In there.' Prior Tuck indicated a cupboard at the rear of the chapel.

'Locked, is it? That cupboard?'

'No. So far as I know, it's never locked.'

'Everyone here is very trusting, it's not like this in most places. But it will be locked until further notice. You say the entire place can be secured?'

'It can,' nodded Prior Tuck. 'The two outer doors can be secured from the inside with bolts as they are now and there are no windows. The only other entrance is the one we used, the stairs down from reception. And that door can be locked and the key made available only to nominated users – it will be kept either in reception or in the cop shop.'

'Good. So as from now, this is a crime scene. I'm going to treat it as suspected murder until we get the result of the post-mortem. I'll secure the crypt and retain the keys in the murder room. No one must be admitted until further notice, I can't stress that too much. If there is a duplicate key, it needs to be removed from circulation. Immediately. Keep it in your cop shop and don't let anyone have it.'

'I understand,' said Prior Tuck. 'I'll attend to it.'

'Right. So that you are aware of what's going to happen, listen to me. I'll arrange for our official police photographer to come along as soon as she can and record the entire scene and I'll ask a forensic pathologist to examine the body *in situ* before it is taken away for a post-mortem. The scene will be examined by our experts too, all as soon as possible. In the meantime I need an office from where I can make secure phone calls. When the teams of detectives start arriving, we'll need a suitable room that will be transformed into a murder room. And we'll need a big car-park. The room needs to be private and secure to accommodate about fifty officers and a load of equipment like computers, scanners and so forth. We have a mobile canteen so it'll need to park somewhere.'

'We've already identified a room you can use,' smiled Prior Tuck.

'Show it to me, but before we begin the heavy stuff, who is our victim?'

'We have no idea,' admitted Prior Tuck.

'You mean he's not known to anyone?'

'Not to my knowledge. We haven't made widespread enquiries at this stage but none of my personal contacts knows him. Somebody on the campus might know who he is once we start looking for witnesses.'

'Well, when we get him into the morgue we'll strip him and I'd be surprised if he doesn't have a wallet or a diary. Or there's always fingerprints and DNA. Leave that with us. Now, before things start to warm up, I could do with a nice cup of tea. Does an abbey like this treat guests to a cup of tea?'

'We treat all our guests as if they are Christ,' said Prior Tuck, gently.

'Does that mean you can turn water into wine?'

'No, but I can arrange for it to be turned into a cup of tea. Follow me.'

'The abbot wants to see me,' I told them. 'I must leave you for the moment.'

'We'll be in the Postgate Room,' Prior Tuck told me. 'Shall I arrange a cup of tea for you, Nick?'

'Thanks, but I might be some time. I'll fix myself one as soon as I can.'

I made my way through the busy corridors and up the stairs to Abbot Merryman's first-floor office. I had known him for some years, becoming firstly acquainted whilst he was the parish priest at Aidensfield when I arrived as the village constable. Mary had also worked at the college as a secretary which involved the abbey and the abbot. He kept fit by playing squash and taking long walks in the extensive grounds where, he had once told me, he would escape from his office to enjoy some uninterrupted time for thinking and planning. I entered his secretary's office after knocking lightly. Mrs Sheila Grayson smiled a welcome.

'He's expecting you, Nick, I'll tell him you're here.'

I heard his response. 'Send him in, Sheila, then no calls or callers for the next few minutes. I'm in a conference if anyone asks. I'll let you know when I'm free.'

He offered me a chair in front of his desk as Sheila brought me a cup of coffee. I accepted it with pleasure.

'Now, Nick, this is not a normal day by any means so perhaps, to start with, you can update me with what's going on in the crypt?'

I explained everything and tried to inform him about the interruptions that would now bedevil both the abbey and the college.

'Murder in the crypt, eh? It sounds like something from a crime novel or television series. Will you be able to stay to help us out? This is hardly a matter for us and I wonder if the regular police will want our input. But if they do want our monkstables to be usefully employed, we must oblige. I am sure there are ways in which we can assist. Now what I'm going to say to you is most important and confidential.'

'You said it was about Simon Houghton?'

'It is. So what is his situation at the moment? Can you tell me?'

'Simon's housemaster and the headmaster are organizing a co-ordinated search. His room is empty and it seems his bed was not slept in last night as the covers are still in place. If he is hiding or asleep somewhere on the campus, such a search seems an ideal task for them – although, Father Abbot, I fear the CID will include the missing boy as a suspect until proved otherwise. I have to say it may not be a coincidence that he has disappeared at this time. There's also the worry that he could be a victim.'

The abbot looked worried as he said, 'Yes, I am aware of that. Acutely aware, in fact. It's for the latter reason that the headmaster has asked me to contact you. We may need some advice and practical help. I should add that this boy's absence is much more serious than a pupil dodging lessons.'

'So there's something I should know?'

'Yes there is, in the strictest of confidentiality.'

'Have you called the county police? I mean officers from Ashfordly?'

'No, we haven't – there's a problem, you see. Perhaps a better phrase would be "there is a matter of considerable deli-cacy" about the entire matter.'

'That sounds ominous.'

'It is and you'll appreciate it is potentially extremely serious. As I am sure you know, we became aware of his absence during the first period this morning and the staff's immediate action was to launch a search of the places he could normally be found, including his own room. We made good use of the teaching staff, his housemaster and the abbey constables, all of whom know their way around the college and also know the boy by sight. All this happened only minutes before I was told about the body in the crypt and there is still no trace of Simon. Am I right in thinking this is the current situation?'

'That's it, Father Abbot, but the body in the crypt is not Simon. The victim is a bearded fifty-year-old adult male, or so it would appear. The missing boy isn't given to theatrical performances, is he? Or dressing up?'

'On the contrary, he's a quiet, shy individual of seventeen. Just before you came into the office, I heard that the search for Simon by our staff is on-going and has been extended over the whole campus – college and abbey combined, indoors and out, with no result as yet.'

'I'm sure the monkstables will do a good job.'

'I don't doubt it. You'll be pleased that Simon's class teacher contacted one of the monkstables right at the outset – it shows they are being taken seriously. Prior Tuck and Father Stutely got things moving very swiftly.'

'That's the sort of challenge they need. A range of tasks and real-life problems to keep them busy. Incidentally, the CID have now arrived.'

'I hope our search is quite independent of their investigation, Nick. We're speaking to friends of the boy to see if they know why he might be absent or where he might be.'

'That's all very positive.' I began to think like a police officer even though I had been retired for several years and wondered just how urgent this was and whether it could be linked to the body in the crypt. As he spoke, I knew that a simple case of a pupil dodging lessons rarely warranted a search party, but in this case there was much more to consider. The fact that a boy had disappeared from the prestigious and world-famous Maddleskirk College had to be treated seriously – many came from important or wealthy backgrounds, both nationally and internationally, consequently kidnapping for a ransom demand was always a possibility.

I asked, 'Are we talking of a possible abduction here, Father Abbot? With a ransom?'

'That must be a strong possibility, Nick. Yesterday, being Sunday, was the senior boys' free day. They can play sport, go for walks and outings, go out with their parents, entertain visitors, take a bus to York or Scarborough, or go into Ashfordly. They can do more-or-less what they wish and our only demand is that they behave themselves and conduct themselves responsibly whilst away from the premises.'

'I know they enjoy considerable freedom,' I commented.

'They do, but it's for a purpose: the idea is to encourage them to take responsibility for their own actions.'

'I wish all families would do that!'

'Taking into account the number of boys who live here, we don't do too badly. Not many ventured out yesterday due to the storms. Fortunately when such things happen, they can be otherwise occupied on campus.'

'So by today – Monday morning – the missing lad should have been back in his room and at his desk for the first lesson at quarter to nine? And that should have been after spending the night in his room and going down to the refectory for breakfast?'

'That's right, but it seems he wasn't back for supper last night.'

'Last night? I know his bed was made-up but he could have done that this morning. So you are suggesting he was away all night?'

'That's what I fear.'

'So would his room have been checked last night? By his housemaster perhaps?'

'Not necessarily, after all, he is seventeen. But if someone had reported his absence last night, we would have initiated enquiries straight away. But that didn't happen. No one had any idea he hadn't returned. It's not unusual for pupils to miss supper when they return late after a day out. Most have enough pocket money to buy a meal, even if it's only fast food.'

'Are you aware of anything that might explain his absence? A letter perhaps? A sudden invitation? Problems at school? Bullying? A victim of child abuse? You've talked to friends and classmates?'

'That's being done as we speak. Boys do absent themselves without us alerting the whole world. This could be such an occasion, but I am not aware of any reason for Simon to absent himself.'

'You seem to have done all the right things, Father. But can we be certain that he actually left the premises? Would he venture out during severe weather? And has he been seen talking to that bearded man who's in the coffin?'

'We can't be absolutely sure about any of that. He could be still on the premises, just not in his usual haunts.'

'In that case I'm sure the searchers will find him.'

'I should stress that he's not in any kind of trouble, Nick, if that's what you're implying. But, as I hinted earlier, there is an underlying problem and I must tell you I did not want to call in the county constabulary to deal with his absence. I know they are aware of it now – it is unavoidable in the circumstances – but I would like his absence to be kept very quiet and confidential. Most certainly I do not want it to reach the media.'

'I fear the death in the crypt is going to ruin all your expectations, Father Abbot. Once the inquiry gets underway with teams of detectives asking questions, there is bound to be media interest – and a missing pupil is relevant. I fear this story will reach the press unless he is found quickly.'

'The monkstables are quite capable of dealing with a normal absence, I'm sure, and doing so without publicity. That is what I would wish. Surely there is some way you can keep his disappearance out of the newspapers and other media?'

As I sipped my coffee, I wondered why the college authorities did not want to call in the local police or their experts from headquarters – or seek help from the press and other media. In most cases when a pupil disappears, every possible source of help is utilised. If the county police – apart from the murder investigation – were to undertake a professional search for a pupil, teams of officers would be deployed and police dogs would be called in to check the huge expanse of the grounds and the surrounding area. Certainly there would be publicity in the press and on radio and television and this would inevitably result in an organized and thorough examination of all buildings, old and new, along with checks on buses and taxis and enquiries in the neighbouring towns and villages. In that way, thousands of extra eyes and ears would be on the lookout for him.

I explained all this to the abbot with due emphasis on the added burden of a murder investigation on the premises. He listened intently but I gained the impression he still seemed reluctant to associate the missing boy with the murder or to involve the media. His attitude pointed to the possibility he was not being completely open.

'You're holding something back, Father. Am I not in full possession of all the facts? Has this something to do with child abuse? Is it something sexual? Involving a monk? Or member of staff? Is there a major scandal brewing behind the scenes that I don't know about? Could that be why he has run away? Or is it why we have a mysterious dead man in the crypt? Is anyone else missing? Teacher? Monk? Another pupil? Someone from the village, a girl perhaps? Someone from the domestic staff?'

'I sincerely hope it's nothing like that, Nick. I have no reason to think it is any of those things, but let me tell you why this is such a delicate matter. And now, to change the direction of this discussion, how familiar are you with the history of Poland?'

'Completely unfamiliar!' I wondered why on earth he had suddenly introduced Poland into the conversation.

'Like many more millions!'

'I think most of us forgot poor old Poland long before it was lost deep within the Soviet empire. But I know it emerged anew in 1968 and is now regarded as a vibrant and progressive nation. The election of Pope John Paul helped a lot. Poland has got some of its old sparkle back.'

'That sums it up, Nick. Now, the Polish royal family was the Waza dynasty which was in power until 1668. The last king was John II who abdicated in that year, and, officially, the line became extinct. That was in 1672.'

'I note you say "officially"?'

'The family line survived, but did so in secret and in exile. Now, with Poland's emergence onto the world scene, there is a move to reinstate the monarchy.'

45

'So you're saying the line did not die out?'

'That's right. Legitimate descendants are very much alive. The family trees have been thoroughly checked by experts. A new King of Poland, descended from the earlier dynasty, is possible. That could – and would – happen if the national desire is there.'

'Really? So how will they manage to resurrect their royal family?'

'There is a young man with pure Polish royal blood in his veins, Nick, one whose ancestry can be traced right back to that time. And his father is dead. He was killed in England some fifteen years ago as the result of a traffic accident.'

'A real accident, or a staged one?'

'That was never determined. The police investigation concluded there were suspicions about the cause of the accident but nothing was proved against the other driver. He was not charged with any offence.'

'That sounds ominous. Are you saying this missing boy is the legitimate heir?'

'Yes, that's exactly what I am saying. It means this young man, or one of his descendants, would be the next King of Poland if the monarchy is ever revived. But there are some people who are not Polish nationals – and others who are – who do not want a Polish royal family under any circumstances.'

He paused as I realized the seriousness of what he was telling me. He continued, 'Let us say these anti-royalists are prepared to take any steps necessary to prevent that happening.'

'So are you saying the future king is the pupil who's missing?' The enormousness of that statement was almost unbelievable.

'Yes. He's one of our boarders. Here he is known as Simon Houghton, and that is the name on his passport. He was born and brought up in this country, so his English is perfect. You'd never know he had any other ancestry. The security services have done a good job in maintaining his disguise.'

'Now I understand your caution!'

'Good – and I cannot over-stress that great caution is constantly required.'

'Well, it seems to have worked for the past seventeen years or so.'

'Yes, but legally the lad is not yet an adult as he is under eighteen. Young Houghton has had that name since infancy and has never been known by any other. That was done particularly so that he cannot inadvertently reveal his true name and future role.'

'So even he doesn't know his own real identity?'

'No. He is completely unaware of who he is. I was informed because we – the community of monks, the college – are acting *in loco parentis*. His mother though is acutely conscious of his true heritage.'

'So does she know he's missing?'

'No, not yet. We thought we should do all we can to find him before we tell her – hence the very thorough search. If we find him safe and sound, she need never know of this adventure.'

'What a huge responsibility. For her and for you.'

'Absolutely. His real name is Wladislaus Sobieski and it must never be revealed to the public in case the wrong people find him. We don't want publicity under any circumstances. Now, you can see our problem.'

'I can and I understand everything now. But could his real name ever be uncovered if the lad himself is unaware of it?'

'The short answer is "yes" and that is the problem. There are agents at work in this country, Nick, and elsewhere. One problem is that more and more people from Poland and other parts of Europe are coming here to settle or to find work and we have reason to believe that some are using such stories as a cover for their real purpose. It is known there are those who are determined to seek out and identify descendants of the former Polish royal family and eliminate them. Such people know that a possible heir exists and they are determined to destroy him. The motives of many are not always supportive of a revived monarchy! I'm telling you this so you can fully appreciate the problem that's confronting us. In view of your experience and contacts, I hope you can co-operate with us in this drama.'

'I must say, Father Abbot, once anyone tries to deceive the press or the police the truth has a nasty habit of emerging. If it is really necessary to conceal or disguise the truth we could say that the hunt for young Houghton is merely a training exercise for our monkstables without naming the pupil who has volunteered to go into hiding! But Detective Sergeant Sullivan is already aware of Simon's absence. At the moment, the media is unaware of it, but if it is shown that the man's death in the crypt is the result of murder, then a continuing absence of Simon will be of increasing importance to the investigation – he'll be considered a suspect or perhaps another victim. It will not be easy keeping such information from the media.'

'Can you offer a solution?'

'I favour honesty when dealing with the media but I see no reason to inform them of Simon's name or home area. We could merely say he is a juvenile so we cannot publish his name. I would be in favour of investigating his absence with all possible help from the media but with absolutely no hint of his background. Perhaps one solution is to inform Detective Chief Superintendent Napier of Simon's background? No one here, apart from you, me and his housemaster knows his true identity, so there is no reason why it should emerge during this investigation – after all, he is merely a seventeen-year old pupil who hasn't turned up for lessons. I am sure Mr Napier will respect our wishes without informing the wider public of the true situation.'

'I still feel there is a risk, Nick, if the wrong people read about the case and begin delving....'

'There is slender hope for us, Father. That fact that Simon is under eighteen means that, in some cases, such youngsters' names are not revealed by the press.'

'That's a good point and it may offer the best solution. Thanks for that.'

'I still think we should inform Detective Chief Superintendent Napier to ensure his co-operation.'

'I will speak to him, but here I must be straight with you: according to the latest intelligence we have received, certain parties are aware that the Polish heir is now masquerading as an English student at an English Catholic public school. And please remember his father died in suspicious circumstances. If this boy's name gets into the national or international media, I fear the truth will emerge. We cannot risk that, murder or no murder investigation.'

'So is his Simon Houghton alias completely secure?'

'Nothing is ever completely secure, Nick. That's my concern.'

'Surely that's all the more reason to behave absolutely as normal?'

'Then I shall speak to the senior detective. So, Nick, despite a murder on our premises, the fact remains that we have to find that young man before someone else does.'

CHAPTER 5

WITH THE MONKS' chanting clearly audible, I left the abbot's office and went directly to the Postgate Room to find Prior Tuck and Detective Sergeant Sullivan. Prior Tuck had been busy. He had found a blackboard, now standing near a lectern, and on the wall behind was a large computer screen bearing a detailed map of the entire campus. Small green areas showed places that had already been searched and declared clear. Facing the screen were about twenty chairs arranged in rows as if awaiting a lecturer and upon each was a pad of paper and a ballpoint pen. Prior Tuck expected his monkstables to make full use of this room as their own assembly point.

'This is the monkstables' operations room,' he beamed, recalling his own police experience as he addressed the detective sergeant. 'The CID murder room will be in SALT – St Alban's Lecture Theatre – near the library. Their equipment and personnel are *en route*. Meanwhile all our monkstables have responded and are searching for Simon. Father Robin has organized them into two-man teams. Father Will in the cop shop will deal with anything that arises and we have both computer and telephone contact with him.'

'Good. So have there been developments with the murder enquiry?' I asked.

'We're awaiting the official photographers, police doctor and the forensic pathologist; when they've finished in the crypt we can move the body. There's very little we can do just now.' Detective Sergeant Sullivan was carrying a mug of coffee as he wandered up and down the central aisle. 'I'm expecting my boss any minute but meanwhile the crypt remains sealed. Your cops are doing a good job.'

'Some were pupils at the college which means they know their way around – and all the hiding places! They're all are very keen. So is there any sign of Harvey?'

'No. I've managed to make a few enquiries, but no one seems to know where he has established his studio, or where he might have gone. He does a lot of his work on his triptych away from here so his studio can't be far away. I'm working on it – we must talk to him as soon as we can.'

'Do we know any more about him?' I asked Prior Tuck.

'I've spoken to the procurator,' he replied. 'Even he knows very little about him. He's a loner, very much a mystery figure and most elusive. He calls himself by one name – Harvey – and won't give his full name or address to anyone, nor will he say where he has based his studio. He's paid cash from funds donated by a benefactor in Cannes, through the abbey accounts. The donation – a large one that covers his fees and expenses – has been banked and the abbey pays him an agreed amount at the end of each month. He insists on cash and signs the receipt as Harvey, but refuses to commit anything else to writing. I must say he works hard; he's not a slacker or a work-dodger.'

'So how do we contact him?'

'By leaving notes on his work-bench in the crypt – he can read! We never know what time he's expected there; he comes and goes without warning and never visits any other place on the campus, except the procurator's office around month end. Even then, he can vary his visits. You can't plan a meeting with him, and have to rely on a chance encounter, or hope he responds to one of those notes.'

'Well, he'll have to change his tactics now.' Detective Sergeant Sullivan sounded emphatic. 'We've bolted the north and south doors from the inside so if he wants access to his creation he'll have to ask me and that won't be granted until we've forensically examined the entire crypt.'

'If he can't get in, he'll ask at reception. He'll be told what's going on.'

'Yes, and I have the key. We don't want him moving around the crypt before we've finished with it. Don't forget he's a prime suspect – lots of his tools would make good murder weapons. We need to examine those and then interrogate him.'

'You're not honestly suggesting he's the killer, are you?' I asked.

'It can't be ruled out, but I'm also aware that someone else could have picked up one of his hammers and used it, then put it back or thrown it down somewhere. That's something we've yet to establish – we'll get more information about the wound once the pathologist has carried out his post mortem. Then we'll try to match a hammer or other tool against it. If it's none of those, we'll have to look elsewhere.'

'There's one more thing about Harvey,' added Prior Tuck. 'He runs a scruffy white van which he parks at the north of the abbey near the kitchens when he's working in the crypt. He usually enters via the north door if he has anything bulky or heavy to bring in, so he'll borrow a kitchen trolley to carry it. The kitchen staff are quite used to him wandering through their corridors.'

'And a description? Do we have a description?' asked Sullivan who was jotting notes on a pad of paper, later to be written up in his official pocket book.

'Of him or the van?' asked Tuck.

'Both.'

'According to the procurator, he's a large man, more than six feet tall and heavily built, more like an all-in wrestler than a sculptor. He dresses all in black – much of it leather, and wears knee-length leather boots with thick soles. Some of his clothing bears chrome studs. He has leather kneecaps because much of his work involves kneeling. He has a very unruly mop of curly black hair with matching moustache and large beard. He reminds the procurator of one of those Goths who go to Whitby to celebrate Dracula's visit. It's hard to tell his age. Late forties perhaps.'

'Well, he shouldn't take much finding, except on a dark night,' beamed the sergeant. 'So what about his van. Has it got his name on it? Do we have its registration number?'

'Neither. It's plain and rather scruffy, quite anonymous. I don't have a record of its registration number but Brother George may have it.'

'Who's he?'

'He's a monkstable and well into his sixties, Sergeant,' responded Prior Tuck. 'He was a hill farmer before joining the monastery and lost a lot of his sheep to thieves. He got into the habit of recording the registration numbers of every car, lorry or van that came anywhere near his farm – and several thieves were caught. He has continued that practice here, especially because there are so many white vans coming onto the site due to the construction work. Building materials are sometimes stolen, and if we get a report of a theft or burglary in one of the site offices, he passes van registration numbers to the county police who then interview the drivers. He's not an ordained priest by the way; he's a monk, Brother George – not Father George.'

'Thanks. He sounds a useful sort of man to have around. OK, at an opportune moment, I'll see what he can tell us. I'm beginning to appreciate your monkstables more and more. I'm sure we can work together on this....'

And at that point, the door opened without warning, crashed against a chair that was rather too close behind it and admitted a huge man with massive splayed feet. Large black shoes with polished toe-caps exaggerated the overall appearance of them. Bald-headed with a dome of white skin but with tufts of black hair around his ears and the back of his head, he appeared to waddle rather like a penguin.

'Ah,' he said. 'Found you, Sarge. Is the coffee on? I'm parched.'

'I'll see to it,' offered Prior Tuck who had not yet had an opportunity to don his police uniform. He was still wearing his black habit.

'Thank you, Reverend, that's a good start. I'm Detective Chief Super Napier,' beamed the huge fellow. 'Now DS Sullivan, I'm sure you have not spent all your time chatting and drinking coffee, so what can you tell me about all this?'

He plonked himself on a chair, issued a huge sigh of relief and continued, 'I must get some weight off, I feel as if I'm carrying several sacks of spuds around with me all the time. So, introduce me to your friends then tell me what I need to know.'

Clearly in awe of the great man, Jim Sullivan first introduced Prior Tuck as the man in charge of the monkstables, giving a brief account of them and then explaining this room would be their base as they searched for Simon Houghton.

'Tuck?' frowned Napier. 'You're not that man Tuck from Northumbria Police, are you?'

'Yes, I left to join the Benedictines, some years ago.'

'I remember you leaving quite suddenly after that child drowned. So what does a prior do?'

'I'm deputy to the abbot.'

'I suppose that means a lot of God-bothering and praying?'

'Among other things. But because of my police experience, I'm in charge of our own force of constables. This is our operations room, apart from being a small general conference room, and we have an office in the abbey's reception area.'

'Oh, well, don't let me get in the way, I'll clear off in a while and leave you to it. Has my team of detectives got another room? I hope there's somewhere suitable. They'll be here soon, forty or so at least. Mebbe fifty. They'll need a lot of space. And they'll want gallons of coffee.'

'Yes, sir,' replied Sullivan. 'We shall be using a lecture theatre called SALT as our murder room – that's St Alban's Lecture Theatre. I'll take you there after we've visited the scene.'

'I'm with you so far. So this must be ex-Inspector Rhea?'

He made no effort to shake hands, so I nodded. 'Yes, that's me.'

'So what are you doing here? I've always thought retired

police officers never returned to their old haunts. When I retire, I'll never want to read about another murder, let alone try to solve one.'

I explained my role as a former police inspector and force press officer, adding that I was founder and trainer of the monk-constables. I explained they were now searching for a teenaged pupil who had not turned up for today's first period.

'Is he a suspect?'

'I doubt it,' was my response.

'Victim, then?'

'I sincerely hope not.'

'Never doubt such possibilities, Mr Rhea. Everyone is a suspect until proved otherwise, and if that kid's done a runner, then he's in the frame. Whatever has happened, he needs to be found and eliminated, and soon. I don't want my men needlessly chasing him around the countryside if there's a genuine suspect lurking somewhere else. So can we place that lad at the scene? At the material time?'

Sergeant Sullivan answered, 'Not at this early stage, sir. We need to establish his movements and contacts over the weekend.'

I now said my piece. 'The abbot wants to speak to you about the missing pupil, Mr Napier. It's very important.'

'He's explained his worries to you, has he?'

'Yes. As I said, I was responsible for helping to train the monkstables.'

'Then you can tell me what's bothering the abbot.'

'I would rather he told you in complete confidence, Mr Napier.'

'Oh, well, I suppose I can fit him in. This is a posh school with rich and famous families here … he's probably thinking of kidnap with a ransom demand. Right, I'll have a chat with him. Maybe you could fix that?'

'I will. The monkstables are searching for the boy at this minute. They're checking the grounds and buildings.'

'I should hope they are, you can't hang about in cases like

this. Those monk-cops could be very helpful. Now, where's that coffee?'

Prior Tuck went to the adjoining ante-room and emerged with a mug of coffee on a tray, complete with milk and sugar.

'Black for me, Reverend,' he said, as he accepted the mug. He drained it almost at one gulp, put it back on the tray and said, 'I don't want to contaminate the evidence by spilling my coffee into this stone coffin you told me about so, now, DS Sullivan, take me to the crypt. How do we get in?'

'We'll go through the door in reception,' Prior Tuck told him. 'I've got the key. The other entrances, north and south, are bolted. We've made the place secure.'

'Good. Lead on. Are we all going?'

'Yes, sir,' replied Sullivan. 'Prior Tuck was first at the scene and he called in Mr Rhea for advice. At that stage, it wasn't evident the man had been attacked, he merely appeared to have died in the coffin. In his sleep perhaps. Then we noticed his head wound.'

'Right, you can each tell me your story when we get there. Then it'll make more sense to me. Any sign of our technical wizards yet?'

'They're all on the way, sir. Scenes of Crime, pathologist, photographer.'

'They should learn to move faster and get here earlier. OK, show me the scene.'

As Detective Sergeant Sullivan took the keys, we followed him into the reception area where I explained to Constable Stutely that we were going into the crypt and that no one was presently in the Postgate Room. He indicated his understanding and would inform us if the technical team arrived.

'You sound as if you've got an efficient private constabulary working here, Reverend.'

'We do our best.'

And so we followed DS Sullivan down the illuminated steps into the crypt as Prior Tuck switched on the lights and led the way, once more using his torch. I was expecting some caustic comments from Napier but the sound of the monks' choir could be heard in the church and he said nothing. He was looking about himself as he entered the crypt, concentrating on his task and absorbing every detail.

'Weird place, nice singing. Monks have their uses,' he muttered, adding, 'Smells musty and damp, I'd say,' and then for us all to hear, he said, 'Prior Tuck, Mr Rhea, lead me into the scene where the body lies, using the exact route you used when you first found it. And give me a commentary on your actions and thoughts at that time. Both of you. If either of you noticed anything out of the ordinary, tell me. I need to know such things. Also I need to know about that sculptor – show me his work area before we leave.'

As they reached the foot of the steps, Prior Tuck began his account, repeating what he had told me about responding to the note currently in the cop shop. He demonstrated how he had approached the so-called coffin curtain, opened it at one side and discovered the body. He described the body as he recalled it, and how he had then returned to the cop shop to summon Father Bowman who was a qualified doctor. He had returned with Father Bowman who had pronounced the man dead. We were shown their routes towards the curtain. Prior Tuck then said he had telephoned me to seek my advice, at that time not realizing the man had been attacked. I provided my own account, adding that I had touched the body on its face and hands to check for *rigor mortis* to satisfy myself that his was a genuine death and not some kind of student stunt. I explained how I had noticed the blood.

'Then what did you both do?'

'I went to inform the abbot,' said Prior Tuck.

'And I went up to the cop shop to ring you because I suspected murder.'

'So where was the sculptor during this time?'

'Over there,' said Prior Tuck, pointing to the workbench. 'He was working on that bench when I arrived, sorting and selecting tools by the sound of it, and by the time we'd finished, he'd gone. We didn't see him leave and he didn't speak to us. He was there when Mr Rhea arrived but left soon afterwards. I've not seen him since.'

'Show me.'

Together we retraced our earlier steps as Napier stood and looked at the incomplete clay proofs, then allowed his gaze to take in the workbench and its arrangement of tools, all on show and ready for instant use. I noted he did not handle anything, leaving everything for forensic scrutiny. We also showed him the cupboard where more tools were stored; again, he did not touch anything. The monks were now chanting *Laetatus sum* – 'They said unto me, let us go unto the house of the Lord'.

Napier addressed his sergeant now. 'Sarge, all this must be preserved as a crime scene, as I know you've done so far, but we need to test every one of these tools for blood or other deposits, if only to eliminate them from our enquiries. That sculptor must be found and must not be allowed in here until we've finished, is that clear?'

'Yes, sir.'

'Right, now Prior Tuck and Mr Rhea, did you do anything else before leaving and locking up the crypt?'

I responded. 'Yes, we searched the entire area, looking for the murderer in hiding or perhaps another victim, or even the weapon. We didn't find anything.'

'No weapon thrown away?'

'Nothing.' I realized we could have missed something that might have been a weapon – even a heavy stone. A thing like that could have been tossed into a dark corner – or hidden among the sculptor's tools.

'We'll search it again with better lights once we've concluded our action at the scene. I must say you've both done well, but now it's our turn.'

'Is there anything we can be doing now?' asked Prior Tuck.

'Not a lot. We'll leave here for the time being and secure the scene until our experts arrive.'

We left the crypt, extinguished the lights and emerged into

the reception as the sound of the singing monks diminished.

'Sarge,' Napier addressed Sullivan, 'we need to form a joint plan of actions to be allocated to our murder team. So what are you two going to do now? Are you going to help us with this investigation?'

'That's the general idea, if we're allowed,' I responded.

'In view of your past experience, I'm happy to have you both on board, Mr Rhea and Prior Tuck. You are both former police officers which means you swore the oath so I can trust you. And that includes your monkstables who are officially police officers and know their way around the place, as well as its daily routine and personnel so they must be useful. But if anyone makes a mess of things, they'll get their marching orders. Of course we do have non-police personnel working on murder inquiries – secretaries, forensic experts and so on, and all can be trusted to do their jobs. I've recently heard of two police forces who are considering their pensioners rejoining as serving officers – they've got a lot to offer society at large. So there we are. We're all one big flexible team!'

'Thanks, we won't let you down. I'll begin by finding out how our searchers are getting on,' said Prior Tuck.

'So what about me speaking to the abbot,' asked Napier.

'I'll call him from here,' I said. When I rang, he agreed to see Napier immediately. Father Will offered to show him the way.

'Now I'll track down Brother George to see if he has the number of the sculptor's van,' I offered. 'Then we might learn more about him.'

As Chief Superintendent Napier prepared to leave with Father Will, he produced one of his rare smiles. 'I can see you fellows know your own minds. I like my officers to show some initiative, but always keep me informed. Remember, that I am the boss as from this moment: this is now *my* patch.'

When Father Stutely returned within a couple of minutes, having delivered Napier to the Abbot's office, I asked if he knew the whereabouts of all the monkstables who were hunting for Simon, Brother George in particular. He explained, not surprisingly adding that Brother George had gone to search the abbey's farm buildings. As an ex-farmer who had also grown up on a farm, he knew all the likely hiding places around farm premises, such as places that might attract tramps wanting a night's sleep or even tired schoolboys. It was about a mile from the abbey church, but I wanted to talk to Brother George, so I took my car.

I was also hoping that whilst I was there I might sneak a quick look at my inherited piece of land. One of its boundaries bordered some fields of the farm although most of it bordered the abbey estate itself. The farm was managed on behalf of the trustees by a husband-and-wife team, Richard and Susie Seaton.

'Good heavens, Constable Nick!' responded Richard, when he answered my knock on the kitchen door. Years earlier, he had managed a farm at Aidensfield where I called regularly to check his stock registers. 'What are you doing here? Not on police duty, I'm sure? Is it about the missing lad? Brother George told us.'

'It is,' I told him. 'I'm looking for Brother George. Is he still here?'

'He's had a busy time searching all over the place, all our sheds and outbuildings, stables and cowsheds. I helped him but he's back in the kitchen now, having a nice cup of coffee and a slab of fruit cake. Then he says he wants to wash up the pots. He regards washing-up as an offering of thanks to God, so he says. Susie is happy for him to do that. Anyway, come in.'

Brother George, sometimes known as Greenfingers due to his gardening expertise, was a jolly fellow with red cheeks, thick grey hair and the gait of a farmer. He had the reputation for creating gardens out of the most barren pieces of land, but he liked to wash up after meals following a heavy day's work – it was his form of relaxation and a way of thanking God for another day on earth. There were times when I wondered if he got in the way of the permanent domestic staff, but seemingly, no one criticized his efforts. When I entered he was sitting at the bare wooden kitchen table chatting to Susie, and both had whopping big mugs before them. I joined them for cake and coffee and after some good-natured banter, I said, 'Brother George, I need your help.'

'Me, Richard and Susie have searched this place from top to bottom, Nick, inside and out, and there's no sign of young Simon. I'm confident he's not been here this weekend. No one has seen him around the place.'

'Thanks; we can cross it off our list. But there's another reason I want to talk to you. I know you've been diligently recording car numbers that come onto the abbey grounds – especially white vans.'

'Yes, it's too easy for a plain white van to get onto our site when all this construction work is going on. It can easily lose itself among all the others. Now we have those archaeologists and they've got a white van too. A camper-van, but white nonetheless. A couple of rogues in a white van can soon nick a few valuables and vanish before anyone knows the stuff has gone. I want to catch them – and their white vans!'

'I can understand that, but I'm interested in the sculptor's white van. Harvey he calls himself, just the one name. We need to trace him, Brother George. We should be able to do it through his van registration number.'

'You don't think he has kidnapped young Simon, surely?'

'No, nothing like that. We just want to talk to him about the body that was found this morning.'

'I've been telling Richard and Susie about it.'

'Well,' I now addressed the couple, 'it was in the crypt not far from where Harvey was working, so we need to find out if he saw or heard anything. He's gone now and no one knows where he lives or where his studio is, so we thought his van number would tell us something.'

'I've got the details in my notebook,' smiled Brother George. He hauled his diary from his pocket, flicked it open at a page in the back and said, 'Here we are, Nick. I might add I checked it – you know when we went to Police Headquarters during training last week? I was curious about that sculptor even then! I asked if the control room could check his number for me. They did. It belongs to a one-man garage-cum-petrol station in Leeds.'

'A garage? In Leeds? So it's not Harvey's own van?'

'I rang them. He hires it. They said Harvey paid cash in return for borrowing the van for a few months. It wasn't a formal hire arrangement. They have no idea who Harvey is, but because he produced the right money in nice fivers and tenners, they let him take the van. No written contract. They told me it was not worth anything as a saleable vehicle and so were happy for him to use it for as long as he wants. He's already paid its market value several times so they're not bothered if its falls to pieces or if they don't get it back.'

'But surely they have his name and address?'

'He gave an address in Hull when he did the deal. Later when they wanted to contact him about renewing the hire, the garage discovered it was a Salvation Army hostel. The manager had no idea who Harvey was.'

'A dead end, then?'

'It seems he's very secretive. Since then I've asked about him here on the campus, but as you said, no one knows where he lives or where he operates from. But he's still got the van and it is taxed, tested and insured by the garage. He still pops in from time to time with cash-in-hand when it's due. No questions asked!

'The procurator says Harvey always wants cash ... no cheque, no money paid directly into his bank account.'

'But even he doesn't know where Harvey lives? Or his full name?'

'I'm afraid not,' said Brother George. 'The only time people see Harvey is when he parks his van behind the kitchens and goes through to borrow a trolley for something heavy. Even then, he won't tolerate being quizzed, watched or approached. He hates people putting him under pressure. He'll simply walk away.'

'Then it's going to take him a long time to get his work of art finished.'

'Maybe that's his intention – a piece of art without an end.'

We had chatted for a few minutes and then I felt I should leave – I wanted to take a surreptitious look at the piece of land I had inherited. It included some old buildings which could be a hiding place for the missing boy. My solicitor had suggested that at this early stage I should not mention my inheritance to any of the abbey officials, trustees or staff because I had not yet signed the relevant papers. It was common knowledge that the trustees had long desired to obtain the land in question but its Scottish owners had refused to sell it. Right now, however, I could justify my visit by claiming I was searching it in the search for Simon Houghton. As indeed I would.

'Can I cadge a lift back?' asked Brother George when I got up to leave.

'You can, but I'm going via Ashwell Priory barns, I want to check them to see if Simon is there.'

'I'll come and help you,' and so Brother George and I thanked our hosts and left, with me taking a short cut towards the south or back entrance to the abbey Estate. On the way we passed close to George's Field and I remarked on the presence of the archaeologists, one of whom had a white camper-van.

'They'll not find anything there,' remarked Brother George. 'I've told them there's nowt to find under that field, but the chap in charge insists on looking. But I should know, I fashioned that field out of some disused land. If there had been summat under there, I'd have found it. Anyway, I've noted the number of his boss's van, just in case he does find summat valuable and clears off with it.'

'Would he do that?'

'Who can tell? Such things are not unknown,' smiled Brother George. 'So, do you think Simon could be hiding in the old barns?'

'I think they're worth a check,' I responded. 'People use them for all kinds of things.'

'I can believe that, Nick. When I had a farm you never knew who was sleeping in your haysheds or nicking turnips from the fields!'

My two stone barns with tiled roofs had long fallen into disuse but remained standing with their roofs intact. They were very close to Ashwell Priory Wood and adjoined each other like two small semi-detached houses. They shared the same roof but had separate large archway doors but no interior dividing wall. Surprisingly dry inside, there was a hayloft at one end of the long building with a ladder in place to give access. It was really a single large barn with two huge entrances but locally everyone referred to them in the plural as Ashwell Barns.

As we drew up before them, Brother George said, 'They're a bit isolated. Simon wouldn't be hiding here, would he?'

'There's only one way to find out.'

CHAPTER 6

I PARKED ON the grassy plot adjoining the barns.

'Do these belong to the abbey?' asked Brother George, his farmer's eyes noting their condition and probably mentally assessing their usefulness.

'No.' I didn't want to tell him the truth just yet, so I said, 'They belong to a Scottish estate. Down the years they've refused to sell the barns and that land opposite. I know the trustees have made offers as they would find the barns and nearby land useful, but the answer has always been "no".'

'Probably there's an old priory buried in those woods.' Brother George pointed to the dense woodland nearby where several trees had blown down in yesterday's gales. 'We've always been told never to look for the ruins as it's not safe. Mind you, if I'd still been farming today I'd have sorted out all that fallen wood and made a few quid from it – folks like log fires, especially ash wood. And I'll tell you what, Nick, I think this district has too many abbeys and priories. If our abbey bought it, what would they do with it? They've already got that old one in the crypt.'

'Religious houses were numerous in the past, but lots were very tiny and depended upon a parent abbey,' I aired my knowledge. 'But I doubt if Ashwell can ever be revived or restored as it's been buried for centuries.'

'Well, I sorted out that patch of land near our abbey and made a cricket field out of it, so I could do summat useful with all this woodland and these barns. Mebbe if folks knew about that buried priory, they would wonder if there was summat similar under what's now the cricket field.'

'It's a possibility,' I nodded. 'We've got archaeologists with us this morning, looking. This place seems full of old ruins.'

'Speak for yourself!' grinned George. 'I'm not past it yet!'

We walked along the frontage of the barns. The doors had long since rotted away, or been stolen, but the interiors were dry and I could see no sign of leaks from the roof or walls. I assumed that circulation of air did something to prevent them suffering damage from damp. There was some litter inside and signs of a long-dead fire that had been used for heat or cooking. Its ashy remains were on the earthen floor between two bricks. Bird droppings suggested that some species roosted in the rafters, or perhaps, like swallows, built their nests there. No doubt hikers and cyclists also made use of this shelter from time to time. The narrow lane that ran past it was a public highway that emerged to the west of Maddleskirk Abbey lands.

'There's a bike over there,' said Brother George, pointing to it. It was leaning against the rear wall but it didn't appear to be the well-maintained kind that was used by serious cyclists or tourists. It was a gents' machine with a very rusty green frame, dropped handlebars and metal 'rat-trap' pedals. It had silver coloured aluminium mudguards, derailleur gears and its tyres were inflated. However, there was no sign of a saddle-bag or other means of carrying a small load. We went for a closer look and although it appeared neglected, its pumped-up tyres suggested it had recently been used. The presence of the bike and the remains of a fire indicated someone might be sleeping here. And there was the ladder leading up to the open floor that formed the hayloft.

'I wonder if Simon's up there?' I found myself whispering, but, as I climbed, I was surprised to see a man sitting on the floor of the hayloft. Heavily bearded, he was squatting on a bed of what looked like a pile of straw and bracken covered with sacks and old coats. Was Simon sleeping under that pile? I completed my climb and without speaking to the man went across the floor to shake the raggy coverings. There was no one else in the loft, but I noticed bits of rubbish lying around, such as old newspapers and wrappings from food. By noisily clambering up the ladder, I had roused the fellow from a deep sleep, but for a long time he did not say a word as he watched my progress.

'Now then,' I attempted to start a conversation but he still said nothing.

Was he Harvey the sculptor? I thought he looked older and smaller than the man I'd seen earlier in the crypt.

I tried again. 'Are you alone in here?'

'Of course I'm alone, you can see I'm alone.'

'Who are you?' I demanded, in what I hoped was a stern, police-sounding tone. Then I thought I recognized him from long, long ago.

'More to the point, who are you?' I detected a faint Irish accent in his voice.

By this time, I was standing over him; then he got to his feet. A few inches smaller than me, he was probably in his mid-sixties, of medium height and slender build with jet black but greying hair grown long and a straggly thick dark grey-black beard. His eyes were black and sharp without specs and he was dressed in a jumble of old green and brown clothes – trousers, a sweater, brown boots and he had a somewhat old and unpleasant sweaty aroma. A jacket and overcoat were hanging on a nail in the wall and on the floor I could see a large wicker basket full of pegs and trinkets. I wondered if he carried it on his head – when I was child we were visited by a tinker who carried his basket of wares on his head. Beside his bed was a back-pack, some packets of cereal, tin plates and dishes, spoons, knives and forks, a pint bottle of milk and other objects such as an electric torch and umbrella.

'So,' I repeated my question, 'who are you and what are you doing here?'

'And I ask you the same thing,' he retorted, his accent

sounding stronger as he tried to defend himself. 'Who the devil are you and what are you doing in my bedroom? Waking me up like this! This is my home. I have squatters' rights, mister.'

'Really?'

'So I have, and I don't like my privacy being disturbed like this. People just barging in—'

'Well, others have ownership rights so I think you should leave. If you are here without permission, you're trespassing.' I refrained my declaring my own rights in these barns.

'Trespassing? I am not, so I am not. I am squatting and I have rights, so you'll have to throw me out, so you will. I am not leaving for you or anyone else. As I said, this is my home. I am a squatter, mister. I have rights. I've been coming here for years.'

'What's your name?'

'I'm not telling you.'

'You realize the owner can obtain a court order to have you removed, by force if necessary, and if you persist in staying here in spite of it, you are open to a fine of a thousand pounds or six months' imprisonment.'

'You sound as if you know the law, so you do.'

'I am a retired police officer.'

At that stage he paused for a few moments, scrutinizing me closely as he weighed my words. Then he surprised me by saying, 'You're that Constable Rhea, aren't you? From Aidensfield. Much older, broader and greyer than when we met before.'

'I am, so who are you?' At that moment, I could not bring our previous encounters to mind. His heavy beard was a good disguise. But that accent? 'I feel I should know you.'

'Look, Mr Constable Rhea, I'm doing no harm, I don't leave rubbish behind, I never light fires or make a mess, all that stuff down below isn't mine, I take all my stuff away with me. I just want to get my head down for a couple of nights, then I'll move on. I'm always on the move. One or two nights here, another one or two somewhere else and so on. That's my life, always on the move. There's never been anyone in here for years; nobody uses these barns, I'm doing no harm, so I am not. Why do you want me out? What harm have I done? I've never done harm, so I have not.'

'I'm undertaking security work for the abbey.' I adopted a calmer tone now that I felt I should know him. 'I'm surprised to find you here. So who are you and what are you doing?' I wondered if he was a villain or escaped prisoner on the run.

'Doing? I'm doing nothing, just sleeping. I sleep here often, like I said. Now it's time I was leaving; I have work to do. You don't remember us meeting?'

'You look like a pedlar, travelling and trading on foot.' I pointed to his basket wondering if he was trying to be too friendly. 'Have you a pedlar's certificate?'

'Tinker, Mr Constable. They call us tinkers where I come from.'

'Here we call you a pedlar. And you need a certificate.'

'I have one.'

'Then it must be produced on demand to a policeman, a magistrate, or anyone upon whose private grounds or premises he is found. I have found you here, on private premises, so I can demand to see your certificate. And if you refuse, or if you don't have one, you can be prosecuted.'

He sighed heavily but delved into one of his pockets and pulled out a battered old leather wallet. He opened it and it was packed tight with money in banknotes; I spotted several £10 notes and fivers along with some coins. From one of its compartments, he pulled out a well-worn piece of paper and handed it to me. It was a pedlar's certificate and it was valid with six months still to run. The certificates lasted a year from the date of issue. His name was Barnaby Crabstaff. For his place of abode, it said, 'No fixed address'. Then I recalled our previous encounters. I passed it back to him.

'OK, Barnaby, now I remember you. You once showed me a nightjar in these woods, one night when I was off duty. It must have been twenty years ago or more – so thanks for that. So are you still doing the rounds?'

'I am, sir, so I am.' Now he was calling me *sir* which meant he respected me as memories of our past meetings began to filter into his brain – and mine! 'I just go around selling my stuff. I sleep here once or twice a year.'

'Without permission?'

'Nobody has ever stopped me, and I do no harm. Just you ask them over at the abbey. The kitchens give me food and drink and they said I could sleep here.'

'The kitchen staff probably think these barns belong to the abbey, but they don't. They never have. All right, Barnaby. I'll not throw you out, but sooner or later, these barns are going to have a new owner and they'll be upgraded and might even be turned into cottages. So long as you look after them, you can stay – until those alterations begin.'

'Thank you, sir, God bless you,' and he held out his hand for me to shake. 'I won't let you down, so I won't.'

'One condition, Barnaby,' I told him as I shook his dirty hand. 'I want you to look after the barns whilst you're here, making sure they are clean and tidy, that unwanted people or animals don't use them, that no one lights fires inside or uses them as toilets … you'd be a sort of caretaker, Barnaby.'

'Would I now?'

'You'll have to take care of them if you stay – and look after the swallows that nest in here.'

'Yes, sir, it will be no problem, so it won't. I'll see to them, sir, so I will, all the times I am here. God bless you, sir.'

'I'll be popping in from time to time,' I warned him. 'I walk through these grounds every day.'

'Yes, Constable Rhea sir, I understand. I won't let you down.'

'Now, Barnaby, we have some questions to ask you. This is Brother George, one of the abbey constables …' By now, Brother George had also clambered up the ladder and was standing to one side as I conducted my interview.

'He looks like a man of the cloth with that dog collar, but he looks like a copper with a white helmet….'

'I am both,' beamed Brother George. 'Now, Barnaby, who does this bike belong to? Is it yours?'

'No, I don't have a bike. It's not mine, to be sure. I didn't steal it, no I did not. I've no idea who it belongs to.'

'We're looking for a pupil who has vanished from the college, a lad of seventeen. Tall and slim, dark hair ... he went out yesterday, we think, and he hasn't come back. Have you seen him?'

'No, not a sign of him, Mr Constable Monk. Is that his bike?'

'I don't know, we have to find the owner. So has anyone else visited the barns that you know about?'

'No pupils have been here over the weekend, and no hikers and such. Only Mr Greengrass, he comes here for our business meetings ... I'm expecting him later today....'

'You mean he's still in business?' I asked.

'Oh, very successful is Mr Greengrass, me and him go back years.'

'Right, if he comes, ask if he saw our pupil over the weekend.'

'Well, he's not been here, Mr Rhea, Constable Monk—'

'All right, we believe you, Barnaby. But we might be back in case the search intensifies, so get thinking about things.' Then I felt I should make enquiries relating to the body in the crypt but without telling Barnaby that a murder had been committed. 'Barnaby, do you get hikers in here?'

'Sometimes, yes. In bad weather. Sheltering mainly, some-times sleeping here. It's them that light fires and leave rubbish, not me.'

'So have any been here this weekend, or recently? Such as a man of about fifty? Small build. Wearing a coloured woolly hat....'

He shook his head. 'Not to my knowledge, Mr Constable Rhea. I came only on Friday, you see.'

'I'm interested in this recent weekend in particular. But you will ask Mr Greengrass when you see him at your business meeting? He might have noticed the lad, or the hiker, or he might know who that bike belongs to.'

'Yes, sir, yes, sir, I'll be pleased to help....'

And so we thanked Barnaby and left him to concentrate on his day's trading.

As we walked back to my car, Brother George said, 'You know, Nick, I'm sure I've seen that bike outside the kitchens when I've been helping to wash the pots.'

'Really? When was the most recent time?'

'It might have been this Sunday after mass. Yesterday, I mean. We have coffee after mass, as you know, around eleven o'clock, and the congregation and visitors are always invited. We have it in the concourse just inside the main entrance to the church but it makes the kitchen busy. I volunteer to wash up the cups afterwards.'

'So you think it was outside the kitchens yesterday?'

'I can't bank on my recollection being accurate as I didn't really take much notice, but I am sure I thought it was rather unusual to see an old bike there.'

'Right, Brother George, you and I are now going to visit the kitchens. I want to check on what Barnaby has just told us and you can ask about the bike.'

Five minutes later, we were entering the kitchens where we were both known to most members of the staff. I spotted one of the cooks that I knew.

'Hi, Sylvia,' I greeted her. 'Can you spare a few moments? We'd like to ask you something.'

'Sure, Mr Rhea, you're a rare visitor here nowadays! Are you both wanting a cup of coffee?'

'No, thanks, we're not scrounging,' I assured her. 'And Brother George isn't here to wash up. It's a minor enquiry. We've just met a character sleeping in the old Ashwell Barns across the valley, an Irish tinker called Barnaby Crabstaff. I recall him from the past so I thought I'd check on him. He says he often pops in here.'

'Oh, him! Yes, he does. He's a tramp or a tinker or something. He comes round this way every few months and sleeps in those old barns for two or three nights at a time, then moves on. He comes to us for food and drink. He's harmless enough, Mr Rhea, although he is a bit light-fingered. He's never nicked money, just cakes and pies. In any case we leave food near the back door for him to collect.'

'The Benedictine tradition of treating every visitor like Christ, eh?'

'Except he never comes inside; we don't encourage him, it's to do with the hygiene regulations.'

'Thanks, I thought he was harmless, but felt I should check. I remember him as quite a pleasant old character and very knowledgeable about birds. But we have another query: have you heard we're looking for one of the pupils who didn't turn up for lessons this morning?'

'Yes, but we couldn't help. Constable Father Little called earlier to ask, but we don't know what goes on in the main buildings – although I did hear a whisper that a hiker had been found dead in the crypt!'

'The CID are there, looking after that crime, Sylvia. Brother George also has a question about a bike.'

'We've not had any hikers or bikers coming here looking for spare food, if that's what you're going to ask.'

'It's not that,' said Brother George. 'Sylvia, yesterday after ten o'clock mass – about eleven o'clock or thereabouts I was washing the cups as usual and I'm sure I noticed a bike outside here? Near the side door.'

'Lots of the pupils have bikes, Brother George.'

'This is a green one, a gents' model, quite old and a bit rusty in places but serviceable. Not a smart bike, but it has drop handlebars.'

'Yes it was outside here, it was a lad who wanted a packed lunch, with an extra helping. He came on the bike to collect it – two sandwiches, extra chocolate bar, two apples, soft drink in a bottle … and off he went.'

'Where did he go? Did he tell you where he was heading?'

'No, he just rode off down the valley towards the back entrance of the grounds, that one near the old barns.'

'On that bike?'

'Yes, he rode away on it with his lunch in a haversack on his back. Nice, pleasant lad, always polite. Tall, dark and handsome. Well bred, as you'd expect. He often does this – you have to book your packed lunch the previous evening and we make it up on Sunday. So he was going off for the day, quite a few of the lads do it.'

'Alone, was he?'

'Yes, quite alone. Not many booked pack-ups this weekend due to the storms on Saturday and then Sunday. In fact, I think he was the only one.'

'Do you have his name?'

'Hang on, we keep a list and tick them off when they collect their packs.' She looked behind the door of one of the cupboards and picked off a single sheet of paper.

'Here we are, Brother George. A lad called Horton. One extra-large packed lunch ordered before mass on Sunday. And it was collected.'

'Horton?' I butted in. 'Do you mean Houghton?'

'Houghton, Horton, it's all the same to us, Mr Rhea. It sounded like Horton to me, I took the booking.'

'That's how Houghton is pronounced by the family, Nick,' said Brother George.

CHAPTER 7

W E WERE PLEASED with the result of our enquiries although they had taken rather longer than expected. When I drove back to my parking space near the crypt, I found it occupied. Likewise, the area set aside for the murder team's vehicles was full, so I emulated Harvey, the sculptor, by leaving my car behind the kitchens where he usually left his van. I hoped none of the monkstables would put a ticket on it although I was half-hoping Harvey might arrive so that I could question him. But there was no sign of him. Brother George and I entered the abbey via the main door into reception and headed for the cop shop where Father Will was on duty. In the background I could now hear the monks chanting the *Te Deum*.

'Ah, there you are.' It sounded as if our presence had been sought. 'They've all gone to SALT. It's going to be used as the murder incident room. Chief Super Napier asked if you could join them when you return – the scientific examination of the body and the crypt is underway. The whole area is still sealed off. At this very moment the murder room is being set up with computers, phones, tables and chairs, desks and so forth, so you might get a job shifting furniture.'

'So where are Prior Tuck and the other monkstables?' I asked.

'Searching the campus – it's rather a cursory search of likely hiding places with a few questions of staff and pupils. They've not found Simon or any trace of him and no one has reported seeing him,' said Father Will. 'This marks the real beginning of the murder investigation and Mr Napier wants to address his detectives and then allocate actions. He's decided to include the monkstables so we've been summoned to the meeting. I'm trying to trace them all as it seems he has a role for us.'

'That's encouraging. I expected we'd be left out of it!' I admitted.

'He knows we can contribute. Things are delayed because they're awaiting the outcome of the scientific examination of the crypt. Refreshments are being provided for everyone, by the way. Lunch for the murder team will be in St Jerome's Room from twelve noon – you can join them, Nick. The monkstables will use the monastery refectory.'

'Things are moving at last,' was all I could think of saying. 'But we have some news of Simon Houghton, Father Will. We'll inform Chief Super Napier but you should know that he booked a packed lunch to take out yesterday. He collected it after mass and then used a bike to ride down to Ashwell Barns. The bike is there now; we've seen it; it's fairly old and battered but still serviceable. But there's no sign of him. Why he would want to ride a bike for such a short distance is not known. We've searched the barns and found a tinker called Barnaby Crabstaff who's been dossing down there for a few days. He hasn't seen Simon.'

'It's odd he cycled there when he could have walked in five minutes,' mused Will. 'Is it possible he met someone at the barns and got a lift from there, leaving the bike for his return journey?'

'That's feasible,' I agreed. 'But as Simon is linked to the murder enquiries, if only for elimination purposes, the forensic team and photographers will want to examine the bike. So if he had arranged to meet someone, who was it? The murderer? A pal? If it was one of the students, he'd be absent too, but there are no such reports. So, did he meet a teacher, member of the domestic staff, a girl? If that's what happened I'm sure we'd be aware of it by now.'

'Unless he met a total stranger?'

'Why would he go off with a stranger?'

'Who knows? It's something we must check. If he has gone off with a stranger, voluntarily or otherwise, we need to know,' suggested Father Will. 'And we need to know the reason. Did he meet someone who persuaded him to accompany him? Or was it pre-planned? And has his housemaster searched his room – not for the lad, we know he's not there, but for clues? Does he keep a diary for example? Letters?'

'The room was checked to see if he was there, that's all,' was my response. 'I doubt if his housemaster looked for his diaries or private correspondence. But you're right, we need to look at them. Leave that with me.'

'OK.'

Brother George now entered the conversation. 'Nick, perhaps you aren't aware of the College system? When a student brings his own cycle he can store it in any of the racks around the campus, and he's responsible for its security. However, when a student finishes here it's customary to leave his old bike behind.'

'Permanently you mean?'

'Yes, as a sort of parting gift. By that stage, though, the bikes are fairly battered, but they may still provide transport for someone without one. So they become runabouts, you jump on and ride it to your destination, then leave for someone to pick up and go elsewhere. Then, every few years, we have a clear-out of bikes that are really done for and Claude Jeremiah Greengrass takes them off our hands.'

'Thanks for that,' I said. 'Well, Brother George, I think it's time we joined the others.'

'You know, Nick,' said Brother George as he walked away. 'I can't understand why our monkstables didn't search those old barns – but even if they had, they might not have realized the importance of the old bike.'

'I think I can explain that. Follow me, we'll call in at our own incident room at the Postgate to see if there are any messages before we join the others.'

And so we did. The Postgate Room was temporarily deserted but a digital map of the campus was on display with more green patches having been added.

'What do you make of that?' I asked Brother George.

'It seems our colleagues are doing their duty in completing their searches.'

'Does anything else strike you?'

He cupped his chin in his hands and stared at the image before him for a few moments, then shook his head. 'No. It's just a map of the buildings and grounds, with areas marked off when they've been searched.'

'Right, but just recently, Brother George, you and I visited two important places, both of which are *not* shown on that map – Abbey Farm and Ashwell Priory barns. Abbey Farm is owned by the abbey but it is rather too far away to be included on the map, and Ashwell Priory barns are not owned by the Abbey, so they are not on the map.'

'Hmm,' he said. 'So when the jobs are allocated, those places not marked on the map could be overlooked – not deliberately, but simply because they are not visible. So we need a more comprehensive map?'

'We do. And we need our monkstables to start thinking beyond the boundaries. Even within the grounds there are lots of people who are not connected with the abbey – building workers, people coming and going on business, visitors, tourists, and now those archaeologists.'

'All to be interviewed?'

'Yes, the CID will want to interview each one of them, And so should we if we want to find Simon, who could be miles away by now – he's been missing for twenty-four hours. So having established that, let's join the others.'

When we entered the St Alban's Lecture Theatre, the place seemed in turmoil. Noisy men and women were organizing the position of furniture, computers, large video screens, internal telephones and maps. The theatre though had been custom-built for lectures aided by computers and photographs, either stills or videos. Despite the high technology, there was a pair of blackboards beside the speaker's lectern and brief particulars were chalked on them – the name of the venue, the name of the detective inspector who had been appointed murder room manager and the date of discovery of the body and by whom. A plain clothes officer approached us.

'Yes, can I help you?'

'I'm ex-Inspector Rhea and I am advising the monk-constables on how to conduct their search for a missing pupil. This is Brother George, one of our monkstables, as call them. We have been asked to join you here. Detective Chief Superintendent Napier will vouch for us.'

'Nice to meet you. I'm Detective Inspector Lindsey, Brian to my friends. As you can see things are bit hectic right now but within a few minutes, all the gear will be in the right position and our teams will be able to take their seats as they await their first address from Chief Super Napier. My job is to make sure the murder room runs efficiently as we can't afford sloppiness or mistakes.'

'Yes, I know. I worked in a lot of murder rooms when I was serving. I'm always amazed at the huge amount of information they generate. Anyway, I'm sure you'll do a great job!'

'I'll do my best. Can I suggest you find a chair somewhere to await events? At the moment the scene of the crime is still being examined and once that's complete our teams will be briefed with actions, tasks that have to be completed and reported back here. Each team consists of two detectives – a sergeant and a constable. I reckon you will know all that.'

'It will be new to Brother George and the other monkstables.'

'They'll soon understand what's going on. You and the monkstables will be expected to continue the hunt for the missing pupil, leaving the murder to us. It will take pressure off our officers, allowing them to concentrate on the crime. There are lots of people to interview, I had no idea this campus was so large and busy.'

'There are several thousand people here during a normal

working day,' I told him. 'Seven hundred pupils for a start ... monks, teachers, other staff members ... now workmen, archaeologists and tourists. But we've just discovered some news about the missing pupil,' I said.

'That's good. Can I suggest you wait until everyone's arrived then all can hear what you've got to say? I'll call you to say your bit. We can then hear what everyone else has been doing and it's a chance to ask questions. There are meal and break periods – we need them – and lunch has been arranged. We don't usually get treated like this during murder investigations but it leaves our mobile canteen free for minor refreshments whenever they're needed – which is always!'

We found seats in the auditorium and settled down and didn't have to wait very long.

A door crashed open and DCS Napier swept in with a retinue of others trailing behind. There seemed to be a lot of plain-clothes officers, men and women. There was the inevitable scramble as everyone tried to find a seat and when Napier was satisfied everyone was settled and listening, he began.

'My name is Napier, sir to you all,' he began without a smile. 'If you have a problem, or want to share a secret, or report a breakthrough in the enquiry, then I will listen. Or you can discuss it with DS Sullivan over there,' – he pointed as Sullivan raised his hand – 'and the gentleman on my right is DI Lindsey, the murder room manager. I expect diligent enquiries and the greatest possible effort from all of you.'

He paused for a moment, then continued, 'Now listen and watch carefully.' He pressed a button on the console on the desk before him and the large screen on the wall behind him burst into life showing a photograph of a wide view of the crypt.

'This is the murder scene: it's the crypt below the abbey church. If you listen carefully you might hear monks chanting, real monks I mean. If you want to have a look at the crypt, talk to DS Sullivan. But not yet, forensics are still busy down there but we have enough information for us to get started.'

He pressed another button and we saw a close-up of the coffin curtain, and then it was drawn aside to reveal the coffin and its occupant.

'A solid stone coffin carved to accommodate one person; coffin's age and origin unknown. Roman, more than likely. It stands on a knee-high plinth carved from the same block of granite and it has probably been here for hundreds of years. There is a custom that it should never be moved and to our knowledge, it never has. The occupant was recently deceased, somewhat whiskery and aged about fifty. He has greying brown hair but he's only five feet two inches tall, a fraction over one and a half metres. A little chap. He had to be little to fit into the coffin. He might have been lying there for less than twenty-four hours. The body has now been removed to the forensic morgue at Middlesbrough General Hospital. The post-mortem has not yet started but this advance information is to get the basics up and running.

'I want you all to note the victim's clothes and facial charac-teristics because you'll be making enquiries to see if anyone recognizes him or has seen him around the place. We need to know who he is and where he comes from. Try the Retreat Centre – did he book in there? Has he booked out? Where is his luggage? Does he have a vehicle? Is it parked somewhere on this site? You know the sort of thing to ask. At the moment we are examining his clothes for alien fibres or DNA. As you can see he is dressed like a hiker and we're examining his boots to see what they can tell us. He is wearing a watch – a gents' stain-less-steel Sekonda with a stainless-steel strap. Inexpensive – maybe costing sixty quid new, less second-hand. We don't know where he bought it. There's scope for someone to find out if we can't identify him. And where did he buy that coloured hat, or those boots? We'll show you close-up images with makers' names of all items of clothing. There was nothing in his pockets, probably removed by his killer with the inten-tion of not having him identified. He has no spectacles and no jewellery, not even a ring.

'We won't know about tattoos or other body marks or injuries until the pathologist gets him undressed and onto the slab, but there is no doubt he died from a vicious wound to the back of his skull, precisely at the top of his spinal column. It fractured his skull and killed him. There is some blood which has oozed from the wound and now lies in the bottom of the coffin, beneath where his head rested. The condition of the blood should tell us how long he's been there. We haven't found the murder weapon but we are examining the tools belonging to a sculptor who has been working in the crypt. The hammer used to kill him will be bloodstained and might also have hair or bone sticking to it.

'We need to establish a motive for his death. Why would such an apparently harmless little chap be wiped off the face of this planet? Who would want to do such a thing to him? What was the motive? We need to establish a motive, that's vital.'

As he paused awhile we were treated to photographs of all the sculpting tools that lay on the table used by Harvey, the camera ranging over them slowly and resting occasionally on each of the stone hammers and mallets.

'So far we've not found any traces of blood, bone or hair on any of the hammers and mallets but each will be subjected to a detailed forensic examination. Similarly, our first examination of the scene has not revealed any blood spots on the floor of the crypt but we shall be further testing the area immediately around the coffin because if the blow was struck nearby, then you would expect tiny spillages or splashes of blood on or near the coffin and on the floor.'

He paused again, then asked of his audience, 'So what does the absence of blood spots on the ground around the coffin suggest?'

'That he was killed in the coffin,' said a male detective. 'Maybe climbing onto the plinth then crouching to look inside it ... whereupon he was fatally struck from behind with a hammer?'

'Then neatly arranged inside the coffin by his assailant?

Sounds possible,' agreed Napier. 'So the assailant's clothing might also bear minute blood spots. I don't think he was killed elsewhere and carried to the coffin as there would have been a trail of bloodstains *en route*. Maybe tiny invisible ones, but they would have been there and visible to our scientific equipment. I tend to agree he was hit from behind while looking into the coffin, perhaps upon the invitation of his killer. So is our victim a historian? Did he come here deliberately to examine the old coffin? What do we know about it? Does it have any significance for anyone? Or any organization? Or is it merely a tourist attraction? Perhaps nothing more interesting than a relic from the past? These are openings for you to consider as you are interrogating witnesses or suspects.'

He paused once more for them to digest his words, then continued, 'Now we need to know who has entered the crypt during the last couple of days or so. We need times, dates and duration. Check the times the doors are locked. Then check again. Were they always locked when they should have been, or has someone been able to persuade a keyholder to surrender his or her key temporarily? Remember, someone has sneaked into the crypt, killed that man and left. Who saw him? Who has keys? Where are they kept, and who is allowed to use them? What are the movements of the sculptor who might be worth a further check in criminal records? I know him from the past. Strange chap.

'And I repeat that the main questions are: who is the victim? Where has he come from and what could be a motive for killing him? And why in here of all places? Why wasn't he hit on the head somewhere outside? Like a dense piece of woodland, the isolation of the moors, or the banks of a river ... but it was here, in a monastery crypt ... in a coffin ... why? It is all very odd, ladies and gentlemen, so you will have many enquiries to make.'

After another brief pause, he smiled and announced, 'Inspector Lindsey will allocate your actions so make a good job of it and I suppose I should say, in a place like this, God be with you!'

After a gentle ripple of laughter, he went on, 'Now there is another thing. A schoolboy aged seventeen is missing from the adjoining college. I propose not to release his name now in case he is located on site. It seems he might have done nothing more than dodge morning lessons and not be connected with our enquiries. I have spoken to the abbot and because he is not yet an adult, I do not want him tainted with involvement in a murder if it can be avoided. He is seventeen, almost six feet tall, very slim build, dark hair cut short, wears spectacles and has a smart accent. You know how people and newspapers can drum up false news about youngsters, especially those from so-called privileged backgrounds. We concern ourselves only with facts. He was last seen on Sunday morning after mass which was here in the abbey church, but he's not been seen since. He didn't sleep in his bed on Sunday night, and didn't turn up for lessons this morning. The abbey has its own private constables who are conducting their search of the grounds and buildings, and making enquiries as we speak. Our two teams will be liaising closely and we hope to get a good photograph of the lad for internal use. The inevitable question is whether or not he is somehow involved in the murder. More importantly, we must establish whether he is a victim who has not yet been found.'

At this point I raised my hand.

'Yes, Mr Rhea.'

'The teams should be aware of the latest information about the missing boy.'

'You've got something? Then fire away, Mr Rhea.'

'It seems that on Saturday he ordered a packed lunch for Sunday, for one person – quite a normal event. He collected it before noon, then rode a bike – not his own – through the grounds and left it in Ashwell Priory barns. The cycle is there now but he is not. I've searched the place.'

Copying Napier's style, I paused before continuing with, 'There are several old bikes around the campus, left behind by former pupils. Anyone can use them. This one could have been left outside the kitchen – if it was, it is quite feasible that the boy noticed it and took it to cover a fairly modest distance. It was easier and faster than walking.'

'Thanks, Mr Rhea. Now we need to fetch the bike here without delay. Sergeant Sullivan, can you arrange that? Examine it for fingerprints or other evidence as we establish its history. And now, unless there are any questions, I will hand over to DI Lindsey who will tell you about the procedures before allocating your actions.'

We sat through the rather ponderous but necessary instructions and rules of a police murder room and advice about interrogation techniques and when that was over, DI Lindsey announced that the police mobile canteen was open for everyone before they embarked on their tasks. This was more than a mere occasion for refreshment – it allowed the teams, some of whom had never previously worked together and those who had travelled a long distance, to socialize for a few important minutes. Relationships would be formed – it was all vital to the good governance of the investigation.

As I made my way to the canteen, Father John Little, Monkstable No. 15, hailed me. 'Ah, Nick, glad I caught you. I think I have a name for the murder victim.'

CHAPTER 8

I DREW HIM to one side, away from the crowd.

'What have you learned?'

'I've been checking the Retreat to see if anyone knew anything of Simon's movements. I took the opportunity to ask about visitors who had recently used the guest accommodation. Mrs Morley – she's the hospitality manager as I'm sure you know – has no knowledge of Simon and she hasn't been told about the murder yet, but described a man who has been staying and who has disappeared – she wondered if he had left early. He's called James Thorpe and he fits the description of the man in the coffin.'

'Well, we can't let her see him to make an identification, he's in the mortuary at Middlesbrough but the murder team has a photo. Maybe we could show her that? It would be a start. What else can you tell me about him?'

'Not a lot. He's been here since Friday and booked his accommodation until this coming Wednesday – full bed and board. He'd booked for the course "The Symbolism of Medieval Church Decorations".'

'Alone, was he? When he made his reservation?'

'Yes, it was a single booking but there are others on the course – ten in total.'

'And where are they this morning?'

'They've gone on a guided visit to Rievaulx Abbey, in a minibus. Father Leonard from the abbey is their guide. They left immediately after breakfast.'

'We'll need to interview them. Was our man missed by anyone else?'

'Yes, some of his colleagues noticed his absence at breakfast this morning and at supper last night.'

'But they didn't register their concerns?'

'No. None thought they should knock on his door just because the bus was waiting. If he wasn't well, they felt he should be allowed to rest. They weren't worried about his absence.'

'You've checked his room since then?'

'I did; Mrs Morley used the master key. All his things appeared to be in his room – clothes in the wardrobe, suitcase on its rack, shoes under the dressing table, toiletries in the shower room – it's *en suite*. We didn't search his belongings.'

'So it appears he didn't intend his absence to be permanent? He wasn't trying to leave without paying?'

'There's no question of that, but his unexplained absence was beginning to cause concern as I arrived as no one could suggest where he might be. Now, sadly, we know. So what should I do now, Nick? About releasing his name, informing relatives, all that sort of thing.'

'Your first action is to inform Inspector Lindsey in the murder room and give him as much detail as possible. He'll deal with everything and allocate a team to deal with your information. At this point, therefore, the monkstables will have to back off that branch of the investigation. It's no longer within our brief. The CID will search his room and belongings, and subject everything to forensic tests. It's a very important step forward. However, although our monkstables have no more duties so far as that man is concerned, it might be a good idea for them to ask around the campus whilst seeking Simon. Someone might have seen Mr Thorpe with or without Simon. We need to know whether the boy was seen around the campus just before he vanished and, if so, when and with whom? Could it have been Thorpe? And has Thorpe been noticed in places that are necessary for his course? Such as the crypt? Or the church? The CID need to know the names of everyone who's been in the crypt during the last three days, and the times and reasons they were there. That information will help us too.'

'I'll attend to that, so, what are you going to do now?'

'I'm going to have words with those archaeologists, ostensibly to see if they've seen Simon, but in reality to find out who they are, where they've come from and what they're looking for. I'll let the CID know what I learn. And we need to visit some of the offices on the construction site to establish whether any of their workmen have noticed Simon on his own or with anyone.'

'Then it's likely we might also come across some information concerning the murder?'

'It's quite possible, but if we do, we must pass it to Detective Chief Superintendent Napier and his teams, no matter how insignificant we think it is. Do that through DI Lindsey.'

'Thanks, I found all this rather baffling at first, but now I see there are clear demarcation lines between them and us. What shall I do when I've passed my information on?'

'Speak to Prior Tuck – he might have a place or two for you to search or some other task that requires attention. It's going to take a long, long time to be sure we've searched everywhere, but Simon is *our* priority. If Prior Tuck can't find something for you to do, come and see me, I'm sure we can occupy ourselves.'

When Father John Little left me I walked across the sports area to George's Field. So far as I could determine, the archaeologists were not partaking in the day-to-day abbey routine.

The students arrived daily in a six-seater vehicle whilst their leader slept in his camper-van in a corner of the field. They provided their own food and the camper-van had a toilet. Throughout the day they chipped away at discoveries in the shelter of their marquee. I was not really sure what they were doing or what they had found. My visit offered an opportunity to find out. As I approached the cricket field, my progress was being observed by a man working at a table in the camper-van;

I could see he held a coffee mug and he had a clear view of my approach. He left his vehicle to confront me.

'Yes?' He was a heavy, stout man probably in his late forties and was deeply tanned. I thought he looked like a shot putter or a rugby player – certainly, there was an aura of physical power about him. Wearing a T-shirt, shorts and sandals, but no socks, he had fair hair but was balding, although he sported a thick beard and moustache. 'What can I do for you?'

'Who are you?' I asked.

'I might ask the same of you,' was his response. 'This is private property.'

'My name is Nicholas Rhea, ex-Inspector Rhea of the North Yorkshire Police and I am currently working with the Maddleskirk Abbey constables. We are seeking a pupil, a teenaged boy who is missing. I wonder if you or your colleagues have seen him?'

'How old is he?'

'Seventeen, very slim and tall, about six feet, dark hair, spectacles.'

'That could fit dozens of kids here,' he said. 'But he's not here, not one of us. Everybody here is known to me; my assistants aren't pupils of this college.'

'And that six-seater?'

'It brings students here on a daily basis from York University; one of them drives it. They're here to gain field experience under my guidance. They're older than your pupil. So, how long has he been missing?'

'Since yesterday around lunchtime. He wasn't in his room last night, didn't come down for breakfast this morning and hasn't turned up for lessons.'

'That happens every Monday morning! Kids dodging lessons!'

'We feel this lad isn't the sort to go AWOL without reason. Teams of constables are out looking for him, searching the entire site.'

'Well, as I said, he's not here and never has been. You're

welcome to ask the youngsters and search the van – it belongs to a friend. I've borrowed it. Search the people carrier and the marquee too. Be my guest.'

'Thanks, I'd better do it for the record.' So I made a quick examination of the van with its cramped accommodation, particularly the sleeping quarters. They comprised a tidily made single bed and a wardrobe full of clothes, with a tiny wash basin and toilet in a corner cubicle. A folding table, two chairs and a little settee filled the small lounge. I noted the vehicle's registration number, then turned my attention to the six youngsters in the marquee, all in their twenties. They gave up scraping earth and seemed eager to help. With their archae-ological tools neatly spread on a ground sheet everything seemed clean and professional. When I asked if they had seen a seventeen year old riding a bike nearby yesterday, all shook their heads. 'We weren't here yesterday,' said one. 'But we didn't see him this morning. We got here about eight, before the general workforce turned up.' Their six-seater vehicle was empty too. I recorded their full names and addresses, then returned for a further chat with their leader. He told me his name was John Wayne Rawdon and gave me his address in Middlesbrough, adding, 'Guess who my dad's favourite film star was!'

'Thanks,' I said to them all. 'I appreciate your co-operation.'

'Sorry we can't be of more help.'

'Maybe you can. May I ask why you're digging here? Sheer curiosity....'

'I'm a freelance,' explained Rawdon. 'I earn my living by lecturing, writing books and articles, taking commissions to search for anything from hidden pottery, coins and entire houses. And I do some part-time archaeological advisory work for museums.'

'It sounds interesting. So what's under here that's so exciting?'

'We're seeking a Roman settlement or possibly a medieval village – an aerial survey suggests there are remains under here so the abbot has given us permission to search. You probably know there are Roman remains *under* the crypt at the abbey; the crypt itself is medieval and there's also an ancient priory just outside the boundaries. In Ashwell Woods.'

'Yes, I know about the medieval ruins but not any Roman remains. But thank you, I won't disturb you any more. I must warn you though to expect a visit from the local CID.'

'I thought you'd accepted we have no teenager either hiding or working here?'

'I have accepted that and know he's not here, but I have some bad news: there has been a murder in the crypt. It's probably unconnected with the pupil's disappearance but the CID are investigating so everyone can expect a visit from them.'

'A murder?' He sounded shocked.

'It's a man of about fifty with a beard and greyish-brown hair; he looks like a hiker. He was found dead this morning. We don't know for certain who he is yet. Maybe you know him, or have seen him around the campus?'

'Oh crumbs, and I thought this was a peaceful and calm place! But no, I can't say I've noticed anyone, but we don't often leave our search area. Everything we need is in our vehicles.'

By now his students were standing around listening to all this and all shook their heads, saying they had not seen the bearded hiker.

I told them, 'This is normally a very peaceful place, but I'm sure you can understand our concern – we have to accept that the missing pupil might be a victim too.'

'So, are we safe working here? Is there a maniac on the loose?'

'I hope not, but your guess is as good as mine. When the CID come to talk to you, you could ask for advice about your future safety.'

'Well, I can't say I know anything about the murder – we don't go to the abbey. We've enough to keep us busy here.'

'How long have you been here?'

'Only since Friday but if this exploratory work finds evidence of buildings underground, we'll return later to carry out a more extensive excavation. It could be a very significant discovery, but at the moment, we've not found anything.'

We parted on good terms. I would provide the CID with the details I had recorded, knowing Rawdon's name and address would be checked along with those of his students. As he rejoined his students I headed for St Alban's Lecture Theatre. DI Lindsey was still there and I reported my findings about the archaeologists and confirmed that Simon Houghton was not among them.

'We'll run a routine check and one of our teams will interview them. Now, you'll be interested in the outcome of our visit to the retreat.'

'You don't waste time!'

'In cases like this, every minute counts. We showed a photo of the deceased in the coffin to Mrs Morley, and she thinks it is the man called Thorpe who was on the symbolism course. We have to be sure, of course, so further checks will be necessary but this is just to get things moving. We haven't fingerprinted his room yet, or tested it for DNA and so forth – that's on the cards for later today – but we have sealed it. When he reserved his place, Thorpe described himself as a lecturer specializing in medieval churches. He got on well with the others and according to them, appeared very knowledgeable about church decorations. Obviously we have to confirm his identity and once we get a positive identification, we can proceed further. What are your next plans, Nick?'

'I'll have words with Prior Tuck to see whether his monk-stables' searches have produced any results. What about that bike in the old barns?'

'We've collected it and it's being checked for fingerprints and DNA. First indications are that it bears Simon's fingerprints – we got a good image from his water glass in the bedroom and it matches those on the handlebars of the bike. We'll need those to be confirmed, but our general feeling is that he used the bike as you suggested, but for some reason decided to leave it.'

'You've done well.'

'It's early days, Nick, but modern technology enables us to get rapid preliminary results even with fingerprint checks. They're not good enough for prosecution purposes in court but good enough to guide us. The pace of crime investigation has accelerated since your day. And time is money. A major investigation costs a fortune so if we can speed up the processes and get positive results, we save the taxpayers a lot of money.'

'OK, I'll have another word with Prior Tuck. We've completed a cursory search without finding Simon but this second one must be more probing. We're checking holes and tunnels within the abbey construction, places where a thin lad could explore or hide for reasons best known to himself, and we are questioning staff and pupils to see if anyone noticed him riding away or behaving not quite normally alone or with someone. The lad can't have dumped the bike and then vanished into thin air.'

'I suggested to Prior Tuck that he checked local buses and taxis to see if Simon got a lift away from here. He assured me he would do that.'

'That's in hand. So are we still pursuing the line that the two enquiries are quite separate?'

'According to Chief Super Napier, they are separate but he admits he can't ignore the possibility of links. He wants your monkstables to be usefully deployed tracing Simon because if they do that, they might turn up some snippet of information that's vital to the murder investigation – like Thorpe! It could be anything – strangers wandering around the site, vehicles seen in the campus, screams of pain … anything.'

'We don't want to muscle in on this investigation, Brian. I'm not in the force now and the monkstables are private constables.'

'But you and your men are all police officers and they're proving helpful to us, Nick, surprisingly so. More important is the fact that Mr Napier is very pleased with them. We're all surprised he has taken to them like he has. He must be mellowing in his old age!'

I decided to go to the monkstables' incident room next because I wanted an update from Prior Tuck. As I was striding towards the Postgate Room, someone hailed me and I turned to see it was DS Sullivan.

'Hi, Nick, glad I caught you. We've just received a preliminary opinion from the pathologist about the time of death of the man in the coffin. I thought you might be interested bearing in mind the disappearance of Simon Houghton.'

'Does this sound ominous?'

'I'm not sure that's the right word but it opens the need for further enquiries.'

'That *does* sound ominous!'

'It's not all that bad! Let me remind you. Simon Houghton was seen on Sunday – yesterday – behaving quite normally. He attended mass which finished at eleven thirty, and he collected his packed lunch from the kitchens, by which time he had acquired a bike. This was around noon when it seems he rode through the grounds to the rear entrance, and left it in those old barns. It would have taken only three or four minutes to get there. Would you agree?'

'Yes, that fits with what we know.'

'Right. This information has just arrived by email. The pathologist's report confirms murder. He has no doubt about that. The victim was found dead about eight o'clock today, Monday. Although it is not possible to be precise about the time of death, he has taken into account statements from the people who attended the deceased. He believes he died some-time before eight on *Sunday* morning.'

'Sunday? It's possible. The crypt opens at five every day,' I reminded him.

'Yes, I know, but who would go there at that time of day? And would they venture behind the curtain? If so, why? We're checking to ascertain who opened the doors on Sunday morning and whether he or she noticed anything unusual. The point is that Simon Houghton was on the site on Sunday until around midday. The man was probably lying dead during that time. Simon is known to have ridden away about twelve noon and has not been seen since.'

'Are you saying Simon could have committed the murder?'

'He booked his lunch on Saturday – that was the routine. He knew he would be leaving the college on Sunday around noon. The murder victim would be lying dead as Simon cycled away.'

'I can understand why you consider him a suspect.'

'We would phrase it to suggest he might have something to tell us. He could have been in that crypt—'

'But surely Simon isn't capable of delivering a blow that would kill a fully grown man?'

'We don't know that, do we? And we don't know whether he was provoked in some way. Or could it be self-defence? Remember a range of weapons was readily available and the victim is not a very big man.'

'I still believe the two incidents are quite separate.' Even though I made that statement, I knew I had no evidence to support it.

Sullivan continued, 'Did the two meet in the crypt for some sexual purpose? What do we know about the sex life of either person? Is Thorpe married, for example? What is Simon's sexual orientation? There's a lot we don't know, Nick.'

'And that means we must find out!'

'Exactly. And your monkstables can help, asking around, being delicate in their questioning....'

'I realize that and I know the way that murder enquiries are conducted. The sex life of suspects and victims is always an important factor.'

'It is. We've drawn time charts. Those of Simon and the deceased overlap considerably. There might be further over-lapping once we get our teeth into the enquiry. The reason I am telling you, is that we may have to merge the two investiga-tions – even to prove Simon is *not* guilty.'

'Well, if that's necessary, I'll go along with your plans and will ask Prior Tuck and his monkstables to do likewise.'

'Mr Napier will talk to you to explain his thinking. I'm sure he will want your officers to continue searching, even extending it beyond the boundaries of the campus. The fact that Simon has not been found dead or alive and left a bike behind, suggests he fled the scene hurriedly. If he killed Thorpe, even in self-defence, say on Saturday night – and one blow from a heavy mallet would have been enough – he could have ordered his lunch before the Sunday deadline and ridden off to make good his escape. It's a scenario we must develop. Mr Napier felt you should be aware of our thoughts. And, Nick, we must be objective about this: we can't avoid the fact that the evidence is pointing in Simon's direction.'

'I can understand that, Jim. I've worked in many murder rooms and they never fail to produce surprises. I'll go and talk to Prior Tuck. Can I tell him all this?'

'I think you should.'

But, as I was preparing to leave DS Sullivan, his boss arrived in something of a fluster.

'Sarge.' Chief Superintendent Napier was panting heavily. 'And Nick. Glad I caught you. We've had a reply from Sunderland Police about James Thorpe. The address he gave is not known in Sunderland and his name does not appear on any Sunderland references – phone book, voters' lists, banks, utility accounts ... It means the victim booked onto his course here at Maddleskirk Abbey by using a false name and address. I find that very curious indeed. So we must ask ourselves why he would do that? Why book onto a course under a false name? Was there something going on between him and young Simon? Something very unsavoury...?'

'So we're no further forward?' I felt I had to say something.

'I think we've taken several steps backwards,' admitted Napier.

CHAPTER 9

'HE HAD SOMETHING to hide, that's obvious,' Napier commented after a brief silence. 'Is he a sex offender? Chasing lads? Right, Sarge,' he turned to Sullivan, 'we'll have to wait and see what his fingerprint check tells us and be sure to arrange samples from his body for a DNA test. We should soon have his real name sorted out.'

'If *James Thorpe* has a record, we'll get a result soon; we took his fingerprints before he went to the morgue,' Sullivan reminded us.

'So we're on course. Now, Nick, what can I do for you? You've got some more news about young Houghton so I've heard. Let's hear it.'

'It's not a lot,' I admitted, 'but I have something,' and I explained about the archaeologist and his team. 'I just wanted to say Houghton's not there, I searched all the vehicles and they've not seen him.'

'What are they looking for?'

'Ruins, Roman or otherwise. They've got permission from the abbot. The leader is John Wayne Rawdon who says he's from Middlesbrough.' I took a slip of paper from my wallet and passed it to him. 'This is his name and address, and the registration number of his friend's camper-van which he borrowed while working here. His students come in daily from York. Their names and addresses are there too. Rawdon is a freelance, by the way, he's not part of a university research team.'

'So are there Roman ruins hereabouts?'

'He said an aerial survey showed unidentified ruins under the cricket field and I understand there was a network of Roman highways not far away. Some experts believe there are also Roman remains under the crypt – that coffin could be Roman.'

'All very historic! Well, I hope he finds what he wants. Thanks for this, Nick, it's useful. Sarge here will task a team to check him out – and his students. We're doing the same with those builders, but they've got dozens of workers coming and going, different ones every day. It won't be easy tracking those who work for cash and give false names. I don't know how the tax man copes with such dodgers ... here today and gone tomorrow, midnight flitters ... but probably not killers. Now, there's something else you can help me with before you continue your hunt for that lad. Do you know the lady who runs the retreat?'

'Mrs Morley.'

'Right, and the lad's housemaster?'

'Yes, he's John Haxby.'

'Then lead me to them. I know you've been dealing with them but I want to check the handwriting on that note left in the cop shop. I know there were spelling mistakes but it's the handwriting that interests me. Who wrote it and when? If Simon Houghton wrote it, did he deliberately misspell certain words to disguise his authorship? That's something you can bear in mind. And by the way, Nick, if you don't find Simon and concern grows that he could still be here on site somewhere, don't be afraid to request a dog team to extend your search. I can justify it as part of the murder enquiry.'

'Thanks, Mr Napier.'

'Right, off we go, we'll collect that note first, and then we must deposit it in our own files for safekeeping.'

At the cop shop, the note had been slipped into a clear plastic cover to protect it. Father Will handed it over.

'We'll retain this,' Napier told him. 'It's going for tests and then it will go into our evidence files.'

'My prints will be on it,' Father Will pointed out.

'Then we'll come and take yours for elimination purposes, Reverend. Any more news for us while we're here?'

'Sorry, nothing. Things are settling down after the first rush of activity.'

'Well, my teams and yours are all hard at work some-where, asking questions, observing, trying to find solutions to puzzles ... that's detective work, Reverend. You're welcome to visit my murder room as I regard you and your mates as professional coppers and trustworthy too. Feel free. Don't be frightened to point out things you think we've over-looked, or which might interest us. You know this place better than we do. However, I want my officers to interview all the monks.'

'The abbot's secretary will help to organize that.'

'Good. Now Nick, off to the retreat.'

As we walked briskly through the campus leaving the monks' choir rehearsing another Gregorian chant, Napier asked questions about life here. He was keen to understand the daily routine, but also how the work-force of men and women, teachers, estate workers, administrative staff and others fitted into a work-place that was based on religion. He said he had always thought an abbey was a place of quiet contemplation and prayer, but now he thought it was more like a busy univer-sity or business complex.

The retreat was an old but handsome house, that had formerly belonged to a wealthy family, standing on the edge of the abbey grounds. For a while after their deaths, it had become a country house hotel but then the trustees had bought it for use as a residential retreat. The abbey boundaries had been extended to include it, adding a chapel and reception area, a library, conference room and quiet room. It was always busy, but, fortunately today the delegates had gone to Rievaulx Abbey on a field trip. When we arrived, it was suitably quiet bearing in mind one of their guests had suffered a terrible death. I noticed a vase of lilies on a plinth before a crucifix in the reception area. Prayers would have been said for the dead man in the chapel and he would be remembered by the monks at masses in the abbey church.

Mrs Morley's office had a bar-style counter which opened into the reception area.

'Good morning, Nick.' Her smile was rather subdued. 'Can I help?'

'Yes, Mrs Morley. I know a monkstable has already talked to you but this is Detective Chief Superintendent Napier. He'd like to talk to you and so would I.'

'Everyone is talking about it. It's such a shock for us with him staying here. Poor Mr Thorpe. He was such a nice man. Who on earth would do a thing like that?'

'That what's we intend to find out, Mrs Morley. And we'll have to interview all your recent guests. Now, before we begin, can we visit his room?' asked Napier. 'I know it has already been examined, but I need to look at it.'

'Your officers locked it and took away the keys,' she reminded him.

'I am merely being polite by asking!' Clearly the atmosphere of this place had affected him. 'You'll have a master key? Ours is in the murder room.'

'I've respected your officers' wishes by keeping the room locked. We have not touched it since he left. I'll take you there now.'

'Thanks.'

I guessed he was testing her honesty but she unlocked a drawer then led the way up the carpeted staircase and along to Room 5. Napier took the keys and opened the door, but did not step inside. He merely stared into the clinically bare room, noting a simple single bed, a curtained rail behind which to hang clothing, a small dressing table bearing a pile of books but little else. It was very tidy with the bed neatly made and clothing hanging on the rail. He did not open any drawers. 'A full search will be done by our Scenes of Crime team,' he explained to her. 'I don't want to contaminate the scene any more than necessary. I see there are books on the dressing table. Are they his own or from your library?'

'They will be his. We ask our guests not to take our library books to their rooms as that's how they get lost.'

'Or stolen,' he muttered. 'And such rules depend upon a degree of honesty. So, if they are his, I would like to know what their subjects are. However, what I am seeking now, Mrs Morley, is something bearing his handwriting. Would he have made notes during the course?'

'It's very possible. Our visitors make lots of notes even though we issue fact sheets galore … but I thought you had come because you might want to clear his room....'

'That won't happen for some time. We need to let our Scenes of Crime experts examine it first and afterwards there will be the question of whether he has family and, if so, will they want to come and claim his belongings. We will go through every-thing in that room, forensically I mean. My dilemma – and it is a dilemma, Mrs Morley – is how much contamination I will create if I start looking for necessary evidence now.'

'Can I help you find what you are looking for?'

'Perhaps. So is it likely he would invite someone to his room?'

'We don't encourage it, there's plenty of private space down-stairs for discussions.'

'But it can't be ruled out? People do disobey rules, so I find....'

'You're right, of course. But I don't know whether anyone visited him in this room.'

'Right, so my next question: has it been tidied by your staff?'

'I can assure you we've not touched it this morning, neither have we cleaned his bathroom.'

'He seems to have been a tidy chap. Where will I find some-thing with his writing on? I can't see any notebooks lying around and I don't want to examine his bags or drawers at this stage … and I can't see any postcards waiting to be posted home.'

'He filled a form in when he applied to join the course, that will be in the file.'

'That should help. I've a sample here I want to check,' and he waved the plastic-enclosed note around. 'I'm going to step inside to check those books as they might tell us about his interests, but don't follow me.'

Immediately through the doorway, he stepped carefully to one side, trying to avoid the normal route used by an inhabitant and approached the dressing table from the side, not from the front. He stopped to read the book titles one by one without touching them, then grunted. All were non-fiction on the objects and adornments that could be found in or near churches, particularly those with medieval origins. There was one entitled *Treasure Trove from Churches and Churchyards*.

He made notes of the titles; he'd get SOCO to check whether the owner had written his name inside any of them. Then he poked his head into the small *en suite* shower room and finally left via the same route.

'The course he was attending is about the spirituality of medieval church ornamentations.' Mrs Morley felt she had to add more to Napier's knowledge. 'The quality of church art in that period was quite astonishing and much has survived.'

'So are they valuable, these medieval art works and ornaments?'

'Some are irreplaceable, Mr Napier. They may not have a high financial value but to us they're priceless. Lots were concealed during the Edwardine Visitations when the child king, Edward VI, ordered papist churches to be stripped. Many hid their wealth before Edward's men arrived and there's a legend that a huge hoard is hidden under this abbey church, guarded by a giant raven. The truth or otherwise is debated during the course.'

'I wonder if Thorpe believed the legend? Was he here to check the facts? Make a recce of the abbey's lay-out,' Napier said as he made his exit, closing the door and locking it. 'I'll return for a more detailed search when the room has been forensically examined. It stays locked until then. Now, before you show me that application form, Mrs Morley, can you tell me if Thorpe was alone when he arrived? And how did he arrive? Car? Bike? Taxi? Bus?'

'He arrived alone and it was a single booking. As he signed in though, he told me he'd come with a friend.'

'Did he say more about this friend?'

'Only that they'd driven down together. His friend wasn't on the course, he dropped Mr Thorpe off and drove away.'

'Where did he go? Any idea?'

'No, he didn't say.'

'Did you see what sort of a vehicle it was?'

'I'm afraid not. I didn't see it, but he said he'd been dropped right outside our entrance.'

'Had he much luggage?'

'Just a back-pack, one of those that hikers use.'

'It was standing on the floor of his coat hanging space,' nodded Napier. 'We'll have a good look at that later. OK, let's have a look at his handwriting.'

She led the way down to her office and found the file for the current course. She quickly found the application form bearing Thorpe's name. In the spaces for the name and address of the applicant were these details: James Thorpe, 31a, Trophy Road, Seaton, Sunderland, SR11 4XT written in hand with a combination of capital and small letters.

'You know this is a false name and address?' Napier put to her.

'Yes, one of your officers told me earlier when I showed this to him. So far as I know, this is the only form he used. I don't know why he would do that.'

'Did you know him as Mr Thorpe?'

'We all did. He told us to call him James.'

'How did he pay?'

'He paid in cash, Mr Napier. Ten and twenty pound notes. He said he had been saving up for years. He paid when he arrived and the bank accepted the notes. Here's the receipt from the bank, and we gave Mr Thorpe a receipt of his own. He seemed quite happy about it.'

'You don't ask for a booking fee in advance?'

'We've never felt the need. He enquired by phone and booked immediately.'

'It certainly looks as if he was determined to conceal his true identity. So why would he do that for a course of this kind?'

'I just don't know. He seemed such a pleasant little man, chatty and open, and keen to benefit from what we offer.'

At that point, I remembered that Harvey, the sculptor, also paid everything in cash ... could there be some kind of obscure link between them?

'That's something for us to work on,' said Napier. 'Now, let's compare this handwriting,' and he placed the strange note beside the application form. 'Quite different. I'd say there are no similarities between them. His writing here is strong and clear, whilst the mystery note's writing is smaller and more delicate.'

'I'd say they were not done by the same person,' I added.

'I don't think we need an expert calligrapher to tell us that, but we'll have them both expertly checked anyway. I'll need that original form, Mrs Morley – can you make a copy for your files and let me have the original?'

'Yes, of course.'

'We're checking his fingerprints and DNA but we'll also need to establish why he came here to look at old ruins. One other thing, Mrs Morley, has he attended any previous courses here? Or shown a special interest in the old legend?'

'Not to my knowledge. When I registered him, the name didn't ring any bells in my mind, nor did it do so when I ran a computer check. And I didn't recognize him when he arrived to book in. But he would only have to grow that beard and moustache to conceal his face ... but having seen that address, it's reminded me that he spoke with a north-eastern accent.'

'I'll get my teams to check him thoroughly. He might have a

criminal record with one of the north-eastern police forces. We'll send photos too. It's vital we get him identified.'

'Is there anything you think we've missed?' I asked Mrs Morley.

'There was one odd thing when he arrived,' she told us. 'The clothing he was wearing didn't look like hiking gear. He wore a jacket, clean plain shirt and smart trousers but later he changed into hiking gear.'

'We'll go through the clothes he's left behind,' said Napier. 'Now, Nick, is there anything you want to ask Mrs Morley – about that missing lad?'

'You know about Simon Houghton?' I put to her.

'Yes. We've had your monkstables here, but Simon never came, although we often get college boys attending our courses. But not him.'

'If you do remember anything about him, for any reason at all, can you let the cop shop know?'

'Yes, of course.'

As we returned to the main building Chief Superintendent Napier told me he was impressed with Mrs Morley's responses, adding that he wished other witnesses were so alert and clear in providing their evidence. He was impressed too that she had pondered over the mode of the man's arrival and agreed it was a very good question. Now it was time to search Simon's room in some detail.

We had no trouble locating John Saxby, his housemaster, who was marking papers in the teaching staff's common room. He suggested we go up to Simon's room straight away.

As we ascended the staircase, I asked whether Simon's room had been thoroughly searched for evidence – I knew it had been examined to see whether he was asleep in bed, or perhaps ill, but I mentioned personal papers and belongings.

'No, we didn't do that kind of detailed search,' confirmed Saxby. 'I just checked to see whether he was here.'

'I think we should search it, Mr Napier.'

'No time like the present,' he said. 'Who knows what we

might turn up – a link between Thorpe and young Houghton perhaps?'

'People often have secrets, as we know. Do we need to be careful where we put our feet? Or how we disturb things?'

'It's not too important, Simon's just a missing pupil, not a murder victim – or so we hope. But let's be careful how and what we search. Handwriting examples are what we need – and a look in his diary. That should settle both our interests.'

It did. When we looked in his daily desk diary we found an entry for Sunday and it said simply, 'Woods'. The handwriting was distinctly backward sloping and when we checked other entries it was always in that form in black ballpoint. It was evident he kept a detailed diary about his various appointments and lessons, even including trips to the dentist or barber and we found entries listing sightings of various birds especially the scarcer ones. One entry for March showed he had seen a buzzard hovering over the college fields, and another recorded seeing a nightjar in Ashwell Priory Woods.

'Is he left-handed?' Napier asked Mr Saxby.

'As a matter of fact he is.'

'Meticulously organized too, judging by his diary-keeping. And, you'll note, his spelling is not faulty.' He laid the police note beside the diary. 'This note was not written by him, that's obvious.'

'I agree,' I nodded, then added, 'There's one point that's just emerged from this. Where was he yesterday? According to his diary, he was in the woods. Which woods? And why? Because he's keen on ornithology? There are bird books on his bookshelf. Or did he meet someone for another reason? Has he a girlfriend for example? One of the maids? It's frowned upon for a pupil to socialize with the domestic staff, especially girls. If he was meeting a girl, he hasn't put it in his diary – probably because such a friendship needs to be kept secret. Unless she wasn't a member of staff? Like the work experience girl in the infirmary?'

'A secret liaison, then? Have any of the local woods been searched?' asked Napier. 'And who could she – or he – be?'

'I'll have to ask Prior Tuck to ask more questions around the college,' and I recalled that I was the owner of Ashwell Priory Wood that adjoined the estate. 'It may be significant that the bike he used was abandoned just across the road from Ashwell Priory Wood. Just the one bike; if he'd had a friend with him there could have been two.'

'Unless his friend met him there,' said Napier. 'If she was a member of the domestic staff, she might not have been working yesterday, being Sunday, so she could have travelled from home along this back lane to meet him at the barns. So are there any girls of his age on the staff?'

'I'm not sure, but there's definitely that one in the infirmary,' confirmed Saxby. 'A teenager on work experience. She's a very pleasant girl.'

'How would he get acquainted with her?' asked Napier.

'Fairly recently, Simon visited the infirmary for treatment to a badly cut hand. I'm not sure how he cut it but the dressings had to be changed regularly – or so he told me. I know he always returned with a happy smile on his face – and a freshly bandaged hand!'

'That information offers possibilities,' smiled Napier. 'You must pursue your monkstable enquiries there, Nick, and let me know the outcome.'

'There was that terrible storm yesterday,' Mr Saxby reminded us. 'Trees down, sheds blown apart, rivers flooded … I doubt if anyone would have ventured out in such conditions. It's probably cleared away a lot of ash trees with that die-back disease. We might have to rename Ashwell Woods….'

'The estate staff have searched them,' I reminded them. 'And we have no reports of a missing girl or any other pupil.'

Napier said, 'Well, whatever's happened, it's my belief that the area needs to be properly searched with police dogs. Remember, we are anxious to talk to Simon. He's definitely in the frame, so I'll call in the team. I'll see that their handler contacts Prior Tuck, and the monkstables can help in the search. I can leave this to the dogs and the monkstables while I deal with other matters. Thanks for all this, Mr Saxby, most helpful. Keep your eyes open for Simon's return. Meanwhile you'd better come with me, Nick.'

CHAPTER 10

BY THE TIME we returned to the murder room with its POLICE – NO ENTRY sign outside the door, it looked like a call-centre with its banks of screens, computers, filing cabinets, a large map of the campus and even a couple of blackboards bearing ever-changing details in white chalk. Most of the detectives, men and women, were out making enquiries whilst others were working at computers. I thought the combination of old and new was fascinating – clearly it was effective.

'Anything exciting, Brian?' DCS Napier asked DI Lindsey who stood beside his own computer as his boss entered.

'Not at this stage, sir.'

'Right, the dog section at HQ is sending a unit, they'll be here as soon as possible. I'll brief the handler when he or she gets here, so what's the current situation?'

'The teams are all out on their actions and we've already had some feedback. The initial computer check on fingerprints found on the bike has thrown up lots of unidentifiable prints but none with a criminal record. Those of the deceased are not among them. The checks need to be confirmed but they're usually reliable. However, I can confirm that some of Simon Houghton's print *are* there – they match those we found on a water glass in his room. The bike remains in our care until further notice.'

'What else is going on?'

'One team has gone for another talk to that archaeologist and his assistants, just to check their statements agree with what they told Nick and we've got two teams interviewing workers on the development site, concentrating on casual employees.'

'That'll involve a lot of work trying to get them to talk! They'll think we're tax inspectors!'

'Apart from that, there's not much else. We've not found that sculptor or his studio, and the crypt remains closed.'

'Keep trying. Is there anything new from the post-mortem?'

'Much of what we have been told confirms what we already thought: the victim died from a severe blow inflicted by a heavy blunt instrument to the back of his skull. Some cervical vertebrae at top of the spine have suffered a lot of damage and the skull is fragmented at that site – it's called the occipital area. It's estimated the victim was in his early fifties but wasn't very healthy. He had a persistent heart condition but it was unlikely to have killed him. The pathologist reckons he would have been aware of it and that he may have been receiving treatment. We've checked at local hospitals but no one knew the name of Thorpe.'

'I'm never sure about that sort of statement, Brian. Heart conditions can kill a lot of us sooner or later, often unexpectedly … but go on.'

'His body is clean and well nourished, and it's evident he looked after himself – neatly cut toenails and good natural teeth. He has a lot of brown hair, greying in places, and sports a Vandyke beard plus a moustache. His body bore no tattoos or other identifying marks or scars from old injuries; there were no operation scars either and no indications of broken bones. We didn't find any spectacles on or near his body. In all, a very ordinary sort of chap.'

'And the blow? Did the pathologist suggest any kind of weapon?'

'He used the old favourite "blunt instrument". That covers a host of possibilities, but the scale of the damage and the shape of the wound indicates something heavy but portable. He even suggested a sledgehammer, but settled for something smaller and easier to wield, such as a builder's hammer or a stone-mason's mallet. The wound suggests the weapon had a square-shaped head not more than two inches broad or wide – about five centimetres – but not a rounded one.'

'He's been very thorough,' I commented.

'He's reliable, Nick,' responded DI Lindsey. 'He takes care over his work. He has more to do on this one though. He says he'll examine the man's hair and beard to see whether they contain any debris that may provide evidence, and his clothing has been sent to the Lab to be examined. It could contain fibres from his killer's clothing or body. It will be a day or two before we get the full results. Neither the pathology team nor our SOCO found anything in his pockets. It's odd that he wasn't carrying anything, not even a handkerchief.'

'Did his killer empty the pockets?'

'It seems so. It would have been done to conceal his victim's identity.'

'He's already done that for himself by providing a false name and address,' I pointed out.

'Even so, I doubt if he would have left his room with nothing in his pockets – no cash, no handkerchief, no notebook or pen, no key to his room … they must be somewhere. We need to find them – but that's our problem although your monkstables might keep their eyes and ears open, Nick? Such things could be hidden anywhere, probably somewhere on campus.'

'Point taken. I'll let you know if we find them,' I acknowledged.

I realized that if his handkerchief and other possessions were missing, it suggested a carefully planned premeditated killing, not a sudden confrontation. However, a person who kills suddenly or expectedly will generally rush away from the scene before the deed is discovered. This killer appeared to be a very calm and deliberate operator – he'd even placed his victim in a coffin! And sent a note.

'A body without any means of identification – other than fingerprints and DNA – always gives our teams something to work on, they welcome a challenge. Now, do we know where we can find Prior Tuck?' asked Napier.

'I can call him,' suggested DI Lindsey.

'Do that, Brian. I want to talk about extending the search for that boy because it might assist our enquiries, but I need to know exactly what has already been done. And, Nick, don't forget to interview the work experience girl.'

'The last thing I heard – about half an hour ago,' said DI Lindsey, 'was that Prior Tuck was concentrating on hidden areas around the Abbey Church but also beneath the older buildings that are still in use, like the crypt. There's a maze of underground passages under the Abbey Church and monastery, even some tunnelling inside very thick old walls. Our ancestors loved secret passages.'

'There are the lofts too,' I added. 'When I was the village bobby at Aidensfield, a boy went missing for hours here at the college and was found stuck in a gap in a loft wall that separated two parts of a building, but he was quite a tubby individual! Boys do go exploring old passages so they need to be searched professionally. Luckily some of our monkstables are former pupils and know all the hiding places.'

'The prior's on his way here now, boss,' announced DI Lindsey.

'Good.'

While DCS Napier went into his own office, I wandered around the murder room as we awaited the prior. I was amazed at the wealth of detail that had already been acquired and displayed on boards and maps. It included everything from the telephone number of the force control room to opening times of the fish-and-chip shop in Ashfordly.

There was a recent aerial photograph of the grounds and from it they had produced an enlarged copy which now showed the names of the builders operating at the new development along with their phone numbers, and those of their site offices. The presence of the archaeology team was included, with their leader's known personal details, and even the monkstables were listed with their official shoulder numbers and names. I was listed there too. There was a colour photograph of the murder victim in his stone coffin with details of his false name and address. His head wound was also indicated by arrows and his height – 5' 6" (c.165cm) – was shown too, with due emphasis on the lack of personal possessions. *Where are his belongings*? That question was written beside his image to remind all the detectives to consider it as they conducted their enquiries. A search had been made of the campus waste bins, but nothing had been found.

All this was vital groundwork; I had witnessed this kind of rapid but accurate response during murder inquiries upon which I had worked when a serving police officer and was constantly amazed at how the CID managed to acquire such detail in so short a time. But this was the key to a successful investigation.

Brian Lindsey announced the dog team was on its way; it had been attending the scene of a burglary at Malton and would be here within half-an-hour or so. Then the outer door burst open and a huge man appeared. He was framed in the doorway like something from a Gothic novel. DI Lindsey leapt from his seat to confront the visitor who was dressed all in black. He had a mop of unruly jet-black hair, a beard and moustache, and a large presence that demanded immediate attention and respect.

'This is private—' began DI Lindsey.

'And I am a very busy man. I have been locked out of my work area. I demand to be admitted. I must continue my work.'

Brian Lindsey did not immediately realize it was Harvey, the sculptor.

'What's your work?' he asked.

'My work? I'm a sculptor. I've been commissioned to produce an important work for this abbey. I've a deadline to meet and now I'm locked out—'

'Ah, so you're Harvey?'

'I am, so who are you? And what are the police doing

keeping me away from my work? I asked at the cop shop and they told me to come here.'

'I'm Detective Inspector Lindsey and this is a police incident room, Mr Harvey. There is no admittance to unauthorized persons, there is a notice outside.'

'So how do I get answers if I'm not allowed in? The monk in the Cop Shop was tight-lipped so I came here like he said. I'm not here to cause trouble, all I want is a simple answer: why am I locked out of the crypt? I don't occupy much space...just a corner near the Lady Chapel.'

'Mr Harvey, I don't think you're aware of what's happened. We've a murder investigation underway in the crypt. We've had to secure it until all scientific investigations have been completed.'

'A murder? In there? It's got nothing to do with me and I want nothing to do with it, so I ask again, how long is the crypt likely to remain closed?'

'I don't know. No one knows at this stage. It will be reopened when we are sure it has been thoroughly examined.' At that comment, Harvey banged his fist on a table just inside the doorway. The noise was amplified by the theatre's acoustics and it caused DCS Napier to rush out of his room to see what had caused the commotion.

'What's going on? Who the hell are you?' he demanded. His size and presence clearly impressed Harvey who halted momentarily, staring at the giant detective, before grinning widely.

'Well, knock me down with a feather!' shouted Harvey. 'It's Nabber Napier!'

Napier halted before the sculptor and stared at him for a few seconds before saying, 'Well I'll be damned! R.V. Carver in person ... who let you out of the cage?'

All the detectives stopped work to observe this interesting exchange. It seemed there were some old rivalries here – and both men were about the same size and of a similarly powerful appearance.

'I've been going straight, Nabber. For years and years. Did my time and learned my artistic skills when I was inside, now I'm out and doing good work. Earning an honest living … creating a life … so you did me a favour, nabbing me for doing-over that rapist who thoroughly deserved the thrashing I gave him—'

'I arrested you for causing grievous bodily harm, RV, because that's what you did. You can't take the law into your own hands, no matter what. Self-defence is permitted in some circumstances and so is the use of reasonable force to prevent crimes, but you went over the top!'

'I was just defending a girl, rescuing her—'

'The way you did so was far from reasonable. I've told you this before! It was a brutal attack, a serious rape, but you attacked someone who was not attacking you….'

'It was a villain who was raping a twelve-year-old girl. He deserved everything he got and I have no regrets even though you had me sent down for five years….'

'The court sent you down, not me.'

'It's all over now, Nabber, let's forget it. I've forgiven you as you were only doing your job. I'm man enough to admit that so tell me about this murder. Am I allowed to know?'

'Come in and sit down, RV, we need to talk.'

'You're not going to nab me for something, are you?'

'I sincerely hope I don't have to. Now, let's sit down – I want our discussion to be heard by everyone here then you will know you've been treated fairly and that you will not be falsely accused of anything. And neither shall I.'

'I'm not sure I like this….'

'Just sit over there, RV, and listen. Gather round everyone. I have known this man for many years, ever since he was a troublesome young tearaway in North Shields and I was a young copper. Am I right in thinking you've done time more than once, RV? Remember I can check your CRO record.'

I could now see how RV had became known as Harvey but wondered what his real name was. I wondered if Napier knew

– he had called him Carver. Was that a pseudonym for his sculpting work? Or was it his real name?

And how much did Napier know about him?

'I've been clean for a long time, Nabber. Twenty years or more, working hard and earning good money. I'm my own boss now, I do as I like and I keep out of trouble. I am making a success of my life and not every juvenile nitwit like I was can boast that.'

'Where are you living?'

'That's not for public consumption, Nabber. My private details will remain private.'

'And am I right in thinking you have a studio somewhere near?'

'I've found a place I can use without people bothering me, but it's only temporary. It's not my home but it is also a secret. So what's all this about? Are you serious when you say there's been a murder? Like I said, I've not done anything wrong, dodgy or illegal so I'm not responsible for it. Why should I answer your questions?'

'You were working on your sculpture this morning, were you? In the crypt?'

'Doing a little, yes. Working on the rough, not the actual image. That comes later.'

'What time did you arrive?'

'Look, I keep asking whether I have to answer these questions. I haven't done anything wrong.'

'Then there's no reason to avoid my questions, is there?'

'Here we go again, a police interrogation when I don't know what the hell you're talking about. This is like Kafka's trial! I repeat – why should I answer your questions? You don't think I've killed someone, do you?'

'I don't think anything. I'm trying to find out. I'll tell you once more: if you've done nothing wrong, you've nothing to fear. When I'm satisfied you may go.'

'I'm not answering because you have not explained clearly. Do you suspect me? Do you think I'm guilty of murder?'

'Listen carefully, RV. A man's body was found in the crypt this morning and it's a suspicious death. We are trying to establish what happened.'

'You *do* think I'm responsible, don't you? How did I manage to walk into this one?'

'Just answer my questions. Did you visit the crypt on either Saturday or Sunday?'

'No, I keep away at weekends, it's too busy with visitors.'

'What time did you arrive at the crypt today?'

'Early, half-six perhaps, maybe a few minutes earlier. I wanted to get some work done before people started coming in. They notice me and then stand over me and ask daft questions as I'm trying to work. I can't cope with it. I don't like being crowded....'

'I know that from the past, RV. You've bolted from me a few times. How did you get into the crypt? Have you a key?'

'No. The monks open up early, five o'clock I've heard. I'm never there that early to see. But the place was open when I got there.'

'What time did you leave?'

'Dunno, seven mebbe. Then I went to my studio but came back to look for a mallet I've mislaid. I got back here about half-past seven then stayed awhile to look for it but couldn't find it. So I thought I'd finish off some other minor stuff while I was here.'

'Which door did you use to enter the crypt? Each time?'

'The south door. Both times. Why?'

'That door is the closest to your work area, I believe? You have your roughs nearby, along with a bench full of tools?'

'I don't like the drift of this....'

'They are your tools, are they? On that work bench?'

'Of course they're mine! Nobody else is sculpting in there.'

'You've also got a cupboard where you keep some tools. In the crypt.'

'Yes, I'm a sculptor, sculptors need tools. I need my tools to be available when I want to use them, just like a car mechanic or a plumber needs tools, or even a surgeon. I know where they are and can put my hand on the one I want even in the dark.'

'You're very trusting, leaving them lying around like that.'

'They're no good to anyone else. I've never lost one – until now. My mallet's gone missing, I use it for carving with stone chisels.'

'And is a stone-mason's mallet part of your normal tool set?'

'It is. It wasn't on my bench in the crypt this morning where I'm sure I left it, so I searched the whole area around the chapel without finding it. Then I went back to my studio to search there in case I'd forgotten where I'd put it – but it wasn't there either. So I came back because I thought it must still be here in the crypt.'

'You keep a set of tools in both places? Here, and in your studio?'

'Yes, I can't be bothered moving all my tools several times a day so I have a complete set in both places where I work. It makes life easier.'

'But only one stone-mason's mallet?'

'I don't do much carving in stone, it's mainly oak now. I don't need two mallets. My roughs are in clay, and I have wood carving tools here.'

'So why did you need your mallet this morning?'

'If you look in the chapel you'd see the estate workers have created a space in the depths of the wall to accommodate my work. When I did some test fittings last week I found the area was a fraction too small for one of the triptych pieces. It was necessary for a tiny bit of stone to be trimmed off around the edge, the left-hand side, so I brought my mallet and a stone chisel down from my studio and did the work.'

'When was that?'

'Last Friday I guess. I got it right, a nice tight fitting.'

'So you came early this morning to look for your stone-mason's mallet after using it on Friday?'

'That's what I said.'

'But you didn't come looking for the mallet over the weekend?'

'No, I've just told you that!'

'So did you search for your mallet as soon as you arrived today?'

'Yes, I looked on my bench and around the chapel. It wasn't a very detailed search, more of a scan.'

'So where exactly did you search?'

'Just the area around where I work, I don't go anywhere else, so my mallet couldn't have got much further than my working area. But it wasn't there and I found that very odd.'

'Then you returned to your studio, searched there without result and returned to make another search?'

'Right.'

'So tell me again, RV, what time did you leave here this morning?'

'After my first visit?'

'Yes.'

'Like I said, about seven. I didn't find the mallet so I went back to my studio to check there, then I came back here and searched again ... still no luck. I returned to my studio, had something for breakfast – cereals – and did another search without finding it so I came back here just now to try again. Now I can't get into the place. I'm locked out.'

'When was the previous time you visited the crypt? Apart from this morning?'

'Friday. There are services in the crypt from time to time, mainly at weekends, so I try to keep away when they're on, but Friday was reasonably quiet.'

'How long were you in the crypt on Friday?'

'Not long. Mebbe from half past nine in the morning to midday, something like that.'

'Did anyone see you there?'

'People come and go all the time, I get students sometimes, art students wanting advice. I had a young lad in on Friday, he's been a few times to see my Virgin Mary; he says he loves her face. Nice lad, interested in what I do. A college boy. Teenager, tall with dark hair. Wears specs. I don't object to kids like that. It's a genuine interest so I don't mind explaining things to kids like that.'

'Do you know his name?'

'No, I've no idea.'

'And was that the last time you saw your mallet here in the crypt?'

'Yes, it would be. I didn't miss it until this morning. I don't think that lad would have taken it, would he?'

'Who knows? Is the head made from wood?'

'No, it's iron, a solid chunk of iron, shaped into a mallet-head. It's small enough to be used with one hand but very heavy, ideal for my purpose whether I'm carving wood or stone. Working with a stone chisel needs a delicate touch if it's to be accurate.'

'And which way did you exit the crypt on Friday?'

'Up the stairs into reception. I go out that way so I can let them know when I've left.'

'And you did not take your mallet with you on Friday?'

'No, I intended to, but forgot.'

'So it was lying in the crypt all weekend, not locked up and an easy target for a thief. You of all people should know you can't trust all the people all the time.'

'I've always left my tools on the work bench and nothing's ever been taken. After all, this is a monastery, you don't expect thieves here.'

'That's very trusting of you, RV.'

'I'm a trusting sort of chap, Nabber. I'm trusting you now, I know you will not be dishonest with me. Not here in a monastery, surely?'

'I have no intention or wish to be dishonest, RV, so now tell me this. When you hunted for your mallet in the crypt this morning, how far did you extend your search?'

'I concentrated on the area where I work, my bench and so on. The light's not very good so sometimes I bring my own. I had a torch this morning, to get into the dark corners as well as under my bench.'

'Did you search the entire place? It's quite large, with all those nooks and chapels....'

'As I told you, I didn't search it all, simply because I would never have carried it there or put it down without thinking. I thought it might have fallen off my work bench or I might have put it somewhere near and forgotten where it was. But I didn't find it. A sculptor's tools are his friends, very important and personal. Barbara Hepworth said that.'

'I'll ask you again, Harvey. Did you search the entire crypt?'

'Only in a very cursory way. I put the lights on and swept all the likely places with my torch, nothing more than that. I didn't find it. So I went back to my studio – and it's not there either. I've told you all this....'

'And you don't think that boy took it?'

'No, I'm sure he didn't.'

'Did you look behind a big black curtain that hangs towards the north of the crypt?'

'No, I thought about it, but while I was here, some people came in and went over to the curtain – they were hard to see, the light's poor and I thought they were monks. I looked behind it some months ago when I first started work here but there was nothing but a stone coffin on a plinth. All carved from one piece of granite ... amazing! How long did it take to do that? I wondered if I could have carved such a thing. One of the monks once told me some time ago that there was a tale that the coffin should never be moved so it was curtained off, but there was no prohibition about entering the place where it is kept. Let's face it, no one could move it without some kind of powerful lifting gear or a tractor. It'll never be nicked by a tourist!'

'Did you look behind the curtain this morning?'

'No, maybe I should have done, but I hadn't been in there recently, so I knew I hadn't left my mallet in there. Unless somebody took it because they fancied chipping a chunk of stone off the coffin ... that never occurred to me then....'

'You said some people came in and went over to the curtain? What time was that?'

'Eight o'clock or thereabouts. Just after mebbe. One was a monk, the prior in fact, and the other was that gentleman over there,' and he pointed to me.

'Right, that's true,' smiled Napier. 'Now, did you see anyone else in the crypt this morning?'

'No, not a soul. Look, what's all this about? Quizzing me like this....'

'RV, listen, I can tell you why they looked behind that curtain. There was a man's body in the coffin and he died from head injuries inflicted by a blunt instrument which the pathologist reckons might be a mallet of some kind.'

RV said nothing. He stared at Napier in deadly silence, his brow furrowing as his dark eyes never left Napier's face.

'You're not suggesting I'm responsible, are you?'

'You'll have to tell me where you were between Friday afternoon when you left and six thirty or so this morning when you first returned to the crypt. A pupil of the college is missing too – he was last seen on Sunday morning. His description fits that of the lad you have just described. You can see why I'm interested....'

'God Almighty, Napper, you don't think I'm responsible, do you? A murder and a missing lad?'

'Then convince me of your innocence. That story about the mallet might be a figment of your vivid imagination. You might have thrown it away—'

But, acting like lightning, the big man rose to his feet, picked up his chair and hurled it at Napier before bolting out of the door and racing down an adjoining alley into some dense trees. It was all over in a matter of seconds. Several police officers gave chase with some tripping over the chair, then reached the doorway at the same time and got jammed, albeit only momentarily. But those precious few moments of disorder as they extricated themselves were enough for RV to run free. Within moments he had vanished into the dark shadows of the dense woodland that cloaked the hillside immediately behind the abbey.

CHAPTER 11

DETECTIVES WORKING AT their desks and computers rushed to the doorway but succeeded only in adding to the confusion. In those few moments while the officers extricated themselves, Harvey had disappeared into the shadows of the woodlands whose branches, in full leaf, brushed the rear of the building. His black clothing enabled him to speedily vanish deep into the shadows. And there was no sound of him crashing through the wood; he knew the value of stealth.

'Get him!' bellowed Napier who was outside. 'I want that man … he must be caught. Don't just stand there like a lot of Charlies!'

'Sir, he'll be lost among those trees,' pointed out DI Lindsey as three detectives gave chase. 'If we follow him he'll hear us and keep his distance. He could be anywhere in that woodland. We'd be wasting our time.'

'We can't just let him go!' snapped Napier. 'Get more coppers on his tail!'

'The dog section will be here soon,' I reminded them. 'It should be possible for them to follow his trail wherever he's gone.'

'We need the dogs to find that missing lad.' Napier's voice had dropped into almost a whisper. 'That man's escape should never have happened … heads will roll! So, where is everybody else? You can never find a copper when you want one!'

'They're out working on their actions.' Lindsey was calm and I think it was his peaceful attitude that allowed Napier to calm down a little as he began to take a measured response to his dilemma. Lindsey continued, 'He hasn't escaped, has he, sir? He wasn't a prisoner; he wasn't violent—'

'He's done a runner, Brian, which says everything! I know him of old,' he snapped back. 'We've got to find him.'

'Did you intend arresting him, Mr Napier?' I asked.

'He was pushing me strongly towards it,' he admitted. 'I was very seriously considering arresting him on suspicion of murder.'

'We'll find him,' DI Lindsey said quietly. 'It's obvious his studio is fairly close, so we'll find him. I don't think it's sensible to swamp those woods with police officers and dogs; their presence will simply drive him deeper under cover. He'll hear us crashing through the undergrowth and he knows where to hide. Let's leave it to those on his tail, and the dogs. His track will be fresh enough.'

'And he does have a white van,' I pointed out. 'He could have reached it by now and be well away from here. Its number is in the monkstables' records.'

'All right, Nick. Circulate that number but get a search organized – I still need to talk to him. As Brian says, he wasn't under arrest so we can't treat him as an escaped prisoner.'

'But we can say we believe he can help us with our inquiries!'

Napier, now much calmer, turned to his detective inspector. 'Recall the teams from their actions, get them to assemble here in, say, half-an-hour, provided they're not in the middle of something that they can't leave. I'll brief them about him then they should all take an early lunch. But it's vital we talk to Harvey. You say the monkstables have details of his van, Nick?'

'Yes. Brother George had the registration number and we traced it to a garage in Leeds, and then linked RV to a Salvation Army hostel in Hull. They say they don't know him.'

'Well done that Brother George! Give the number to Brian Lindsey, tell him what you know and we'll put out an alert for

RV and his van. God, that was an awful moment. No copper likes a prisoner to escape.'

'He wasn't a prisoner, sir,' Lindsey reminded him gently.

'He would have been if I'd quizzed him just a little longer. He has to be a prime suspect, Brian – we've placed him at the scene and he's admitted he's disposed of what could be the murder weapon. Do we honestly believe he's lost it? Thrown it away more than likely. What more evidence do we need? You saw him blow his top; that shouts of an inability to control himself. Now we must ask what he knows about the disappearance of Simon Houghton. Are we talking of a kidnapping? Followed by a ransom demand? We've got to consider all that. The man's a villain. Remember, I know what he's capable of doing.'

'We also need a motive,' I suggested. 'We haven't established a link between Simon and the murder victim, have we, apart from the timing of these events? The question of timing is important – do Harvey's movements in and out of the crypt coincide with what we know about the victim's presence there and his time of death, not forgetting the disappearance of Simon Houghton? We know that he also visited the crypt on occasions. He liked the Virgin Mary's face!'

'The timings are all pretty damned close, Nick, we need to analyse them in detail.'

'Is there any evidence that Harvey has been behind the curtain?'

'No evidence, but he must have searched behind it if he was genuinely looking for his mallet! Could he be lying about that? If so, why? If he did go back there he must have seen the body. Can we believe he didn't look behind the curtain or into the coffin? I think he's lying. And another thing, Nick, we need to check his handwriting against that note.'

'So you've lots of new actions awaiting your detectives, Mr Napier. I'll get out of your way and update Prior Tuck and the monkstables.'

'Any help will be appreciated!'

'If they're still seeking Simon in the grounds and buildings, they might have seen Harvey galloping away or noticed his van on the move. And I want to revisit the old barns to see if we can pick up Simon's trail from there.'

Napier sighed heavily. 'You'll need the dogs for that, a missing pupil is more important that a witness absconding during questioning. We'll find Harvey, so I'll direct the dog unit to you. Where will you be?'

'I'm going to update Father Will and then I want to find Prior Tuck so I'll return to the Postgate Conference Room. Prior Tuck might be there and the constables' searches should be complete by now. But we must extend our enquiries – quite simply, we need to know where Simon went after leaving that bike in the barns.'

'OK, Nick, keep asking! And keep in touch,' and Napier turned abruptly on his heel and returned to the murder room as his subdued staff followed him inside.

After briefing Father Will, he told me that Prior Tuck had recalled his monkstables and volunteer searchers and would now be addressing them in the incident room. I hurried along and entered just as Prior Tuck hammered on his desk and called for silence.

'Ah, Nick, just in time. Find a seat and you'll see what we are doing.' He turned to address his audience, who I realized, included staff from both the College and the Abbey, including the abbot and headmaster. 'Thank you all for your efforts in the search for Simon. Now it's time to pool our knowledge. I'm going to start with our monk-constables. Father Bowman?'

One by one the eight officers gave their detailed reports as a co-opted secretary recorded their reports on a Dictaphone and also highlighted their areas of search on the whiteboard. It was invaluable as a visible display and, as the meeting progressed, it showed that every part of the abbey had been searched twice by different teams, but with no positive result. Local bus companies and taxi operators had been contacted but none had reported seeing anyone matching Simon's description at the material times. Staff members and even the contractors had been interviewed with no sightings. Prior Tuck now addressed me.

'Nick, have you any comments at this stage?'

I referred briefly to Harvey's flight, adding the CID were continuing inquiries into the murder and were interested in any information we discovered.

'There are lines of enquiry to pursue,' I suggested. 'One involves people who should have been on the premises today or yesterday and who have not turned up. We must include the contractors and employees working on the construction sites, staff members, whether permanent or part-time, domestic staff and freelancers who would normally have been here today or Sunday. They need to be cleared of any involvement. That's something we could do to help the murder inquiry whilst continuing our search for Simon.'

'That's not going to be easy,' offered the headmaster who was sitting quietly in the back row. 'We have hundreds of people on campus every day and that includes visitors whom we don't know.'

'We must do our best and not be afraid to ask questions, and ask again if we are not satisfied.' I was adamant. 'If anyone is known to be absent, we want to know why and where they were. Anyone without a feasible explanation must be questioned in depth, more than once if necessary. And if we are still not satisfied with their answers or feel they are evasive, then we must inform Detective Inspector Lindsey in the murder room. His officers will then question them. And don't be afraid to ask Brother George if you need the registration numbers of any vehicles seen on the sites.'

'Some construction workers wouldn't be operating yesterday, being Sunday,' pointed out Prior Tuck.

'Thanks, Father Prior. We'll bear that in mind. So what about domestic workers? Teaching staff? Clerical workers, estate workers?' I asked. 'And I've heard that Simon might have been secretly seeing a girl who works in the infirmary – a schoolgirl on work experience. Technically, I suppose she's not a member of staff and so he's not breaking any school rules. I don't have her name yet but we need to find her and ask what she knows.'

'Some domestic staff are required to work on Sundays – pupils are here around the clock. The personnel department is checking all records and we will locate and interview that girl. So far as casual workers on the site are concerned, timesheets will tell us a lot. After this meeting, I will allocate actions to each of the constables. It shouldn't be too difficult or time-consuming to carry out staff checks but I fear the tracing of casual visitors won't be easy – unless Brother George produces more car registrations from his vast collection!'

'So what do you suggest next, Nick?' asked the headmaster.

'Before I make my suggestions, there is one matter than needs attention,' I pointed out. 'Has Simon's mother been informed?'

'Not yet.' He shook his head. 'It's early days. We're hoping to find him. We don't want to cause undue concern if he is unharmed and likely to turn up.'

'It's a difficult decision but it might be no more than a pupil dodging lessons,' I admitted. 'I have no idea whether she is the sort of woman to make a fuss, or to allow us to take things more quietly.'

'I'm sure she knows not to risk any adverse publicity about Simon,' the abbot now entered the discussion without revealing the reason for his statement. 'However, she can be very determined – and she has a great deal of responsibility for ensuring the safety of her child.'

'So have we,' muttered Father Bede, the headmaster.

Because this search was steadily becoming inextricably linked to the murder investigation, I decided to help the chief superintendent's officers by adding, 'There is something the monkstables can do to help both inquiries to move forward. I suggest the officers extend their searches to nearby villages.

Teams comprising of two each should visit Maddleskirk village, Elsinby and Aidensfield and, if necessary, place posters on notice-boards. They should make enquiries in shops, post offices, pubs and places of public resort. We need to get the villagers talking about Simon and persuade them to contact us if they've noticed anything unusual. At the same time, we could ask whether anyone has noticed a boy and girl together. And we could provide a description of the murder victim in case anyone has seen him. We should provide the phone number of the cop shop too. Do you agree, Prior Tuck?'

'A good idea, Nick,' he replied. 'I'll make the arrangements and will organize transport. They're all small communities so shall we say a couple of hours in each village? Then back here to give a full report?'

'Thanks, Father Prior, that's great. Now,' I went on, 'there is another slight problem. If Simon returns of his own accord when we have all dispersed, how will we know? He could creep back unnoticed and lock himself in his room.'

John Saxby, Simon's housemaster spoke up. 'I'm making a point of visiting his room every half-hour. If he returns, that's where he'll go. I've left a very large handwritten note on his bed ordering him to report to me the moment he returns. Clearly if that happens, I'll inform you immediately.'

'Do you know Simon very well?' I put to him. 'Is there anything we've missed?'

'He spends a lot of time on his own,' John Saxby reminded me. 'It is not unusual for him to go out alone on a Sunday. He enjoys spotting birds and exploring the countryside. Some think he's a twitcher, but he's not *that* keen. He knows a lot about wild birds without being manic about them. He enjoys the out-doors walking the moors or exploring rivers. He's not a swot or book-worm, he likes the outdoor life. He's a really nice, decent lad, Nick, and to disappear like this, without a word to me or anyone else, is out of character. It worries me deeply.'

'The role of that young girl in the infirmary is becoming very important,' observed Prior Tuck. 'One of us must speak to her. I think I know the girl you mean. I'll arrange an interview.'

'Thanks,' I said, turning to John Saxby. 'So, John, can I ask what your worst thoughts were when you learned of his disappearance?'

'Kidnap. It happens overseas, children and indeed adults are kidnapped for ransom, and it can happen here. Most of our students are from rich or important families. I've been expecting a ransom demand.'

'There's still time.'

'I know, which is why we mustn't give up our search. He can't have vanished into thin air so let's hope our abbey constables can trace him. But there is something, Nick, which may or may not be important. When I searched his room, I noticed a couple of batteries in his wastepaper bin. Torch batteries.'

'Used ones, you think?'

'I think so.'

'Which means he intended using a torch during his outing yesterday?'

'Just what I thought. I couldn't find a torch in his room so thought he expected to be out late or in an area where he might need light during daytime hours.'

'You mean he might go underground?'

'It's a thought.'

'Have you somewhere in mind apart from under the abbey and college?'

'We've checked those. Could it be a local cave perhaps? Seeking bats? An old building. Some kind of underground chamber? Like those beneath this abbey, not forgetting the ruins of Ashwell Priory....'

'Ashwell Priory?' I asked, wondering if the girl was with him.

Before I could question him about the old priory which was now my property, Prior Tuck said his monkstables were ready to be given guidance about their duties in the surrounding villages. We needed to get them on their way without further delay.

'Let's concentrate on the villages just now. There's not a lot to add to what I said earlier,' I told them. 'If anyone asks what you are doing, explain it's a training exercise for the abbey's new police officers. It's a case of saturating the villages with news that Simon has disappeared – tell them Simon could be hiding somewhere, perhaps with a girl, in their village. Provide a description of both, display them in shops, pubs, church and parish notice boards, the post office and so on. Get people talking. And don't forget to add a description of the man in the coffin – without telling them he's been murdered – we're seeking him too. We're not issuing photos as we don't want the youngsters to be recognized and the girl must remain anonymous, Simon too. By all means call him Simon – but omit his surname. Even after you've left, people will discuss it and we might elicit something useful.'

I paused for a moment to allow them to absorb this information, then concluded by adding, 'Make sure to leave a contact number. And tomorrow, if he doesn't turn up, repeat the procedure. If and when he is found, remember to inform those villagers. Now, any questions?'

'And if we do find him, what then?' asked Father Gilbert White, known to all as the White Friar.

'Bring him back with you.'

'And if he doesn't want to come?'

'Arrest him on suspicion of stealing the bike in the old barns.'

'Oh, crumbs!'

'That might be enough to change his mind. We need to talk to him, to know what's behind his odd behaviour, where he's been and who with.'

After a few comments and questions, the officers boarded the waiting mini-bus that would deliver them to their locations and collect them later. Then Brother George approached me.

'Nick, can I make a suggestion?'

'Of course, that's what we want. Ideas.'

'The one man who knows the tunnels, corridors, lofts and

hiding places in this complex better than anyone is Father Will Stutely. He's been staffing the desk in the cop shop but I think he could be more usefully employed showing the searchers around the hidden parts of the campus. He was a pupil here. I could staff the desk while he does that.'

'Right, let's do it,' I said without hesitation, then added, 'I'll contact Father Prior and suggest those monkstables not engaged in the village searches meet in the conference room in, say, twenty minutes? That gives them time for a quick break for lunch. Then we can arrange yet another thorough search under the guidance of Father Will.'

As I returned to the Postgate Room, I wondered if Harvey was also making use of underground tunnels, corridors and other hiding places. It would be most gratifying if we found him too.

CHAPTER 12

WHEN FATHER PRIOR and his remaining officers reassembled in the Postgate Room, I saw that the abbot and the headmaster had joined them.

'You've something to tell us, Nick?' asked Prior Tuck who, as the man in charge of the monkstables, was responsible for the next stage of our search.

'Yes, it's important. There is yet another hunt in progress around us – it's linked to the murder investigation and concerns Harvey, the sculptor, a large black-clad man you might have noticed at work in the crypt. He's fled, so there's now a search for him.'

I told them about Harvey running from the murder room. 'He could be hiding somewhere on the premises or nearby. Keep a watchful eye open, he's easily recognizable. Report any sightings to the murder room.'

Father Robin asked, 'Is he a suspect?'

'I can't say.' I tried to be honest. 'All I can tell you is that he was being questioned by Detective Chief Superintendent Napier when he bolted before anyone could stop him. He ran into those woods on the north of the campus – he could still be hiding there or have got away somewhere else by now. I believe you all know about his white van? If you see him or his van, don't approach him, he could be dangerous, but let the murder team know as soon as possible.'

They all agreed to do whatever was necessary to deal with this unexpected development. At this stage, I felt it was time for me to back away from the operational aspects and sit on the sidelines as an observer, or perhaps a consultant if needed. After all, Prior Tuck, not me, was in charge, but he said, 'Before I allocate this afternoon's duties, Nick has news of another development.'

'Thanks. I've been told that Father Will can offer suggestions for extending and perhaps concentrating our searches. By the way, a team of police dogs will be *en route*, when they've dealt with another matter. We shall use them to search for Simon, although the murder teams are anxious to deploy them too – especially in their hunt for Harvey.'

Father Will rose to his feet. 'Thanks, Nick. As some of you know, I used to be a pupil here and I quickly learned it was part of one's education at Maddleskirk to find secret places no one else knew about. I am referring especially to any of the monks or teaching staff not knowing about them! Let me give examples.'

He moved towards the whiteboard and pointed. 'Consider the clock tower, nineteenth century with a Norman base below ground level. It's accessible from the school library cellar via a maze of passages. Even if you could find a way through, they're too narrow for an adult to use. Men of former times were smaller than modern people – even a medium-sized boy could get stuck. There's said to be a complex code that can guide you through, if you can decipher it. I've never found it.'

From the map I realized they could lead to the cellar below the crypt but he moved steadily through the diagram to highlight further hidden doors, cellars, steps and tunnels. I was surprised there were so many of them still on record.

'One channel emerges into the monks' choir in the church,' he told us. 'From the choir stalls, the entrance looks nothing more than a flat heavy stone but from beneath it can be pushed upwards and to one side if you are strong enough, to lead into the choir. Catholic priests of medieval times were pretty good at creating hiding places. There are not many in the modern parts of the abbey but old sections do contain hiding places and they're the ones that need to be searched – urgently. They were overlooked during our initial searches, not out of carelessness but simply because few know they exist. I'll be pleased to guide anyone. And, of course, if anyone knows of any others, you must let me know.'

There were murmurs of agreement – certainly the first searches had been rather superficial, being based on the theory that Simon might have fallen asleep or have discovered somewhere quiet from where to watch the birds. Possibilities that he was either ill, or had been trapped somewhere, had not been diligently considered.

'We can work from this plan on the wall. I will indicate some of the places that need to be especially examined. I am sure you know the way around the main centres of the campus. Ask if you have problems.'

'Fine,' agreed Prior Tuck.

Father Will continued, 'There is one other place that needs this kind of attention and it is not part of this campus and therefore not shown on this plan. I am speaking of the ruins of Ashwell Priory and its woodland. I know it has been searched already by the estate workers and staff, but because we haven't found Simon, I think we need to try again. I will deal with that proposal in a moment.'

Then he highlighted with bright orange ink the sections of the college and abbey to which he referred. As Prior Tuck watched, he named a monkstable who would investigate each part and report back within the hour. One of them would also be detailed to visit the infirmary to talk to the schoolgirl and all were warned again not to place themselves in danger if they confronted Harvey. If there was any indication that Simon was ill or had been trapped or injured in such a secretive place, the alert must be raised and official rescue plans implemented immediately. He instructed them not to attempt any search alone in dangerous places – if deep and dangerous holes or tunnels were to be explored, it must be done with lights, ropes and teamwork.

'Now,' continued Father Will, as he turned to face Father Mutch, 'Father Matthias Miller? I believe you have caving experience?'

'It was a long time ago, but yes, you're right. Please ask me if you think I can help in any specific case.'

'Thank you, but I have a special task for you.'

Father Mutch, as Father Miller was known, bore shoulder number 16 and was a former champion weightlifter. Before becoming a monk, he had once, with his teeth, hauled a double-decker bus for a hundred yards. Now in his mid-forties he had settled down as a monk, was a capable chef, a very good baritone and his hobby, since retirement from exploring or mapping caves, was reading detective novels. One of his oft-recounted successes since becoming a monk was to rescue a motor cyclist who had crashed into a deep ditch with the machine crashing down upon him and pinning him down. Father Mutch happened to be passing, saw the incident and with his bare hands and sheer strength hoisted the machine off the injured man and then carried him to safety.

We all waited as Father Stutely moved onto his final suggestion – the task for Father Mutch. He pointed once more to the plan on the wall, but now indicating the road that led from Elsinby to the rear entrance of the campus. It was, in effect, the southern boundary of the entire estate but the road was rarely used, except by local people. It was more of a lane than a road although it had a sound tarmac surface – in fact, local people called it Back Lane. At the far side of it lay the ruins of Ashwell Priory, the old barns and the former holy well. All were mine! I didn't mention it as I wanted to retain my secret for as long as possible. But could Simon be lost or trapped on my property? A long shiver sped down my spine.

'Just across this lane lies the ancient estate of Ashwell Priory. Lost under repeated landslides of rocks and fallen trees are what remains of the priory – quite a substantial amount in fact, including some old cells. There is also a large expanse of deciduous woodland with a few conifers flourishing among them, and in the hills to the western end is the former holy well of St Valentine, once a place of pilgrimage, especially for young lovers. It's now a pond and needs to be searched too.'

He paused and I interpreted that as a hint that Simon might have ventured there with his secret girlfriend. But Father Will did not elaborate. He continued, 'I'm sure most of you know about this place but for adventurous lads those ruins have always presented a challenge. It has long been out-of-bounds to students, but, of course, that's never stopped them.'

As I listened, I realized I had no idea of the extent or condition of my old ruins and had never explored them, not even when I was a policeman in the district. As he continued, Father Stutely suggested that a substantial part of the old priory had survived beneath avalanches of earth, rocks and trees.

I spoke now, 'You mean there are entire buildings under there?'

'There are indeed,' agreed Father Stutely. 'Those hidden places in Priory Wood were a challenge. Exploration of the ruins is very exciting for boys ... especially after a storm such as the one last night.'

'I thought it was nothing but ruins!' was all I could think of saying.

Father Mutch stood up and addressed us. 'Those who explored the ancient tunnels and cellars found a veritable labyrinth, despite restrictions imposed by the college, but the old Priory was, and probably is, one of the greatest secret challenges of college life. Neither the teachers nor monks say anything about it because to do so might be an encouragement. You enter through one hole and emerge from another which can be several hundred yards away, using a complex system of passages and ruined walls – an underground maze.'

'Dark and dangerous too,' added Father Stutely.

'I had no idea that went on!' I added. 'Even when I was the village constable at Aidensfield, I never heard those tales!'

'It is not generally known, Nick; it was kept a close secret but I think elder brothers passed the information to their siblings.'

'So, are you suggesting Simon might be there?' asked Prior Tuck. 'Trapped, or worse?'

'It's increasingly likely.' Father Mutch spoke for both monks and sounded confident. 'His bike was in the barns which are themselves out of bounds. The police have confirmed he used it so we know he got that far. I know the first search, on the surface, didn't find him but we can't ignore the possibility he could be trapped somewhere underground.'

I reminded them, 'He mentioned woods in his diary, shown in the space for Sunday. Yesterday.'

Father Will entered the discussion. 'That could be significant. Is there any way we can get access to the passages? Things have changed since I was a pupil.'

Father Mutch said, 'Landslides have obliterated lots of entrances and passages. I haven't been in there for years, but that sort of thing never stops adventurous lads. And there'll be fallen trees and landslips from yesterday's storm.'

'We'll need guidance, but we'll also be trespassing,' Prior Tuck reminded his troops. 'Besides, I don't get the impression that Simon is particularly adventurous.'

'He's a young lad,' I told them. 'He's as likely to get into trouble as any other. But we wouldn't be trespassing if we search for him, Father Prior. Police, fire, ambulance and indeed ordinary people can trespass to carry out lawful acts such as rescuing people and animals, saving lives, preventing danger and so forth.'

'So we don't need permission from the owners?'

I was almost tempted to admit that I was about to become the new owner but with some difficulty held my tongue.

'That's right,' I told the gathering. 'We can take whatever steps are necessary to achieve our purpose without fear of being accused of an illegal trespass – which is not a crime, merely a civil tort.'

'Well, that's one hurdle crossed,' beamed the prior. 'So, Father Stutely, what sort of problems are we likely to meet?'

'As we all know, the old priory was a Carthusian establishment, one of only two in England. The other is Mount Grace Priory on the western edge of these moors.'

'Why is that relevant?' asked Brother George.

'It's to do with the type of buildings. In most monasteries monks lived a communal life. They all slept in the same dormitory, ate together in the same refectory, worked in the grounds and walked in the cloisters and so forth. That meant that their communal areas were large, as you can see if you visit most of our ruined abbeys. If a tree fell down today and smashed the wall of a ruined abbey, the chances are that no one would be hurt. There'd be damage to the ruins but hopefully no injuries.'

'I'm not sure I understand your point,' admitted Prior Tuck.

'With a Carthusian monastery,' pressed Father Stutely, 'each monk lived his life in isolation, spending almost his entire time in a tiny cell, permitted to leave only to attend mass. Lots of cells were arranged around three sides of a cloister, rather like a giant honeycomb, and each was large enough only to accommodate one monk. He had a living room downstairs and a bedroom above, plus a small oratory. He was not allowed even to see one of his fellow brethren and so his food was passed to him through an angled hole in the wall.'

'And your point?' queried Prior Tuck once again.

'If just one tree or a high wall collapsed in such a monastery, it could trap several monks. Their cell walls would crumble, roofs would cave in. Because of regular landslides and crashing trees over the years, new tunnels would be created among those old cells and voids could develop. It's a honeycomb under there, ideal for trapping someone. There could be injuries and more structural damage than in any other type of monastery.'

Father Will said, 'In truth, a genuine troublesome labyrinth aggravated by neglect?'

'Completely,' interrupted Brother George. 'So you're saying some of those old cells still exist under all the debris?'

'Yes, I am,' said Father Stutely. 'They have survived despite the damage. It's a testament to the original builders but it means the place is riddled with tunnels, often with dead ends. And don't forget there was a mighty storm on Sunday night with trees and rocks dislodged ... and floods ... water from the wishing well flows under the old ruin too and its route could be blocked, with flooding as a consequence. Need I say more?'

'I never went that far inside!' muttered Father Mutch.

'Some of the derelict cells could make ideal hides for bird watchers,' smiled Brother George. 'But, before we risk our own lives in there, have we any evidence that he's definitely inside?'

'Nothing positive but several clues,' I had to admit. 'The indications are that he was going out for a day watching birds. On top of that, we are certain he used the bike. Why leave it so close to the woods if he was heading somewhere else? We think he also took a torch. That's significant, I feel. It all makes sense – the storms mean he could be trapped somewhere below ground.'

'Dogs will make a thorough search,' suggested Brother George. 'When I was farming you could rely on Jack Russells to flush rabbits out of their burrows....'

'The police dogs can reach places we can never hope to reach and their sense of smell will quickly find a human, dead or alive,' I assured them.

'You're not suggesting he's dead, are you, Nick?' asked the abbot, his voice registering his alarm.

'It's something we must be prepared for. There was a new landslide yesterday, I noticed the freshly uncovered earth on the hillside this morning....'

'That's terrible!' The abbot sounded and looked extremely worried. 'We must pray for him to be found. So will police dogs carry out the search without the press being notified?' he asked. 'He has been missing for more than twenty-four hours now.'

'Yes, we can ask the handlers not to publicize their work. They can always call it an exercise.'

Prior Tuck took command. 'Gentlemen,' he said, 'it's time for action. I have allocated each of you a specific search area with

Father Will, Father Mutch and Brother George being advisers. Nick, if you can ensure that the police dog and its handler arrive in time to help, they could meet us near the old barns.'

'I'll make sure they do.'

'Right, we'll start without them. Father Mutch, we will need torches and equipment. Can you get some from your stores?'

'I'll see to it. I'll meet you all there.'

CHAPTER 13

Prior Tuck was firmly in command and before leaving the Postgate room he showed us a map of Ashwell Priory. He had found it in the library and it was large enough to help our search. It showed the buried ruins, the former holy well and the extent of the surrounding woodland plus the old barns.

Explaining that he knew something of large-scale searches due to his police experience in the wilds of Northumberland, he indicated that his men would begin their overland search at the east end of the priory site. They must form a long straight line across the width of the search area and always remain within sight and hearing of their neighbours to left and right. The stores had equipped them with stout footwear, hiking gear and sticks with which to probe the ground and they would progress steadily towards the west. Nothing would be over-looked and if any searcher found something of interest he must call out and halt the advancing line. As they progressed they must repeatedly call out Simon's name in case he could hear them – even if he was trapped underground, it was hoped he might realize help was nearby and call out to guide them. Father Will Redman would take his turn on duty in the cop shop to deal with telephone calls and enquiries; police dogs would carry out the underground searches.

As the eager monkstables left their operations centre, I said I would join them later because I was now going to the murder room to inform Detective Chief Superintendent Napier of our plans and to get updated on the murder hunt. As the eager monkstables marched across the campus like a squad of soldiers, I entered the murder room to find DI Lindsey in charge. Both DCS Napier and DS Sullivan had left to organize a search of the northern woodland for Harvey, leaving the teams to continue their questioning around the campus.

I told Brian Lindsey what we were doing and mentioned the girl working in the infirmary, saying a monkstable would inter-view her when the opportunity arose. Clearly, she was not missing – we'd have been told if she was. I asked him to direct the dog team to the old priory site and ask for me.

'PC Elaine Newton is the handler's name,' he told me. 'Obviously, their other job has taken longer than anticipated, but she'll be here shortly.'

'I thought your boss might want them to hunt for Harvey.'

'He thinks the safety of the missing pupil is more important,' I was told. 'He's sure Harvey will turn up in due course. Mr Napier knows Harvey of old and says he'll turn up full of apologies – he is known for absconding when he's under pres-sure and always returns like a naughty puppy. But we must search hereabouts; we can't ignore his dash for freedom!'

'So long as he doesn't attack someone,' I ventured.

'Mr Napier has stressed he's not violent even if he did attack a rapist, he's just a big clumsy man, surprisingly so for a sculptor. The boss says the fact he's done a runner doesn't mean he's guilty of murder but we still need to clear him of all suspicion.'

'I understand. So any news of the victim? Has "Mr Thorpe" been positively identified?'

'Local detectives are visiting the area around the false address he gave but no one admits knowing him. We've got nothing yet from his fingerprints but the CRO check should give us a lead, the result should soon come through. However, his alias "Thorpe" has no criminal record. There may be some-thing recorded under his real name if we can discover it. There's a lot of activity going on behind the scenes, Nick.'

'Can I ask about Thorpe's movements before his body was

found? He must have had contact with other people, spoken to someone whether they were attending the course or not. There's always a social element to these things. Have we confirmed how he arrived here?'

'Other than Mrs Morley saying he got a lift from a friend, we know nothing more. She didn't see the friend drop him off. We've checked local buses and taxi firms, and he didn't use them and we're satisfied he has no transport of his own. None of the checks of vehicles on the campus has thrown up his name. The DVLC has no record of a vehicle at the address he gave and our searches of his room and clothing haven't revealed a wallet or any money. The search of his clothing in the coffin revealed nothing either – all his belongings seem to have been removed.'

'He must have carried some money!'

'We know he paid for his course on arrival – in cash. That behaviour is quite normal if he was trying to be anonymous. But if he carried a lot of cash it might have been noticed by an unsavoury character – and that suggests a possible motive for his death – robbery.'

'That makes sense.'

'On Friday he attended a lecture in the library at three o'clock. It lasted about an hour and there was refreshments afterwards. We think he left the library shortly before five and returned to his room, then he later turned up for supper in the dining-room of the retreat centre. That was at eight.'

'And the other attendees?'

'All the other course members were there too. After the meal, they sat around in the lounge chatting and showing photos of some of their discoveries.'

'All fairly normal for that kind of event, eh?'

'Absolutely. Then, shortly before ten Mr Thorpe bade everyone goodnight and went to his room. Alone.'

'So he's had no meetings with anyone? No long walks in the evening?'

'That's something we don't know, Nick, but it appears not.

He came down for breakfast on Saturday morning and attended a lecture from nine thirty until ten thirty, and then joined a group that went to Whitby Abbey with a tour of the area afterwards. They returned late that afternoon and had supper at seven thirty. Thorpe was there but no one has seen him since.'

'And Sunday?'

'No one reports seeing him on Sunday. Sunday was a free day but it is expected that visitors will attend mass at ten, and join the monks for coffee afterwards. Lunch is provided for those who wish to remain on the campus and places like the libraries and sports facilities are open to all. The fact no one saw him on Sunday didn't cause alarm – some people do make use of the centre as a base for exploration. They treat it like a B&B and do their own thing. It is quite feasible to go off on one's own without causing concern, especially on a Sunday.'

'Was he a Catholic?' I asked.

'We don't know. There is no indication he was – there was no missal or other Catholic artefact in his room or upon his body. Being a Catholic is not a condition of acceptance for the course.'

'And his body was found this morning.'

'Right, Nick. Timing a death is not a precise science. Even though the pathologist thinks he was killed early on Sunday morning, he could have died on Saturday night or any time on Sunday. He can't be more specific except to express a belief he died very early on Sunday. But that is just an opinion, not a fact.'

'So have your teams managed to find out anything about the archaeologist?'

'We haven't done in-depth research into him – he's not entered the frame and our initial enquiries suggest he's genuine enough. There's nothing remarkable about him. The particulars he gave to the abbot's office when he applied to carry out his excavation have been checked and verified. He's a well-known independent operator; we've also checked his helpers. They're all students at York University, all listed in the records with no convictions. So no problems there. They come and go each day in a people carrier, Rawdon remained alone on site over the weekend to finish off some important tasks. He's not sure when they are going to leave – it depends on what they find. And we know his van – borrowed from a friend – is taxed, tested and insured. Its registered keeper is Leonard Larkfield from Newcastle-on-Tyne. We've been to his address – which is genuine – but Larkfield isn't at home. His neighbours don't know where he's gone. Apparently, he's often away for long periods.'

'Thanks for all this, Brian. It helps me when I'm dealing with our monkstables. I'm going to Ashwell Priory now as they begin their concentrated search for Simon.'

I decided to take my car across the valley and leave it there in case I needed it. As I passed through the gently downward sloping valley I could see the wooded area that contained the ruined priory. My two barns were prominent against the background of trees and hills and I could just discern movements of the white helmeted monks as they began their search. I drove onto the area in front of the barns, parked, and decided this was a good place to await PC Elaine Newton and her police dogs. I had a good view of the mainly deciduous woodland being searched and I wondered if any progress was being made. Perhaps it was too early to expect a result? My initial impression was that many trees appeared to be unstable, including some suffering from ash die-back. Several had crashed to earth during last night's storms and were lying at awkward or even dangerous angles against huge boulders and stronger trees. Was it feasible that Simon could be among them? And still be alive?

Then I heard a voice hailing me and someone tapped on the driver's side window. It was Barnaby Crabstaff and he shouted, 'Hello, Mr Rhea, have you come to look for more nightjars?'

I climbed out and immediately saw Claude Jeremiah

Greengrass descending the ladder from Barnaby's flat – or hayloft as we might describe it.

'Not nightjars this time, Barnaby. We looking for that student I mentioned to you. There's still no sign of him.'

'Now then, Constable Rhea,' as unkempt as ever with long hair and a grey beard, Greengrass had now joined us, still wearing his old ragged army coat. 'What brings you here? Not checking on us, I hope – you know, me and my pal here have just been talking about old constables and troublemakers, and then you turn up. Amazing. Have you been eavesdropping?'

'Give over, Claude! Who would want to spy on an old rogue like you? You'll be retired now—'

'Retired? How can I afford to retire, I have to make a living. I don't get a pension like coppers do. I'm a busy general dealer, Constable Rhea, and me and Barnaby like to have business meetings now and then. Which is what we were doing when you turned up.'

'Claude, I have far better things to do than worry about your dodgy business ventures. So what do you know about this missing pupil? And have you seen a big dark-haired fellow dressed in black? We'd like to find him as well.'

'There's nobody here but us....'

'You can search the barns, Mr Rhea,' invited Barnaby.

'We've a team of police dogs arriving any minute, we'll get them to search properly,' I told the old fellows.

'You're not looking for stolen property, are you?' asked Claude. 'Because nobody's daft enough to dump it in those woods. It's not safe in there, besides it's all fenced off. Then there's tumbling boulders, falling trees, landslides and all them dark and dangerous tunnels with floods … you take your life in your hands if you go in there, storm or no storm.'

'Underground tunnels? What do you know about them, Claude?'

He stood before me, blinking like a startled owl but he said nothing.

'Claude, I'm not interested in your smuggling operations,

past or present. I'm not a police officer any more, I am here to help find a missing pupil and that big man dressed in black. So if you know anything, I hope you'll help me.'

'Help the police? Me?'

'I'm not a policeman any more, Claude. This lad has been missing since midday yesterday, he might be trapped or lying injured. We must find him.'

'Will there be a reward if I find him?' Those cunning old eyes blinked again. 'Me and Barnaby know these woods like the backs of our hands.'

'Do we?' Barnaby sounded startled. 'I never go in there, Claude, I've told you that. It's not safe. All those tunnels and running water and trees falling down even when there's no gales ... rocks tumbling ... I keep well clear of the old priory.'

'Aye, well, mebbe so, but I live at Hagg Bottom, it's far enough away not to know of such goings on, but I used to explore these woods as a lad, Constable Rhea, and that tells you how long ago it was. I knew every cave, shelter, rabbit run, badger track, foxhole, pheasants' nesting areas, water course ... but I couldn't get into any of them small spaces now, I've expanded here and there.'

'What do you mean by shelters, Claude?'

He blinked hard again. 'Did you say a lad was missing?'

'A youth of seventeen, Claude. He's not a child, so where could he be?'

'Would that be his bike, Mr Rhea?' asked Barnaby. 'That one that was here until those chaps took it away this morning?'

'We're sure he rode it here, Barnaby. It's not his but when a pupil leaves the college, he usually leaves his old bike behind for others to use. No one claims them so anyone can use them. He probably spotted that one outside the kitchen and helped himself to it. That's how the system works. He didn't steal it.'

'Did he not?' and Barnaby's eyes open wide.

'The college sells 'em off eventually,' smiled Claude. 'There's allus a good market for second-hand bikes. I do 'em up and polish 'em; they earn me a few quid.'

'Well, someone has to get rid of them, Claude, so you're doing a good job.'

'I do my best, in spite of nosy coppers. Anyway, why would that lad want to ride that bike down here, then leave it? What's he want, coming into these woods? Especially on a day like yesterday? They're out-of-bounds to students anyroad.'

'He's a keen birdwatcher, Claude. I think he might have been hoping to spot something interesting, like a nightjar, just as Barnaby showed me one many years ago. So if that was his intention, where would he go?'

'Hiding somewhere,' offered Barnaby. 'If you come to look for rare birds, you need somewhere quiet to hide and plenty of time to spare.'

'There's plenty of good places in them woods, Constable Rhea,' Claude joined in. 'Ancient ruins underground, old cells the monks used, little stone houses all buried now but some surviving – they're the shelters I mentioned. If you know your way in there, you could hide for ever. It's like a giant mole-run.'

'That's right, Mr Rhea,' nodded Barnaby. 'But you'd be daft to go into those woods in storms like yesterday's.'

'Those cliffs behind the wood aren't safe either,' added Claude. 'Boulders keep coming loose and crashing down, felling trees as they go. It's usually after heavy rain, all that ground becomes unstable. You'd never catch me going in there.'

'Well, we've a party of monkstables searching for him and they have an experienced guide.'

'They'll need him!'

At that point, I heard the sound of a motor vehicle. It turned towards my parked car. It was a blue and white van with POLICE DOG SECTION emblazoned on the rear panels, and I noticed the protective grilles behind the front seats.

It parked and a petite young policewoman emerged with her short fair hair tucked into her uniform cap. She seemed to be in her late twenties. She approached me.

'Are you Mr Rhea?'

'I am.'

'I thought there was a party of private constables here too?'

'They're searching the woods over there,' I told her, waving my hand to indicate the woodland beyond us. 'I'm here to take you to them.'

'Thank you. I'm PC Elaine Newton, and in the van are my two German Shepherds, Sherlock and Holmes. From our K9 department as the old joke goes!'

At the sound of their names, the dogs barked and rocked the little van until she ordered them to be quiet.

'I'm pleased you've arrived,' I said, 'These gentlemen are Claude Jeremiah Greengrass and Barnaby Crabstaff, both local and both have knowledge of the area we have to search.'

'Did you hear that, Barnaby, he called us gentlemen!'

'He's referring to me, Claude,' laughed Barnaby.

'Oh, I thought you had some monks helping?'

'We have. They are the private constables you mentioned, they're already searching the woodland, with expert guidance,' and I gave her a full account of Simon's disappearance. 'But they're not searching underground. You should soon hear them approaching, they're at the far end of this wood at the moment.'

'So where do you suggest I begin?' she asked. 'I'm to search underground.'

'Like I said to Constable Rhea before you arrived, miss, there's lots of underground tunnels, shelters and such in these woods. They're in the middle bit where the old abbey used to stand … it's covered with trees and rocks now. You'd never know there were buildings underneath, but the whole place is riddled with alleys and underground routes big enough for a young slim lad to find his way around. Mind you, he'd have to crawl on all-fours and in pitch darkness in some places.'

'The dogs will cope. I've got some spare personal radio sets in my van,' she told us, 'which are tuned in to the Talk Through channel so if it becomes necessary we can keep in touch with anyone underground.'

'Thanks, they'll be useful,' I told her. 'I'll take you to meet Prior Tuck now, he's in charge of the monk-constables – he is a monk but was once a police officer in Northumbria. He'll know how to deploy the radios. His officers won't be searching underground for a while as they have to clear the surface areas. Now, Claude and Barnaby, can you show Elaine to a suitable underground entrance whilst I find Prior Tuck and tell him what's going on?'

'I've never been known to help the police but I can make an exception in this case,' beamed Claude. 'Did I ask if there was a reward if we find him?'

'You did and there isn't.'

'No harm in asking. Now if I'd had my Alfred with me, he could have joined those police dogs and showed 'em a thing or two about hunting; he was brilliant at finding rabbits and things underground.'

'So where is he?' I asked in all innocence.

'In that place where there aren't any dog licences but plenty of pheasants and bones,' he grunted, slightly embarrassed by the emotion that was clear in his eyes. 'I thought about replacing him but there's only one Alfred. He'll be watching us from his doggy heaven – isn't that somewhere near the Dog Star?'

'No,' said Barnaby, 'on the Isle of Dogs.'

'Alfred would never have survived in London!' snapped Claude.

'He hasn't survived here,' countered Barnaby.

'But he's here in spirit, isn't he, Claude?' smiled Elaine. 'And he's going to help us find Simon.'

CHAPTER 14

J UST AS WE were leaving, a small and rather ancient blue Mini-
Traveller arrived and I realized it was driven by Oscar
Blaketon with Alf Ventress at his side. It must be a classic motor
vehicle by now! I wondered what on earth my former sergeant
and ex-PC Ventress of Ashfordly Police were doing here. Then,
very swiftly, I understood – they had helped me to train the
monkstables and no doubt wanted to see how they performed
in this first difficult test of their skills. Clearly news of our activities had reached a wider public.

Greengrass groaned aloud. 'What's going on? Are all these ex-
coppers spying on me? I've never seen so many coppers in one
place...even the monks around here are dressed like coppers....'

'They've come to see how their students are performing,' I
told him.

Oscar Blaketon came straight to me and asked, 'Am I right in
thinking our students are busy with a murder investigation?'

'Murder?' shouted Claude. 'Nobody said anything about a
murder!'

'There's been a suspicious death in the crypt beneath the
abbey,' I told him. 'Detectives are there now. This is a
completely separate issue – our monkstables are looking for a
missing pupil. So, Oscar, how did you know about this?'

'I've still got some good contacts both in the job and outside,'
grinned Blaketon conspiratorially, as he tapped his nose with
his finger, as if telling us to mind our own business. 'I'm
surprised the press aren't here.'

'I don't know whether they've been in touch,' I admitted. 'The murder enquiry might attract them, but I've heard nothing and they'll not be interested in a schoolboy who's dodging lessons.'

'Nobody tells me anything these days ...' muttered Claude.

I explained events to Oscar and Alf and referred to the arrival of PC Elaine Newton with her two Alsatians, adding that Claude and Barnaby were going to guide us to the best entrance so we could search underground if Simon was not found on the surface.

'Can we join in?' asked Alf Ventress.

'The more helpers, the better, especially those with police skills,' was my response.

'That's us,' acknowledged Blaketon.

'Fine by me,' added Ventress who followed with, 'Come on, Claude, don't keep your old pals waiting.'

'Old pals?' he stormed. 'Who are you calling old pals?'

'Give over, the lot of you.' I tried to halt all the jesting and jocular teasing. 'Let's get started. By the way, we have the use of two police personal radio sets, which might come in useful as they're linked to the police dog van radio.'

'Good, then let's join the others.'

'Claude, if you and Barnaby are going to help, remember your old antagonists are not in charge of this operation. We're all working together but the man in charge is Prior Tuck of Maddleskirk Abbey.'

'Friar Tuck? Wasn't he a pal of Robin Hood?'

'He was, but this is Prior Tuck.'

'Aye, right, if you say so, then you'd better lead on.'

'First we must find him to tell him of our presence and make him aware of how we can help,' suggested Blaketon. We all joined Elaine who was waiting with her dogs near a hole in the wire fence that surrounded Ashwell Woods; the dogs were at heel, awaiting her commands.

Once we were through the fence, Claude took over. 'Follow me,' he said, then led us into the trees.

We located the prior and his searchers who were about halfway through their examination of the woodland. We explained we now had the dogs and it was our intention to concentrate underground beyond the range of mobile phones.

'Fine,' he said. 'We'll finish the overground search, then if we don't have any success, we'll join you.'

'We have the use of police radios,' I told him. 'We can keep in touch.'

'I wouldn't know which button to press,' he laughed. 'I'll find you all, this isn't a very large area and we're all making plenty of noise.'

'Now it's your turn, Claude,' I told him.

We followed Claude and Barnaby into the dark green depths of the wood, avoiding fallen trees and boulders and Claude reminded us that we were walking over treacherous ground, some of which was hollow beneath our feet. It was a difficult trek but Claude and Barnaby knew the safest route. Then Claude halted.

'Now Constable Rhea,' he said, with uncharacteristic seriousness, 'I'm standing directly above the centre of the cloister. To the north, east and west under here there are rows of old cells with the remains of the monks' tiny gardens, all buried under tons of rocks, earth and rotten trees. Behind me to the south, is where the old priory church is buried, badly damaged I must warn you. But I'll bet it would be recognizable as a ruined abbey if it was excavated.'

'One day perhaps,' I said, more in hope than expectation.

'Right,' continued Claude. 'The hillside behind that wood will need to be stabilized if people start coming here in numbers. It's unstable now and liable to produce an avalanche at any time without warning. I think there's a water-course under here too, the flow from the old holy well sometimes emerges near where we are now. To the south of the church is another row of half-a-dozen cells – it is their walls, badly damaged but still surviving, that form two underground tunnels.'

'You'd make a good guide, Claude. How many cells are there in total?' I asked him.

'Twenty-five mebbe. Summat like that.'

'You do know a lot about it, Claude, and all so very useful.' He glowed beneath Elaine's praise.

'Aye, well, I've lived here man and boy for more years than I care to remember. You learn your way around as a lad, and never forget.'

Elaine now asked, 'If I can find an entrance to the underground maze under our feet, can the dogs make a complete search?'

'I would say they can, so long as they don't get trapped. A lot of those tunnels link up but there are some dead ends. Very narrow in places an' all, due to fallen rocks and stuff. And there's allus water about, deep in some places. Anyroad, I'll take you to a good entrance.'

He led us to the remains of a massive oak that had toppled over many years ago and the roots of which stood upright from the earth like a giant wheel against the leafy background. The lower end of the roots disappeared into the earth and he showed us lots of apparently bottomless holes that had resulted from the tree's fall. He indicated one of them, the largest.

'When I was a lad, I used to crawl down there,' he told us. 'It opens into a network of tunnels, some with gaps that let the light in and some being part of the old cells. There's flowing water in some parts but the waterways can soon get blocked with rubbish and falling soil, so the water has to find other ways out. Sometimes it doesn't, and so you get a flood, sometimes deep, sometimes shallow.'

'Won't things have changed since you were an adventurous lad?' I asked.

''Course they will, but those cells were so well built they'll still be standing there, providing the framework. It's the same conditions, just moved around a bit. These dogs will have no trouble down there.'

'That's good news,' smiled Elaine.

'It's the best entrance,' nodded Claude. 'There'll be more entrances and exits they can use, but I'm not going down there now, I'm past that kind of adventuring. The dogs will do it far better. But before you send them in, I'll shout to see if Simon can hear us.'

He bellowed into the echoing depths of the hole but there was no response.

'Right,' he said. 'It's up to you now, Elaine.'

As she despatched Sherlock and Holmes into the dark hole with a command to seek, Claude, Barnaby and I set off to locate more entrances. In such a large area it was possible there were more entrances and dead ends, but Claude seemed to know his way around. Barnaby merely followed like a lost sheep. As we worked, we could hear the approaching monkstables in the trees; they were checking every inch of ground and calling out to satisfy themselves that Simon was not hidden nearby. Only when satisfied, did they move forward. We became aware of Prior Tuck heading our way with Oscar and Alf beside him, but he raised his arms to signal they had not found Simon.

Then Elaine's radio crackled into life. She responded. It was Blaketon calling on behalf of Prior Tuck. I could hear his voice, 'Elaine, Prior Tuck suggests a rendezvous and a good place would be right where you are now. Can you remain there until we arrive?'

'Will co,' she responded.

'I'm enjoying this,' beamed Claude. 'It's better than selling scrap bikes.'

And then we heard a dog barking somewhere deep underground.

'Quiet please! And stand still!' shouted PC Elaine Newton. 'Listen....'

Everyone stood still and listened. We heard the deep barking again, a double woof clearly underground but I found it impossible to gauge the direction from which the barks came. Clearly the dog was deep below the surface and a long way from where we were standing.

'That's Sherlock, he's found someone!'

'You know that?'

'Dogs have different voices, just like humans. And that's definitely Sherlock. Two barks tell me he's found someone alive! He must have separated from Holmes down there. Holmes must still be seeking. I hope he hasn't got lost.'

'Will he also bark?'

'No, it's Sherlock who's barked, which says everything, even to Holmes.'

'What will he do?' I asked. 'Holmes, I mean? Will he stop searching?'

'No, he'll continue to work as Sherlock remains where he is, guarding his discovery and continuing to bark twice at intervals. He'll keep doing that until I order him to stop, or until we locate the target,' said Elaine. 'Hopefully, Holmes will join him but he will not bark – unless, of course, he finds somebody else! Then he will also deliver a double woof.'

Instead of cheering loudly at the news we lapsed into silence at what she was telling us in such a calm, matter-of-fact way. Then Sherlock barked again, twice. But we all noted there was no human voice from those depths.

'Can you tell where they are?' asked Claude. 'It's a dangerous warren down there. Some dogs can get lost just like humans. I've spent hours digging terriers out of rabbit holes.'

'We can't dig down to find him without knowing exactly where the dog is. And we don't know where or how deep below the surface he is or how dangerous it is down there....' Barnaby was standing at my side, wringing his hands.

It was Claude who said, 'The lad might not be able to help ... if the dog says he's alive, he could be unconscious or badly injured.'

His words jerked us all into remembering that this exercise might not have the successful conclusion we all hoped for, but then I had an idea.

'Barnaby, you remember when you showed me the nightjar, all those years ago....'

'I do, Constable Rhea, indeed I do.'

'Do nightjars still come to these woods?'

'Oh, they do, sir, yes they do. Every year, regular as clock-work … they'll be here now but they only fly at dusk.'

'I'm sure Simon would know all that if he's a keen bird watcher … and he asked for extra food in his packed lunch. Obviously he expected to be late back—'

'I think it was him who once asked about the nightjars,' frowned Barnaby, as he tried to recall the occasion. 'It was a young lad from the college, tall, with dark hair and specs. He'd never seen one, he told me, when he was out walking down here – not recently, a week or two ago.'

'Where was he going?'

'He said he was heading for the woods, so I told him the nightjars only came in spring and went back to Africa by October. I think he often came down here after that, always alone.'

'Did he know where to find one?'

'He seemed to know they came to this wood. They don't visit many woods around here, although I believe some get into Dalby Forest near Pickering and there's organized parties there who go looking for them at night…'

'What's a good time to see one?'

'At dusk onwards, Mr Rhea. Once it starts getting dark they'll be flying around catching moths and flies.'

'And at daytime?'

'At nesting time, they sleep on the ground, you'd never notice one on its nest or sitting among dead leaves, but after nesting time they'll roost in the trees, sitting lengthways along a dead branch, very hard to see, Mr Rhea. Well camouflaged.'

'Do they come back to the same place year after year?'

'I'm not sure about that, Mr Rhea, me not being an expert, but I do know that they can be seen in these woods at this time of year, if you're lucky. Before they go back to Africa.'

'Did you help the lad to find a suitable place to wait and watch?'

'I told him where the birds could be seen, yes, and told him to hide because they are easily scared if you get too close, but I said not to go into the holes under rocks around here ... but I didn't wait around with him as he wanted to be alone.'

'But clearly you had a lot of contact with him, Barnaby?'

'Not all that much, Mr Rhea. Sometimes I'd see him coming down here on his bike and he'd leave it in the old barns while he went bird-watching, telling me he'd borrowed it....'

'You told me you'd never met him and had no idea who'd brought the bike here.'

'I didn't want to get him into bother, Mr Rhea, if you understand, with you being a policeman and that mebbe it not being his own bike....'

'All right, Barnaby, I understand. And I'm not a policeman now. Anyway, it seems there is someone alive underground not far from here. How can we reach him? Can we get into those passages and, more to the point, can we get him out?'

'I'd say not, Mr Rhea. Too narrow for adults – dangerous for dogs and children, falling rocks and things, unsafe roofs, deep holes, pits, dark places....'

'You don't make it sound easy, Barnaby.'

'It's downright dangerous, Mr Rhea, and I told him to keep out, that was another time when I saw him. I did tell him, Mr Rhea, truly I did.'

As we chatted, the others stood and listened, not entering this two-way conversation between me and a tramp I'd known for years. Barnaby and I seemed to have a sort of understanding and, in truth, I liked the fellow. But if he thought he was in trouble of any kind, he would produce devious answers; interviewing him was a case of gaining his momentary trust and that was never easy. He seemed to spend his entire life defending himself against continuing but imaginary accusations.

'Barnaby, you are not in trouble of any kind and neither is Claude. All we want to do is find Simon and we think you can help.'

'You'd be best searching that side of this old ruin,' and he pointed towards the south.

'Why's that?'

'The best place for seeing nightjars is that patch of woodland over there.' He pointed to an area below the cliff. 'That's where I suggested he search. I told him he'd have to find somewhere secret and hidden, and I told him to look in the branches as it was getting dark but not to scare the birds off.'

'Was there a hide nearby?'

'Just some parts of the old ruin, Mr Rhea, old cells, knocked about a bit but with gaps for windows, overlooking that bit of the wood … good hides … you could find a way to them if you were small enough…'

'Where are they?'

'Over there as well.' He pointed again towards the cliff behind the woodland, a lofty embankment faced with bare earth that had been so recently exposed by a landslide. It was about fifty metres from where we were standing and it was evident that a massive oak and some smaller trees had toppled down as the ground had collapsed beneath them. The shifting trees had carried tons of earth, rocks and even huge boulders onto the roof of the hidden priory which, in places, had collapsed beneath the sudden impact, shock and tremendous weight.

'That big oak and those little 'uns all came down yesterday, Mr Rhea … and some of those rocks … new falls, they are.'

'You mean he's somewhere down there?'

'He could be, that's all I can say, but I think it's likely.'

'Did you see him go down any of the openings? There's quite a few – it's difficult knowing where they lead to.'

'No, I never saw him after he walked away from me, but I warned him not to go down into the old priory, so I did.'

'I'm sure you did, Barnaby. So I repeat my question: how do we get in to find out if he's there.'

'He is there, Mr Rhea.' Elaine had no doubt in her mind. 'My dog tells me and dogs cannot lie. Even if Simon can't speak to us, Sherlock is telling us that he – or someone else – is down there. Alive.'

Barnaby stood at our side looking thoroughly miserable. He shrugged his shoulders and I could see tears in his eyes. 'It wasn't my fault, Mr Rhea, it wasn't, God knows that. I did warn him....'

I placed my arms around his thin shoulders. 'No one is suggesting you're to blame, Barnaby. You're not. But we must find out where Sherlock is, then set about getting Simon and the two dogs out.' I now addressed the others. 'Has anyone any idea how to do that among those unstable rocks and trees?'

'I don't know, God above knows I don't know,' sniffed Barnaby. 'I wish I did. I wish I could help—'

'You've helped a lot, Barnaby.' I patted him on his back. 'I mean that.'

By this time, Prior Tuck had moved closer with his monk-stables as they continued to inspect the ground beneath them. They were close enough for me to address Father Will. 'Father Will, you are a caver, I believe?'

'A retired caver, I think! It's not going to be easy, even for the most experienced of cavers. We are not dealing with a solid rock roof and well-used routes, we're talking of an unstable ceiling full of dangerously loose earth and rocks, uprooted trees, probably water somewhere along the route ... we need experts.'

'At this moment, we haven't got experts: you're our expert. So what can you suggest?' I tried to remain calm as I felt a tense situation building up.

He thought for a while and then said, 'We need someone to enter the passages with a radio, a torch and something to drink or eat, with a rope trailing behind so someone else can follow. We need to find a way through the labyrinth so we can carry out the rescue. Then, once we've found him we've got to get him out. That won't be easy especially if he is unconscious or injured. And we must be aware we are at risk from further roof falls. Our mere presence could trigger them off.'

Father Will's caution created a few moments of silence as we all began to understand the awesome task that lay ahead.

'Can't we dig down to him?' asked Claude, anxious to be useful.

'No, the pressure of digging and any movement above the place he is lying could cause the ground to collapse and bury him. Or a falling rock could crush him.'

Father Prior took control. 'Father Will, do you belong to a cave rescue team?'

'No, Father Prior, it became impossible due to my monastic responsibilities.'

'But do you know whom to contact? We need an expert to guide us as we could do more harm than good if we try to get him out.'

'I'm still in contact with my former colleagues through newsletters.'

'Good. Then can you call some of them to see if anyone can come to guide us or even work the depths?'

'I'll ring from the cop shop. Immediately.'

'I'll drive you across the valley in my car,' offered Blaketon.

And so we had to stand around for a few minutes whilst Sherlock continued to bark at intervals to remind us of our responsibilities.

'Can you tell from Sherlock's barking whether it is a person he's found and not a badger?' I asked Elaine.

'Oh yes, it's definitely a person. He wouldn't bark for a badger.'

'Is the person dead or alive?' I knew the answer but needed her reassurance.

'Alive, definitely. But the person could be asleep or unconscious. One bark means a corpse.'

'How can we trace the victim's whereabouts by using the dog?'

'If the injured person is able to communicate, we could send a length of white rope tied to the dog's collar; if the person is able, he could detach it and attach it to himself, then we would recall the dog. Or we could order the dog to stay. A person experienced in caving or mining would then descend and follow the rope – there are phones that operate underground and other devices from which we could get a fix. In this case, we can't do that right now. We might, if we had more time before dark.'

'It's not possible to get a fix on Sherlock's barking, is it?' asked the prior. 'If we could, we could begin to dig or excavate … very, very carefully of course.'

'It's obvious the tunnels are wide enough and high enough for Sherlock to find his quarry,' I added. 'That makes it seem to me that a small person could crawl through to him.'

'A small person might reach him, but we've still got to get him out,' said Elaine. 'You can't rely on dragging a casualty along a tunnel, especially someone who might be badly injured. We have no idea what conditions are like but know it will be dark, wet and cold. From what I know, the only way to get him out is to dig down.'

'But that creates its own extra dangers,' I reminded them.

'I think,' said Father Prior, 'that we must establish his position as closely as we can in the circumstances – I am sure we have, or can acquire, the technology to do that and then we can start to excavate as closely as we dare.'

'A good idea,' said Claude. 'I once saw a Jack Russell dug out of a rabbit warren like that – we go in by another entrance, listen to Sherlock barking to get the directions established and bingo, the lad will be saved. It worked with that terrier.'

As the banter went on around us and as the time began ticking away with worrying speed, I wandered away from the rescuers who were now standing around and chattering to no useful avail. We needed actions, not words. Sherlock maintained his barking every few minutes with encouraging responses from Elaine but I was acutely aware we were making absolutely no progress. From a short distance I looked upon the rescue site hoping against hope for some inspiration that might get things moving. Even if Father Will turned up with a contact phone number for a rescue specialist, it would take time for him or her to reach the area.

I became increasingly concerned that darkness would envelop us. We must execute an immediate manoeuvre if our mission was to be successful. As we awaited Father Will, I sought somewhere quiet to think – and think hard. As I walked down the lane for about a hundred yards, I found an elevated but safe piece of land on the edge of the woods and climbed onto it to get a wider and better view of the rescue site. From this distance, there were clearer signs of the problem. I could see the new scar down the cliff-face where the recent landslide had deposited tons of rocks, trees and soil on top of the old priory that was now imprisoning the boy.

Had he been trapped by that new fall? Or had he stumbled into a situation that had been there for a long, long time?

I descended from my vantage point and hailed Barnaby Crabtree.

'Barnaby, can I talk to you again, over there?' and I indicated the path of land I had just vacated.

'Sure, Constable Rhea,' he said, and I climbed back to my vantage point with him close behind. 'What are we doing?'

'See all that fallen earth, rocks and stuff, Barnaby?'

'Sure I do, Constable Rhea. Quite an avalanche – and it came down only yesterday. I heard the rumble, I'm glad I was nowhere near it.'

'Barnaby, I want you to think carefully and be honest with me – you are not in trouble, I am not trying to catch you out or get you into bother – but when you told Simon about the bird hide so that he could conceal himself to see the nightjars, was it under there, under where all those rocks and trees and sliding earth came to rest only yesterday?'

I hoped he wouldn't think I was trying to get him into some kind of trouble and was relieved when he responded. 'Yes, it would be about there, Constable Rhea. Under there somewhere. Not in other parts ... In fact one of those trees that slid down the hillside is the one where the nightjars would have been roosting....'

I began to feel my heart pounding. 'Barnaby, we must be sure about this, so do you think Simon could be under that part of the wood? It's very important that I know.'

He looked at me and I could see tears of fear in his eyes. 'Yes, Constable Rhea, I'm sure of it. I shouldn't have told him to hide down there ... if he's anywhere, he'll be down there....'

'So we need to get him out, don't we? And that means we must find him soon! Where was the entrance to the hide before the landslide?'

He hesitated, and I thought he would not answer for fear of being blamed.

'Will you show me?'

He nodded again and walked towards it with me following. I don't think any of the others had observed our short diversion and at this stage, I did not want any of them to accompany us. This was between me and Barnaby. He led me to a huge outcrop of rock on top of which there grew a massive beech tree the roots of which encircled the rock as if holding it in position like the tentacles of a giant octopus. The landslide had missed it even though much of it had come to rest nearby.

'Under there.' He pointed to a dark, narrow entrance which appeared to disappear deep into the earth beneath the rock; it was the sort of hole that I would have thought was a fox earth or badger sett.

'How far down does it go, Barnaby?'

'It used to lead right beneath the surface, Constable Rhea, turning back on itself but branching out in all directions into several different passages, with the walls of the old monks' cells still standing with no roofs...a real warren it was, you had to know your way in and out.'

'Do you think it's still open?'

'No,' he said, with more than a hint of finality. 'No, the land-slide has made the roofs collapse. You can see the dents in the old floor of the wood that cover them ... maybe a dog could get in here and search ... but if the lad's in there, he'll have to be dug out.'

'Barnaby, you're a treasure.' I shouted Simon's name into the hole but got no response, so I told Barnaby, 'I'm going to see if that police dog can go in through this entrance.'

With Barnaby following, I returned to the throng who were still awaiting the return of Father Stutely and sought Elaine.

'Is Sherlock still underground?'

'Yes, and still speaking to us to say there's someone down there.'

'Can I ask him to test another entrance? Can you recall him? Or Holmes?'

'Yes, of course, Mr Rhea. I'll recall Sherlock. I still don't know what's happened to Holmes. Sherlock might give us a clue as to where he's been, depending which way he comes out.'

And then Father Prior came to my side. 'You look excited, Nick, it shows in your face.'

'I think Barnaby could have found Simon for us.' In view of the circumstances, it was a bold statement so I explained my theory. Father Prior listened intently and nodded.

'I understand what you are saying, Nick, well done. What do you suggest now?'

'I would like Sherlock to go down here to see if this is where Simon went in. I must admit that when I heard Sherlock speak earlier, he sounded a long way off. If this landslide has locked Simon in, he could be much closer than we realize – and Barnaby does say this is the site of the hide Simon would have used to watch the nightjars from underground.'

Elaine recalled Sherlock from his earlier success and this time indicated the hole beneath the beech tree on its massive rock. 'Seek,' she commanded.

We all stood, watched and listened as Sherlock's wagging tail vanished from sight somewhere among the debris. The wait seemed interminable. Then he spoke again with those two distinctive barks. This time, they sounded much closer.

'He's in there,' Elaine sounded delighted. 'He's not far away either.'

'All we have to do is get him out,' said Prior Tuck.

He relaxed just a little as I saw Father Will returning with Oscar Blaketon.

'Sorry to be so long,' apologized Oscar. 'We had to make lots of calls.'

'And all without success,' admitted Father Will. 'Would you believe the rescue team is already out on a job in the Dales, so everyone's committed. It seems a team of cavers are missing down one of the caves near Ingleton, flood waters trapped them yesterday, another result of the storm.'

'I think, under the circumstances, we can manage,' I offered. 'We have all those diggers and earth moving machines on the construction site, with a lot of willing hands, I am sure. We can make good use of them and their operators....'

'A good idea, Nick. Leave it with me,' smiled Prior Tuck, and he set off to discuss the problem with one of the site supervisors. As he left I could see Elaine gazing around the site with a look of concern on her face.

'Problems?' I asked.

'Holmes still hasn't returned,' she told me. 'I've not heard a whimper from him. It's not like him, Mr Rhea. I hope he hasn't got himself trapped down there. The problem is he won't bark unless it's a person, dead or alive, which means we have no idea where he is and what he might have found. I've tried recalling him but he hasn't responded. I am now very worried – for both Simon and Holmes.'

CHAPTER 15

ELAINE PRODUCED A dog whistle from one of her pockets and hurried to the entrance hole that had been first used by both dogs. She halted beside it and called Holmes's name then blew hard on the whistle, its pitch being so high that I could not hear it. But it was Sherlock who responded with two barks; she recognized his voice and ordered him to remain on guard. He barked again in response and I had to admit his voice did not sound very far underground. I recognized the hope in his bark, and so did most of the others.

'He's OK, he knows what to do but I'm worried about Holmes. We should have heard something from him. I'm going to try some of the other access holes.'

I motioned to one or two helpers who set off with her, but advised them not to follow. If she was going to try and locate the dog guided only by his sounds, she would need as much silence as possible. And so we all hung back and gathered on the roadside, awaiting the return of Prior Tuck. Most of us felt we should be doing something positive rather than just standing around, but there was nothing anyone could do. Hopefully, Prior Tuck would return with a willing contractor who could help to extricate Simon and at least one police dog. For what seemed an eternity therefore, we waited and waited although it was probably not more than twenty minutes at the most. I moved to a bank of higher sloping ground within the wooded area so I could look across towards the construction activity within the grounds. Brother George joined me as we gazed across the scene before us – a graceful church fronted by sports fields and surrounded by woodland, and before it a conglomeration of vehicles, huts and part-buildings which was producing noisy drilling, clatter and loud music. It was not a peaceful image.

During those few moments Brother George stood at my side, I gained the impression he had something important to say. But he kept quiet as the noise from the construction site filled the air. There was constant movement as the sophisticated machines carried out their complicated and specialized roles. A dizzying number of white vans buzzed around too, apparently aimlessly. I knew they were not wandering around without purpose – they would be fetching and carrying necessities and personnel, bringing in new supplies, or removing unwanted rubbish, or equipment that had completed its functions on site. And all the time there was movement by workmen as they went about their tasks.

I did not wish to interrupt Brother George's contemplative silence as I wondered if he was praying, but conversely I wondered if he wished to talk to me or whether something was troubling him. As we stood quietly, I could see the knot of helpers and monkstables chattering among themselves. The panorama could be an industrial scene anywhere in England, not a peaceful living abbey full of monks in the depths of the North York Moors.

During the time I had been the village constable at nearby Aidensfield, and since purchasing my own house in Maddleskirk – a period of some fifty years – the expansion of the abbey and college had never halted. New buildings were constantly being added and one of the valued aspects of its presence was that people living in the vicinity could take advantage of its facilities. It was like having a benevolent uncle living nearby. The newly constructed sports centre, with its swimming-pool, indoor tennis, badminton and squash courts and the gymnasium, was available to members of the public, adults and children alike. They gained admis-

sion when they became members of the Maddleskirk Abbey
Sports Club. The public could also attend concerts either in
the church or at the sports centre when its indoor courts
became an auditorium. Even the school theatre offered invi-
tations to the local people for plays or films. Looking upon
the huge campus from this distance made me realize it was
far bigger and infinitely busier even than its neighbouring
village of Maddleskirk. It really did need its own private
police force.

These thoughts occupied my mind as I found myself
thinking of the contrasting ruined priory. In its heyday, before
its destruction by Henry VIII and before his successor, Edward
VI ransacked Catholic churches and destroyed their treasures,
that old abbey would have been a similarly busy and important
place. The modern Maddleskirk Abbey was an amazing
recovery from those dark days, second only to its sister abbey
at Ampleforth. In the silence of those few minutes while Elaine
tried to re-establish contact with Holmes and we awaited a
response from the contractors, I was trying to comprehend the
impact of the Reformation upon my life and the lives of others.
In simple terms, much of it had been glossed over in the history
books but old records revealed a sorrowful period with faults
on the side of both Protestants and Catholics. As I stood in deep
contemplation, one result of those times lay directly beneath
the damaged woodland behind me – but we had no time to
worry about the past.

Our present dilemma was to find and rescue a young man.
With Brother George at my side, I gazed almost unseeingly
across the landscape as I awaited the return of Prior Tuck. I
noticed in the far distance that an anonymous white van was
moving slowly in front of the south door of the church. It was
a long way from my vantage point but its slow movement
attracted my attention. It was not unusual – contractors' vans
were constantly moving around the site – but this one
continued past, then turned away and moved down the slope
which would take it towards the part of the campus where the

construction workers were busy. At that distance – I was probably half-a-mile away – it looked like a Ford Transit, but, as I
watched, I was reminded of the white van used by Harvey.
Could it him? Had he returned to the murder room and been
re-interviewed by DCS Napier who had dismissed him this
time? The contrite return of Harvey had been forecast by the
CID but was it actually happening?

I continued to watch as the van headed in our direction.
Then it vanished behind a partially constructed accommodation block so I regarded the incident as one of those many
miniscule daily events that could be expected here. It was of no
consequence. Because all the monkstables were gathered in the
woodland awaiting the return of their prior, none would have
noticed that van – except Brother George. But he was still
saying nothing.

With more serious matters to occupy me, I tried to concentrate on the job in hand. Then someone called, 'Here he comes',
and that voice broke the spell of my silent observations. I could
see that Prior Tuck was on his way back in Oscar Blaketon's car
followed by a procession of other vehicles.

All the monkstables and other helpers had congregated
beside the road, not far from 'my' barns. Then I could see the
convoy of vehicles and diggers heading our way from the
construction site. There were a couple of white vans among
them with sundry other cars about to join us. I called to Elaine
to alert her.

'Anything from Holmes?' I asked.

'Not a whisper, Mr Rhea. Not a sound....'

'So Sherlock is still down there?'

'Yes, I would have thought he would have responded if
Holmes had whimpered or made any kind of noise, but he's
not said anything. He will be guarding Simon right now.'

'What news of Simon?'

'Nothing. I'm so pleased these men are coming, we need to
get down to him wherever he is. I do hope it's Simon and not
someone else!'

'Reinforcements are on the way.' I pointed to the procession of oncoming vehicles and their crews. 'We'll soon have all the casualties out.'

'I could always radio for police assistance. Shall I do that now?'

'Let's see how our friends cope,' I suggested. The truth was I didn't want the police to arrange the rescue of Simon and the dog for that would surely create local publicity, which was precisely what we did *not* require. Until now the press and even the villagers had no idea that a murder investigation was on-going at the abbey. It was very low key probably because the forensic evidence had not yet been fully assessed and the hunt for Simon had accounted for a lot of the activity. None-the-less, I felt we had to keep the proverbial lid on this rescue operation by dealing with it ourselves. So far, my contact with the media in both incidents was nil.

As I watching the oncoming convoy, I felt sure we had the personnel, skills and equipment necessary to complete our operation. After all, it was not like a mining disaster where several men could be trapped deep underground with the imminent threat of flooding or collapsing roofs. Despite the imminent help, though, Elaine looked very worried and despondent.

'Do you think I should radio my inspector?' she asked me. 'We've always been told not to be afraid of seeking assistance.'

'Let's see how things work out,' I suggested. 'I know your colleagues would not wish to be diverted for something that might be over in a few minutes, or even before they get here.'

'Yes, you're right. But I do worry a lot....'

I wondered whether she was speaking for her dogs or Simon, or for all three, but, as we watched, the convoy of diggers and vans halted on the lane close to our location. It reminded me of an army convoy going into battle. I noticed the white van I'd seen earlier had now joined the tail-end of the convoy along with some other cars. It seemed as if everyone was heading this way....

Prior Tuck clambered out of Blaketon's vehicle and headed my way so I left Elaine and Brother George to go and discuss tactics. She returned to the hole in the ground into which she had first despatched both dogs and called Holmes's name. He did not respond so she moved to the new entrance in an attempt to establish contact with Sherlock. Certainly his voice sounded louder and closer when it came from this new hole but again, there was nothing from the other dog. As I watched events unfolding I had no idea how or where to commence the rescue operation and hoped that someone amongst us would know what to do. I was acutely aware of the impending dangers and the entire operation threatened to be very exhausting, tense and nerve-racking.

But Prior Tuck was in charge. I went to meet him as another man wearing spectacles, a hard hat and a bright yellow jacket joined him. From the gathering of monkstables and others who had assembled nearby, I motioned to the two, Father Wills and Father Mutch, to join me – I wanted Father Will Stutely and Father Mutch to be present due to their caving experience and Father Will Redman because of his architectural knowledge. I guessed the prior would be aware of all the valuable experience he had at his disposal.

I felt that Father Redman could be useful if the question of stresses and strains on underground timbers, walls or roofs required expert assessment. Indeed he might know a lot about underground conditions too.

Prior Tuck appeared to be totally confident as he took charge of events. He came to speak to my little group and said, 'I've been offered a selection of vehicles, equipment and experts,' he announced. 'We're not sure what's required so we've brought a choice. Once we've determined what we should do, the other vehicles and operators can return to work. Now, let me introduce Joe Sampson, he's the site surveyor and has offered his services.'

'Good afternoon.' In his bright yellow jacket, Sampson, a tall fair-haired man in his late forties, spoke with a cultured accent.

'Pleased to meet you all. So can someone explain to me exactly what the current situation is, then we can see what can be done.'

'Nick?' asked the prior having been away for a while.

'Sure.' I gave my name then offered a full and detailed explanation, bringing events up-to-date with the current situation and not forgetting an account of recent problems. I called on Elaine to explain what she had done and how things had escalated. I concluded by saying we felt sure that Simon was somewhere beneath the most recent heavy landslide, pointing out there were several entrances including one close by. Elaine had already indicated that at least one of the police dogs was beneath that point. I stressed that we believed Simon was with that dog, probably still alive but unconscious adding that we had had no communication from him. I also referred to the skills of the three monkstables now at my side. Meanwhile, Brother George had wandered off and had returned to the patch of higher ground that gave him an elevated view across the campus. Something was still demanding his attention but he did not seem inclined to share it with anyone. I puzzled over his behaviour – it was as if he was cutting himself off, wanting to be away from all the turmoil and activity which might not produce a good result.

'First, let me examine the location alone,' requested Joe, oblivious of my worry about Brother George.

He mounted a secure rock to elevate himself above the crowd and continued. 'All of you please remain here, I don't want a crowd of people tramping across the roofs of these passages, as any one of them might collapse and that would create another blockage. Heavy falling stones could kill the boy or animal. We need to take every precaution.'

And so we remained in our small gathering but gathered at the roadside very close to my barns. I suddenly noticed the abbot among the crowd, and was then surprised to see DCS Napier at his side, and, even more surprising, in the background was the dark figure of Harvey the sculptor. So it had been his white van! No one spoke. It was almost as if the sound of voices would break some kind of spell. Elaine joined us, momentarily suspending her hunt for Holmes but at Joe's request, she did speak as she called Sherlock and we heard his bark from beneath us. In the silence, Joe did not walk on top of the landslide but skirted it gingerly, sometimes stooping to check some minor point with his bare hands and at other times listening carefully with his head on one side. From time to time, he asked Elaine for another guiding bark from Sherlock. He examined the first entrance by which we had thought Simon had entered the underground maze, then shook his head.

He returned to address us. 'It would be dangerous to dig down from above the area where we believe Simon to be. The landslide has dislodged heavy rocks and sodden earth, and if we excavate downwards from the surface we could disturb the overlying materials and whatever's beneath. The whole thing could collapse and bury him. The network of monks' cells will have created a fairly stable system of passages as Simon has managed to get so far underground. And so has Sherlock even if we are uncertain which of the entrances Simon used. Sherlock used the distant one, over there' – he pointed – 'but there is one near this location. So, gentleman, if we can't dig downwards then we must enter from the side, shoring up our tunnelling as we progress. Now, I am told there are three monks with caving experience and architectural expertise?'

The two Wills and Mutch indicated their presence with raised hands.

'Which is which?' asked Joe.

'We're both called Will,' said Will Stutely. 'But I am Will the Caver, and my colleague here is Will the Draftsman. He knows about stresses and strains in earthworks and buildings. And this is Father Miller who is both a caver and a weightlifter. He's pretty good at shifting blockages, I can tell you. And we can get the Abbey estate workers to help with the digging.'

Joe continued, 'That all sounds very promising! My colleagues and I are skilled at erecting buildings after excavating foundations, but we are not accustomed to digging underground where people or animals might be lying injured. So we need advice. Will the Caver, what do you recommend we do?'

'I agree we should enter from the side and not the top; we need lighting once we're in there and we will also need a narrow stretcher and first aid equipment.'

'Would you be prepared to enter any tunnel we either discover or create?'

'I would, but after first inspecting it for myself.' Monkstable Stutely made the sign of the cross on his forehead and chest.

And at that stage, Harvey surprised me by stepping forward, having worked his way without being noticed through the crowd towards the point of action. 'I'll volunteer to go underground,' he offered. 'I know I'm big and clumsy, but I have caving experience too. And strength.'

'Good. So we have volunteers! Wonderful,' nodded Joe. 'It's time for action.'

'I'd also want a moment or two to ask God to protect me, Simon, the monkstables and the other rescuers, not forgetting the dogs!' said Monkstable Stutely. 'As we go deeper, we'll need to shore up our tunnel. Whilst it won't be too difficult reaching the target area if mechanical diggers are used, it will be far more difficult extricating an injured or unconscious person if trapped by heavy rocks or fallen timbers. If we move or disturb anything we might cause further falls. And as Father Will said, we'll need floodlights.'

'We've got some,' nodded Joe. 'For our sites after dark. We can use them.'

'Good,' smiled Will Stutely. 'But we must act with speed now.'

Joe said, 'At this stage, I am against using mechanical diggers because they could cause more landfalls. I'm afraid it's down to the good old-fashioned picks and shovels.'

'I'm capable of cracking rocks open,' volunteered Harvey. 'Even big ones with pickaxes....'

'I'm delighted at this response,' said Prior Tuck. 'But we have estate workers who are handy with picks and shovels ... they can do a lot to help. Under guidance.'

Joe nodded his agreement. 'I'll keep a JCB and a smaller digger here in case there are heavy boulders or fallen trees. Right, that's settled. I'll retain those vehicles and despatch the others back to the site while you organize the workers with their picks and shovels. Then we're in business.'

'The sooner we get started, the better,' said Prior Tuck. 'Whilst Joe is organizing his side of things, Brother George, can you contact as many estate workers as possible and tell them they are needed here with their wheelbarrows to shift the spoil and dump it? Tell them to bring plenty of picks and shovels and whatever lights they can find. It's better to have more stuff than we need, far better than not having enough.'

'Leave it to me,' said Brother George who had remained quiet and isolated during the discussions.

'I'll drive you up to the estate office,' offered Oscar Blaketon.

'Whilst I'm there,' said Brother George, 'I'll organize refreshments. I fear this might be long haul.'

'Splendid idea,' agreed Prior Tuck. 'And now we must decide how to deploy the remaining monkstables. Gentlemen, the noise and activity that is going to be generated here within the next few minutes is bound to attract curious bystanders and even the press. People will come to see what's going on and they could get in the way. So, can you form a barrier around the working area to prevent any access by unauthorized persons – Father Robin, perhaps you can oversee that?'

'Of course.'

'If anyone asks, tell them it is an exercise ... you can say we are rescuing a trapped dog and we're doing it as realistically as possible.'

And so the task of locating and rescuing both Simon and Sherlock began in earnest. But I was very interested in why both Harvey and DCS Napier had decided to attend this operation. Did it mean someone else had been arrested for the murder?

CHAPTER 16

So THE DELICATE rescue operation got underway. Elaine ordered Sherlock to remain with Simon from whom there had been no sign although Sherlock confirmed his presence when requested by his handler. His barks were immensely valuable as the rescuers carefully began to remove tons of earth, rocks and trees around the place the boy was thought to be trapped. Even then, there was no reaction from the other dog.

The rescuers were already proving very adept and their gentleness reminded me of archaeologists as they removed the earth and other debris inch by inch from a precious relic, always careful not to disturb or damage anything of value. Large trees were sawn into manageable logs with chainsaws, heavy rocks were gently teased from the ground by miniature diggers and tons of earth were removed by the bucketful and carried off in dumper trucks as the rescue got underway.

As there was nothing I could do at this stage, I stood and watched from a respectful distance and could see that as the men worked, so they gained confidence in themselves and their machines. Nonetheless, any delicate work was undertaken by hand. I was impressed by their care and gentle workmanship and the knowledge and leadership skills of Joe Sampson.

A small crowd began to gather because the activity could be seen from the estate and a few houses in the locality. It was inevitable bystanders would arrive and, as it was after five o'clock, many staff members had come to watch before going home. The monkstables were preventing spectators from unintentionally interfering with the operation.

Then I realized we had forgotten something. No one had brought a stretcher. I made my way through the spectators towards Oscar Blaketon.

'Could I ask a favour?' I put to him. 'Your car's handy so can you drive up to the infirmary?'

'Something wrong?'

'No one's brought a stretcher, or arranged for the ambulance to stand-by. I thought we should have them on hand if and when needed – like now! We could borrow one from the infirmary, can't we? The ambulance can come later once we've got a clearer picture of events.'

'My trusty old Morris Traveller will cope, Nick. You stay here as you could be needed. I'll see to that.'

And he left to go upon his errand.

I was alone for a moment or two, standing apart from the growing crowd as I watched Oscar Blaketon's gallant old vehicle head across the valley then I saw Brother George heading my way. He had been prepared to join the underground rescue attempt but Prior Tuck had advised against it, doubtless because of George's age. Already, the rescue attempt was underway as the noise of machinery filled the air. Prior Tuck was in firm control.

'He said this job was for younger people, Nick! I can take a hint!' said George. 'But I'd like a quiet word with you. With no one overhearing us.'

'Fine, let's take a walk.'

Recalling George's moments of thoughtful solitude, I wondered what was troubling him, so we strolled in silence over to my barns. The frontage was now a car-park. I reasoned that our detachment from the rescue effort would be hidden from curious sightseers. I found a low stone wall for us to sit upon and asked, 'So, Brother George, what can I do for you?'

'I've something to say but hope you don't think I'm being silly.'

'I'm sure I won't think that! It's a good idea to share some-thing that's worrying you. How can I help?'

'You've seen the maps on the walls of the murder room?' he began.

'I have. The detectives managed to locate a lot of them in a very short time – no doubt the monastery library helped.'

'Right, now the cricket field is clearly shown—'

'George's Field, your field in other words?'

'I don't own it,' he corrected me. 'It's just named after me because I created it out of an abandoned overgrown area full of rubbish. They didn't call it Brother George's Field in case I became ordained, then it would have to be changed to Father George's Field, or even Prior George's Field, or Abbot George's Field or just Abbot's Field.' He grinned cheekily. 'Or even Archbishop's, Cardinal's or Pope's Field ... but I know I shall always be Brother George.'

'So what's your point?'

'You know that excavations are under way in a corner of it? And that the search area resulted from an aerial photograph? A helicopter pilot flying over it is supposed to have noticed the outlines of foundations beneath the surface and photographed the site. A common occurrence. Then, fairly recently, the archaeologist got permission from the abbot for an exploratory excavation.'

'That's what I heard,' I nodded. 'He's a freelance called Rawdon and his team of six are students from York University.'

'Yes. I was there when Detective Chief Superintendent Napier confirmed he'd checked his identity and purpose. There were no problems. Rawdon has no convictions and neither have any of his students.'

'Right, Brother George, and also Mr Napier would have asked the local police to check his home address and back-ground. Clearly, they did so and there were no problems. Rawdon is not in the frame for the murder, as we say.'

Brother George eventually came to his point. 'I must tell you this. This morning very early, I went into the library to have a look at that aerial photo. I'm not happy with the situation which is why I hunted out the original map that I used when creating the cricket field. A copy of the aerial photo is in the library having been donated by Rawdon. I looked at it this morning.'

'Go on.'

'That aerial photograph is a fake, Nick.'

For a moment or two, I was unsure what he was trying to explain, so I asked, 'How can it be a fake? How do you fake such a photo?'

'Oh, the photo is genuine enough. It is a real aerial photo-graph of a field with evidence of former buildings or some other structure like an old road beneath the surface. That's not in doubt. But it is *not* a photo of George's Field, Nick. That's my point.'

'How can you know that? A field is a field....'

'No, it isn't. Fields have identities, characteristics. Believe me, Nick. That photo does not show George's Field. It shows somewhere else, but I don't know where. As you know, all digital photographs are automatically dated and timed by modern cameras. This one is no exception. It is dated four years ago – on Wednesday, 20 May to be precise, and it is timed at ten minutes past three in the afternoon of that day – but of some unknown field. There is no location marked and no map reference. It was the Feast Day of St Bernardine of Sienna, that's how I remember it. Bernardine, by the way, was a man's name. He was a Franciscan monk and renowned as a preacher in Italy.'

'All fascinating stuff, Brother George, but what has this got to do with that photo being a fake?'

'Wednesday is sports afternoon at Maddleskirk College, Nick. That day – 20 May – was the final of the college's inter-house cricket tournament. St Aelred's was playing St Aidan's on George's Field that afternoon. It was a fine, dry and sunny day, I know, I was there. At that time, the south-east corner was occupied by the pavilion, and even if we had not been actually playing a match, the outfield would have been cut, the site of the pitch selected with the crease marked, boundaries and so on highlighted with white lines. There was always a roller on hand too, parked behind the pavilion ... none of those things is on the photo submitted by that man Rawdon. They would have been, if it was genuine.'

'So, to your knowledge, has George's Field ever been photographed from the air? Indeed, is it known whether it sits on top of an ancient ruin of some kind?'

'That possibility has never been suggested, Nick. Having worked on that field and seen a dowser at work there, looking for water pipes, I know there is nothing of the kind beneath the surface of George's Field, and neither are there any ancient foundations.'

'You sound very sure.'

'I am very sure, I'm positive, Nick, and there's evidence to support my statement. The field was photographed from the air by one of the ex-students who was given a lift over it in a helicopter. His photo is on file in the library and there are no signs of ancient walls or stonework under the ground. If there had been, the outlines would be visible on his photo.'

'Well, that seems positive enough.'

'That's why I find this very worrying, particularly with so much going on now. Something is very wrong, Nick. Very wrong indeed.'

I wasn't quite sure what he was driving at because, as a result of the disputed photograph, an archaeologist and his team of volunteers had come to excavate and research the area. They must have thought the photo was genuine. According to checks made by the murder team, Rawdon and his volunteers had no criminal records and nothing was known against them. To all intents and purposes, it was a perfectly normal archaeological excavation. So why would someone go to such lengths to excavate George's Field – what could they be looking for? Why search for something that was patently not there? Even more curiously, why go to the extent of faking a photograph and gathering a team together to hunt for something for which no genuine proof existed? Or was it all due to someone's carelessness – or even a genuine mistake?

'What do you read into this, Brother George?'

'I'm no intellectual, Nick, neither am I a detective or even an historian. I'm just an old retired Yorkshire farmer who happens to have become a Benedictine brother and I find it all to be very baffling.'

'You must have had a reason for telling me.'

'I've heard you telling us during those training sessions that detectives and police officers rarely believe in coincidences.'

'That's true, yes.'

'Well, we've had a murder here, then a missing boy – and now a research team working from a fake map. All at the same time. I can see how the missing lad might not be linked to the murder, especially if he's trapped. He was doing nothing more than any normal lad would do. We used to call it bird-nesting, he might call it bird watching, but it still leaves us with an unsolved murder along with a man in our grounds who seems to be doing something very odd. And he did not come alone, Nick. I'm not talking about those students; I saw him arrive. I was working in the garden and saw Rawdon arrive in the van. It dropped someone off – that person, a man I think, went into the retreat and Rawdon drove the van away. It went towards the cricket field, Nick, and parked there. I find it all very suspicious, really I do.'

'That confirms what Mrs Morley said about Thorpe's arrival. She said he'd been given a lift by a friend.'

'We know Thorpe was murdered, but what do we know about Rawdon? Nowt!' stressed Brother George.

'Napier must be told of this, Brother George, but do you think Rawdon could have made a serious mistake? Selected the wrong map from wherever they obtain such things?'

'If he had, he would have realized his mistake by now, packed up and gone home. He's been here long enough to realize that. Nick, I know there is nothing to be found under that field, and he is still excavating. Or pretending to.'

I began to walk around in a large circle as I tried to see some kind of logic in Brother George's observations, then I halted.

'Come on, Brother George, tell me the rest.'

'I'm glad you used to be a policeman, Nick. We had a lot o' time for our local village copper, but coppers don't know everything, do they?'

'No,' I admitted. 'But they are usually capable of learning very quickly.'

'Right,' he said. 'Now, I know nowt about computers but I had a word with Father Will early this morning. Will Redman, that is. He knows about them and does most of his research work in the library about ancient abbeys, their architecture and so on. And what's likely to turn up in their grounds or even in old graves. So I told him I was worried about that archaeologist.'

'So what did he do?'

'He put that chap's name into the library computer. Searched the web, as he called it – not that that means owt to me. But he came up with his name.'

'Because Rawdon's a well known archaeologist?'

'No, because he's a well-known treasure hunter, Nick. He goes off hunting in all sorts of places with one of those metal detectors. Do you remember that hoard of Anglo-Saxon gold that was found on a Dales farm four or five years ago? Thousands of pieces ... worth millions they reckoned, shared with the farmer who owned the land.'

'I read about it, yes.'

'It was this chap who found it, he's a very successful treasure hunter, earns his living by doing it. He got a share after the inquest – and he's found loads of other stuff up and down the country.'

'Do we know exactly what other stuff he has discovered?'

'There's a lot of it listed on the computer, Nick, but I can remember only odd bits. One was a silver chalice he found in

Rievaulx Abbey grounds and then there was a ring discovered near the edge of the pond at Whitby Abbey. He has got the knack of finding things.'

'You think he's seeking buried treasure in your cricket field?'

'What, with a load of students? Whatever he finds he'd have to share it with them. I don't reckon he's that sort of chap, he wants it all so he works alone. By all accounts he's not one for sharing, so the reports said. He had a right battle with that farmer when he found all that gold on his land – he wanted the lot for himself. It was all in the papers at that time, now it's all shown on the web. Anyway, there's no buried treasure in that cricket field – I couldn't tell you how many pupils of Maddleskirk College have had a go at prospecting there and not found even a dropped penny. I think Rawdon's pretending to search and it's his cover for wanting to be inside the Abbey grounds legitimately because he's here for some other purpose. The question is – what?'

'So we've an unsavoury character looking for treasure in the grounds, someone who has sneaked in with a very dodgy photograph. In fact, Brother George, his presence could be classed as nothing more than trespassing which means the abbot or someone on his behalf could ask him to leave. His behaviour is not a criminal offence though – unless he steals something or causes criminal damage.'

'Or kills somebody,' said Brother George in his slow and calculated voice.

'Is that what you think?' I was quite shocked to hear the old gentleman suggest such a thing, especially as he was now a monk, albeit not ordained.

'Greed is one of the oldest motives in the world, Nick. It's one of the seven deadly sins – covetousness.'

'You've been thinking hard about this, haven't you?'

'Aye, I have.'

'Right, you're sure you saw a man leave the van and go into the retreat?'

'I am, I was working in the garden like I said.'

'Would you recognize him?'

'I thought it was that chap in the stone coffin, Nick. Not very tall, with a beard, but when he arrived he was wearing smart clothes. In his coffin he looked like a hiker, but his face on the photos was the same, I'm sure about that.'

Brother George's story supported that of Mrs Morley but required immediate investigation. Clearly there was more he wanted to tell me but at that point, I noticed DCS Napier heading in our direction.

'Brother George,' I said. 'You must tell Mr Napier everything you've just told me. He's on his way.'

'OK, I'll do that, I need to get it off my chest,' was all he said.

'Is this a private conference or can anyone join in?' asked Napier as he drew closer. 'I've come for my car, Nick. I'm returning to the murder room. I came over to see what's going on just in case there's anything that might be linked to my murder enquiry. I must say I can't link that missing lad with the dead man in the crypt even though we think Simon had been in there looking at a pretty face on the triptych.'

'That's something of a relief, I can tell you!' I issued a long sigh of exhaled breath.

'I'm also inclined to discount his disappearance as being in any way associated with the murder. And, thanks to the monkstables we know Simon is genuinely missing and on the point of being rescued – I can concentrate on other matters now. I hope he gets out alive. Keep in touch.'

'While you're here, Mr Napier, Brother George has something very important to tell us which I think is highly relevant. But before you speak to him, did you know Harvey is among the searchers?'

'Yes, and we've talked. In fact, he called at the murder room on his way here and wanted to explain why he ran off like he did. He does it whenever he feels pressured. He's done it before. I interviewed him at length and there is no way I can arrest him or charge him with the murder. He apologized for running off which I accepted and, because this is a Catholic abbey, I gave him a penance and suggested he came here and helped in the rescue operation. That's his penance.'

'He's quite a character,' I admitted.

'He's a one-off, Nick. He was a young violent tearaway but he's reformed. I know him well enough to believe him. I've no evidence against him except he was in the crypt twice during the time the victim was lying there and there's no scientific evidence against him. Now, Brother George, what do you want to tell me?'

For the second time, Brother George gave a full account of his researches to which Napier listened intently without interrupting the narrative. George told the story just as he had explained it to me and it was interesting to hear Napier ask questions very similar to those I had asked.

Then Napier said, 'One of our teams interviewed the archaeologist and his students earlier today. Their stories have been checked and are true. They come from York University, studying archaeology, and their stories tally with what the university authorities have told us. They arrive daily in a university mini-bus and leave at five each day.'

'They ended their stint on Friday afternoon about three, then returned this morning,' I told him. 'None of them was on this campus at the time of the murder, we're sure of that, but their leader was – he camps in his van and remained here alone over the weekend, working to complete a section that he considered important. Have your men checked his background?'

'His full name and address have been checked, Nick, and they match the information in the correspondence between him and the abbot when he was seeking permission. We checked with the Institute for Archaeologists and he's listed as a member even though some people describe him as a treasure hunter. The van belongs to a friend called Larkfield. It hasn't been reported stolen and Rawdon has no criminal record so we can't check his fingerprints against CRO records, nor have we taken any DNA samples as he has not come into the frame as a suspect. In short, Brother George, we have no reason to suspect the archaeologist of any illegality.'

'It still seems very odd to me, Mr Napier. How do we account for Rawdon's presence with a fake map? He must have known it wasn't the right one,' Brother George stood his ground. 'So what's he up to?'

'It could be the result of human error,' suggested Napier. 'I haven't asked about that as I had no idea it was a fake until you suggested it. I guess he was supplied with it and came here not realizing it wasn't actually the map of the cricket field. Clearly he has reason to believe there are hidden remains and equally clearly, he has obtained permission to search the field for them. He's done all the right things and is no more under suspicion than any workman on the construction site. And if you think he is the killer, Brother George, why hasn't he disappeared? Fled the scene?'

'To make it appear he is entirely innocent?' suggested Brother George.

'That would require extraordinary nerve! So you think he's guilty?' Napier pressed.

'It's not impossible if greed is the motive.' Brother George spoke quietly and with some conviction.

'What evidence have you for thinking that?'

'The treasure hidden beneath the stone coffin,' replied Brother George. 'It's said to be worth millions. It's not just a legend protected by a raven – it's genuine.'

'Nobody has said anything about that to me! Anyway, no human power can move the coffin and you can't get machinery into the crypt to do the job, there's no access. How can you be sure it's not merely a spot of ancient folklore? Remember, Brother George, we are professional detectives and must base our results on hard and proven evidence, not theories or fairy stories. However in view of your concern, and the fact you've raised some valid questions, along with the fake photo, we'll investigate him further. He needs to be eliminated from our enquiries. He's a noted treasure hunter, not an archaeologist?'

'That's right,' said Brother George. 'Thank you for saying

you'll investigate him. But don't forget all those tunnels that run under parts of the Abbey and crypt; some of them give access to both the church and the crypt. I think both those chaps were up to summat, then one of 'em got killed.'

'All right, Brother George, I'm getting the message! This needs more work. Now I must return to see if my teams have uncovered anything of interest, so leave the archaeologist to me. Pop into the Murder Room any time, both of you, we value your input.' And he left.

'What do you make of that?' I asked Brother George when Napier had left.

'I think I've got him interested in my story so I hope he'll do something.' He smiled. 'If he doesn't, I'll dig deeper and produce the evidence myself!'

As we concluded our conversation, Oscar Blaketon returned with the stretcher and used Napier's empty parking space as more sightseers' vehicles had arrived. Happily, the duty monkstables were in control and the high wire fence was keeping most visitors at bay. We returned to the scene, helping Oscar to carry the stretcher and we placed it close to the centre of operations. Then we sought Prior Tuck. He was standing not far away but near enough to observe all the action.

'We've got a stretcher,' I told him. 'Narrow with wheels; ideal for this. The ambulance will follow. So, have there been any more developments?'

'Not really,' he sounded just a little unsure of both himself and the merits of this exercise. The men had been working a long time without any result, and his posse of monkstables had also been on duty a long time. Neither group was accustomed to this kind of pressure when at work. I felt they all needed a fillip or a breakthrough of some kind.

'Things are going well?' I suggested, having noted considerable progress. From my amateur viewpoint, it seemed that most of the recent landslide had been removed and deposited at a safe distance, but there was still no sign of a passage or ancient cell walls.

And then, as if on cue, there came an almighty roar of voices with cheers and shouts. 'Hello,' said Prior Tuck. 'Methinks we have a breakthrough!'

As the workmen relaxed their efforts, the rest of the search party – including me and Oscar – were allowed into their inner circle to inspect the result of their efforts. The protective ring of monkstables remained in place as the crowd of onlookers was clearly wishing to see what had caused the cheering, but they were all held at bay. As we approached, we could see the results. The workmen went off for a well-earned break and their boss, Joe Sampson, remained to explain things.

'Quite literally,' – he indicated with his waving arms and hands – 'the lads have skimmed off the top of the old priory cell block at this point. Thanks to some wizard workmen operating our machines, we have removed and dispersed all the recent debris and a good deal more without causing any more damage or danger. It's only a small patch that we've cleared, and there is much more debris on other parts of the old priory, but if you follow the direction I'm pointing, the important thing is that we have exposed one of the ancient corridors. Thanks to the monastery librarian we have a ground plan and that open corridor gives access to a passage that in turn leads to other cells and surviving parts of the structure. We can go in now!'

'Is it safe?' asked Prior Tuck.

'As safe as it can be. I must say the stonework is in surprisingly good condition, a real tribute to the medieval builders. From here we can walk upright into several parts of the main priory. However, I'm sure that around some of the corners, and out of our vision from here, there will be blockages with tree trunks, rocks and so on. And they could represent new dangers. But the good news is that whilst our diggers take a much needed break, we can enter the complex in reasonable safety.'

'Do we know where Simon is in relation to this point?' asked the prior.

'Not with a hundred per cent certainty. We can ask Elaine to
get her dog to speak to us again, as he's been doing for most of
the time – he will be hoarse by now – and then we'll need a
volunteer to enter and carry out a very careful search.'

'Father Stutely is our caving expert,' smiled Prior Tuck. 'He's
slimmer than Father Mutch! I'm sure he'll volunteer. I see
Elaine's over there.'

He pointed, shouted and raised his hand, and called, 'Elaine,
can you come please?'

She and Father Will Stutely arrived at the same time. Prior
Tuck updated them, then asked, 'Elaine, can you get Sherlock
to speak again? He must be absolutely sick of barking at us …
If you go to that big entrance hole the workmen have
produced, your voice might carry further. But before you do so,
is there any news of Holmes?'

She shook her head. 'If he was trapped he should be able to
communicate with us, but if he's been killed by a rockfall or
something …' Her voice faded away.

'We must be positive,' whispered the prior.

'Yes, I know. No barks could mean he's found a dead person
or something important which he's guarding till we find him.
And he must be too far away to hear me asking him to speak.
I'm not sure what he's trying to tell me.' She sighed. 'But whatever it is, he's guarding it. I feel sure he must have spoken
without us hearing him above all the noise out here.'

'But Sherlock will continue to speak?'

'He will.' She spoke with confidence.

Before Father Will entered the maze that was now partially
revealed before him, he asked Joe, 'Have you a long length of
white rope or a piece of cable? I need to fix one end to my waist
if I'm going in there. Then if I find Simon or the dogs someone
can follow my trail, otherwise we're going to have helpers
wandering all over the place and getting lost themselves.'

Joe called one of his workmen. 'Eddie, can you get a reel of
white rope? There's one in the van over there, the one we use
when fixing and tracing deep sewers and drains.'

'Right, boss.'

'Now, Elaine, while he's doing that, can you get Sherlock to speak again? We need to know precisely where Simon is if that's possible.'

'I might have to go inside,' she warned us, with a slight tremor in her voice.

'Fine, so get yourself fixed up with some white rope and a hard hat, then we'll let you in!'

And so after the magic worked by tea and cake, the team returned to work, this time accompanied by Father Will in a hard hat instead of his white helmet, and Elaine without her police cap but with also with a hard hat. She carried a powerful torch from her police van, and had found another walkie-talkie radio. When everyone was ready, Elaine and Father Will moved as close as possible to the entrance, each with a long coil of white rope attached to their waists and anchored on reels close to the entrance.

'Ready?' asked Father Will.

She nodded and said, 'I do hope we find them. Can someone stand near my van to receive calls from me over the radio? We need someone accustomed to using them.'

'Count me in,' smiled Oscar Blaketon. 'Alf and I will volunteer for that, won't we, Alf? We'll become the control room for the exercise!'

'And I will say a silent prayer or two as we go deeper inside,' said Father Will Stutely to Elaine. 'Can I suggest we remain as close as possible? It will get darker as we go deeper but I have a torch,' and he produced one from the pocket of his police tunic. 'Time to go?'

Elaine nodded.

'Quiet, everyone,' called Prior Tuck. 'They'll need silence once inside.'

As Elaine entered beside the monkstable, she called out, 'Sherlock', and was rewarded by a double bark that sounded a long way off and echoed slightly. But it meant Sherlock was still by the side of the boy although it did not reveal whether he was unconscious, trapped or merely lost. Simon did not speak.

'We'll soon find him,' I heard Father Will tell Elaine as they moved slowly along the darkening passage and into the network of ruined cottage-style cells.

Then a strange thing happened. Prior Tuck's voice rose above the gentle chatter of the audience and the remaining helpers and monkstables lapsed into silence.

'Everyone, pray silence for a moment. I want all the monkstables to offer two minutes of silent personal prayer for the success of this operation, and then immediately afterwards I shall ask everyone to join in a prayer known to us all – Pater Noster, otherwise known as the Our Father. We shall say it in English.'

Amazingly everyone became still and silent as the searchers moved slowly into the depths. Heads were bowed as people considered their own thoughts. After a couple minutes, Prior Tuck began the Our Father with everyone joining in.

And in the silence of the moments that followed, they all said 'Amen'.

By then, Father Will and Elaine had disappeared with only their long white tails of rope indicating their progress ever deeper into the dark, dank labyrinth.

CHAPTER 17

I WASN'T SURE how long we were expected to remain quiet, but we watched in silence as the rescuers disappeared into the darkness of the ancient buried corridors. From our vantage point, the reflected light of their bobbing torches marked the progress and we could see some old cells that were close to us. They glistened with dampness between patches of bright green moss which must support various kinds of subterranean wild life. The onlookers began to whisper to one another, but the sense of tension remained as we all settled down for what might become a long and nervous wait.

As my eyes became accustomed to the exposed areas of gloom, I could see there was water in the passage they had used. Some of the footway seemed to be standing in several inches with the other parts being thick with mud and uniden-tified debris. I began to wonder if any of the areas further inside were flooded, if so to what depth? Were there dangerous pits and pools? It was probable that any drainage system would have become blocked after centuries without mainte-nance, with the ever-present water finding its own levels and outlets.

So far as we could tell, Elaine and Father Will had not confronted any problems as they continued into the depths occasionally calling the names of Simon and the dogs. At our distance we could not hear whether or not they received replies but were aware of their voices gradually diminishing in volume. I wondered if they would be able to hear any sounds from the network of walls and corridors but the searchers were now beyond the buzz of the waiting crowd.

Prior Tuck remained at my side. Suddenly he said, 'Nick, we don't have a doctor on site. Really we should have one here, there may be injuries.'

'You have one or two in the monastery, I believe,' I responded.

'Yes, Father Raymund qualified. I'll contact him. He's not one of the monkstables but I shouldn't have any trouble finding him.'

'He sounds ideal. How do we get in touch with him from here?'

'I'll ask Father Alban, he's one of the monkstables standing over there. I prefer to keep Father Miller here in case we need his strength in a rescue attempt.'

Father Alban Dale, one of the monkstables and a slightly built man in his early fifties, had been very quiet throughout the day's events. I knew him to be a thoughtful man who enjoyed nothing better than a quiet pint in a traditional English village pub. One of his ambitions was to visit every Marian shrine in Britain and Ireland and compile a book about them, and it was his determination to achieve that aim that took him into many village inns for his meals and a pint of local ale. There were stories of him being challenged by local drinkers to games of darts or billiards – his dog collar attracted that kind of attention. He would accept such challenges and then go on to win every game – he was a former champion snooker and billiards player, a keen darts player. He had also been known to lead singing sessions in some pubs.

'Father Alban,' Prior Tuck called to him. 'Can you find Father Raymund and ask him to join us? Explain what it's all about and say we need him to stand-by as a doctor – and it's time to chase up the ambulance.'

And so, with Oscar Blaketon sitting in the driving seat of the police dog van with Ventress at his side, both listening for any communications from Elaine, we all settled down among an ever-increasing crowd of spectators. Now that Father Will and

Elaine had disappeared from view and were out of ear-shot we began to talk more freely. A powerful atmosphere of expectation and hope enveloped us as eventually the topics for conversations were exhausted and long silences followed. A natural sense of anticipation followed as we awaited news. I wondered how the team would cope if they encountered a blockage anywhere but was confident they would summon help if necessary. I could hear the call-signs of the occasional radio signal being transmitted to the police dog van but it was too far away from me to hear anything. I thought the calls would be from Elaine as she kept in touch with Oscar to announce they were proceeding deeper into the labyrinth without any problems and without any more positive news. It was a pity we could not map out their route from above, but that was impossible. As the tension increased, I walked away from the gathering, not to distance myself from any action that might follow but to reflect on what I was witnessing. After all, I had a very great interest in this location.

As the new owner, I would become responsible for maintaining the old site and making it safe even if its visitors were trespassers. I knew enough about the law to realize that landowners owed a duty of care to everyone who ventured onto their property, including those not invited. It could be an expensive asset! I had no money to maintain it even though, according to my solicitor, there was a cash inheritance of around £55,000 and a house in Scotland. Maybe I should sell my Scottish interests? But something as simple and basic as the installation of safety features and a new security fence would require most of my available cash. As I tried to anticipate how I would cope with my new responsibilities, I was aware of someone approaching me. It was Abbot Merryman.

'Nick, I saw you there looking thoughtful so I thought I'd have a quick word. I've just spoken to Prior Tuck and he's updated me. He tells me the monkstables have played a very significant part in this and in the murder investigation. As you'll understand, I have to compile a written report for our trustees, so I wondered what your reactions are? I only need it verbally at this stage, because the trustees have already started ringing for my comments! I am amazed at how rapidly word spreads!'

'Who is spreading the news?' was my immediate reaction.

'One of our trustees lives in Maddleskirk, Nick, and he was told by a friend who works for the college. I have to provide an accurate account of Simon's disappearance and the murder investigation.'

'So much for trying to keep this story under wraps,' I said. 'Rumours and wild stories are easily generated – I'm surprised no newspaper or local radio station has been on to us.'

'They have. I've already taken a call from a news agency in York. I dealt with it – told them it was nothing more than a training exercise for our fledgling constables. That appeared to satisfy him as he knew about the monkstables because he'd covered the story at their inception. He asked no further questions and wished us luck. Surprisingly, he didn't mention the murder.'

'Good, well, I can update you from my own point of view and I'll begin by praising all the monkstables – I know the task isn't over but they've done extremely well so far,' and I outlined the entire operation as I had seen it, hoping I had not omitted anything of importance.

As I talked to him, the small crowd of onlookers moved to encircle the police dog van where Oscar Blaketon and Alf Ventress were virtually running a minor police control room with regular input from Elaine and Father Will. We could all hear their progress so we were not standing around and awaiting results; those closest to the van could hear the best.

'They're all captivated,' smiled the abbot. 'This is real, not a TV drama.'

'Father Prior is in charge.' I felt I should stress that. 'He's got the monkstables performing crowd control. But now for something quite different, Father Abbot. Have you time to listen to something important, perhaps almost under the seal of confession?'

'Of course, Nick. What on earth's happened?'

We walked away to distance ourselves from any listeners but I was not sure how to begin. I did not want to take up too much of his valuable time but felt he should now be aware of my inheritance. Satisfied we were out of hearing, I began. 'Father Abbot, suppose I mentioned the abbey's relationship with the owners of Ashwell Priory, and all that goes with it – the woodland, the holy well, those old barns....'

'There's hardly any relationship, Nick, certainly not a meaningful one. The owners won't talk to us. They don't maintain the site and it was we who erected that wire fence to keep our trespassing students safe. The owners don't visit the area or acknowledge our correspondence. You know their history? That they are an old Scottish Protestant landowning family.'

I paused for a few moments.

'Yes, Mr Cheslington told me. Father, suppose I told you that I'm going to be the new owner of Ashwell Priory Estate? Only a few days ago, and as a complete shock, I received news of an inheritance. It was a bolt from the blue. I had no idea I had Scottish ancestors, let alone those who were estate owners. Mr Cheslington, with whom I believe you are acquainted, is acting on my behalf.'

He stared at me as if I had confessed to the murder of Prior Tuck and I heard a brief expulsion of his breath. 'Are you serious, Nick? You've taken the wind right out of my sails.'

'I'm serious, Father.' I told him about the original owners' family line becoming extinct, and how I had been traced as the eldest male of an obscure line of cousins. All the religious restrictions placed on the inheritance of Ashwell Priory had been wiped out with the end of the main family line, leaving me as the surprised beneficiary.

'I don't know what to say.'

'I thought you ought to know, in confidence. You've treated me with respect in telling me about Simon's true family, so I am now returning the compliment.'

'What are your plans?' he waved his hands around in a grand gesture.

'I have absolutely no idea. I've not had time to think about it, but seeing all this carnage has made me realize that I could have inherited some serious problems and responsibilities.'

'Are you actually the owner of this now?'

'I don't know,' I admitted. 'I'm not sure whether I became the owner at the moment the original owner died, or when my particular circumstances were determined, or when I sign on the dotted line. All I can say at the moment is that I have not signed anything but expect to do so next week.'

'I don't really know what to say, except perhaps congratulations,' admitted the abbot. 'I'm stunned. Thank you telling me, it gives me time to adjust to the idea that, at last, Ashwell Priory has returned to Catholic ownership as it was in the beginning. I am presuming you are aware of our long term interest in it?'

'I am indeed, Father Abbot, but now that I am its owner, I am not sure how I shall deal with it.'

'I'll keep this to myself of course, but once the paperwork is complete, perhaps you'll get in touch? That's if you want to discuss it further! After all, it is really nothing to do with me or the abbey trustees but I hope you will keep in mind our interest in that patch of land.'

'I'll keep in touch,' I promised. 'I might want your help and advice.'

As we ended our conversation, there was a burst of activity at van as its radio burst into life with Elaine's voice. All further conversation was terminated as we hurried closer to hear what was happening.

I heard Elaine's distinct voice. 'Sierra Two Five to base, are you receiving? Over.'

'Receiving, go ahead. Over,' replied Oscar. Everyone lapsed into a deep silence at this exchange. Blaketon had turned up the volume so that everyone, including the bystanders, could hear what was being said.

'Sierra Two Five to base, we think we have found a body. We cannot be certain; we cannot reach it without moving a lot of debris. It is in darkness and beyond the effective reach of our lights. Over.'

'Do you need assistance? Over?'

'Not at this point, we need to examine it from a closer range, but we have found Holmes.' The relief was clear in Elaine's tearful voice as she added in a lower voice. 'He is guarding his discovery and did not speak because it is not living.'

'Keep your radio open all the time,' suggested Blaketon as all around him lapsed into a deep silence. 'Can you give us a verbal account as you make your approach? Talk naturally to your colleague, we shall hear both of you.'

I wondered why the dog had not 'spoken' when making this awful discovery but perhaps he had, and perhaps he had been too far away, or too deep inside the ruins for any of us to hear him. With these thoughts, I lapsed into silence as did everyone else, all focusing on the van and its crew of police pensioners who were staffing the radio.

Listening to Father Will and Elaine discussing their moves and plans was eerie in the extreme and highly emotional. They had to move a lot of branches and tree trunks, stones and mud and it was slow progress. Then Father Will's voice came through loud and clear. 'Sorry for the false alarm,' he breathed. 'It's not a body Holmes has been guarding. It looks like a dead body, but in fact it's a stone statue of a young man or boy, about three-quarters life size and in surprisingly good condition.'

'A statue? Is it moveable?' asked Oscar.

'Yes, but it will be heavy and we wouldn't want to use the stretcher.'

'Have you further details?'

'Not many, but it is beautifully carved and seems to represent a saint.'

'The missing St Luke ...' whispered the Abbot. 'I wonder if there is a winged ox near it?' I had no idea what he meant by that comment. St Luke and a winged ox?

Oscar Blaketon broke into my thoughts as he spoke into his microphone. 'We'll have it examined when it is recovered. I'm sure we can prevail upon our construction helpers to fetch it out. It needs to be removed as it's probably causing an obstruction and might cause difficulties when we bring Simon out. I'll arrange some means of transporting it out of there. Are you able to continue your search in the meantime?'

'Yes, we can step over it. We are now resuming our patrol and are proceeding towards our objective. Sierra Two Five out.'

Oscar Blaketon turned in his seat to look at the crowd now gathered around him. He saw me with the abbot.

'Did you hear that?' he asked of anyone who might respond. The sense of relief was clear in his voice.

Many in the crowd shouted 'Yes' and some added 'Thank you'.

'It sounds very hopeful,' said Blaketon, as Joe Sampson stepped forward.

'I can obtain a small hand trolley that will cope with that statue. It's very like those you'll find on railway platforms to carry suitcases. A porter's trolley. It can also be carried by two people as it has handles at each end. Would you like us to recover it? We have torches and we can follow the white ropes until we find it. I'll seek two volunteers from my crew.'

'Thanks, Joe. That's another problem solved,' breathed Prior Tuck.

Joe was rewarded by a round of applause from the crowd and whilst the discovery of the unknown statue had galvanized the observers and participants into action, it was Father Prior who reminded us, 'And now we must concentrate on Simon and Sherlock – with some assistance, I am sure, from Holmes.'

The contractor rushed off in one of the firm's vans to locate the trolley as Father Raymund arrived with Father Alban at his side.

'Anything?' asked Father Raymund.

'Only a stone statue so far,' responded Father Prior.

I asked, 'What's all this about St Luke and a winged ox?' but my voice was drowned by an interruption from the radio in the dog van. It was Elaine.

'Sierra Two Five to base, are you receiving?'

'Go ahead,' said Blaketon.

'We've found Simon.' But it was evident Elaine was in tears as we all heard the barking of her dog.

CHAPTER 18

THERE WAS A long expectant silence as everyone listened to the conversation being relayed via the police dog van. Oscar Blaketon asked, 'Sierra Two Five, have you further details of the casualty?'

Father Will answered. 'Hello, Mr Blaketon, this is Monk Constable Stutely,' and his voice was echoing in the confines of the corridor somewhere beneath our feet. 'The casualty is definitely Simon Houghton. I recognize him. And I can assure everyone that he is alive....'

At this announcement a great cheer rose from the crowd.

Father Will continued when the excitement had died down, 'This is the situation: Simon is unconscious, he's very cold and wet and is trapped by his left leg, a huge tree trunk has crashed through the roof and pinned him to the floor. He's covered with other debris. We're not sure whether his leg is broken or if he has other injuries. I think the soft mud might have prevented more serious injuries, but I suspect he's suffering from exposure, dehydration and very deep shock. He can't move and we need to extricate him without delay and get him into the infirmary. Do you have an ambulance?'

Blaketon called to the crowd, 'Is the ambulance here?'

Prior Tuck responded. 'Yes, Mr Blaketon, it's ready and waiting. Father Raymund needs to examine Simon before he's moved. Is that feasible?'

'I heard that,' responded Father Will. 'Before we do

anything, we must shift the debris and move the tree trunk that's pinning Simon down.'

'I'll send Father Miller along with Father Raymund.'

'And I'll send a couple of my men,' added Joe Sampson. 'The roofs and walls need to be checked.'

'I'll go in as well.' The giant figure of Harvey the sculptor stepped forward. 'I used to be a weight-lifter.'

'Thanks, Harvey. There isn't much room to manoeuvre in here, it will soon get very crowded,' said Father Will.

'We'll take things step by step,' responded the prior with a hint of strong confidence. 'We mustn't rush into this and create further problems. Joe, we need your men in there with a chain-saw, but it's vital Simon is medically examined where he is. Monkstable Miller, Father Raymund and Harvey will get to you as soon as they can but don't let the place get over-crowded.'

We had all forgotten the time until I noticed Father Prior checking his watch.

'We must finish before dark,' was all he said to anyone who may have been listening and, as the volunteers began their tricky task, he moved closer to the dog van with its radio. Someone should be in overall control and I could see he was preparing to accept responsibility for the rescue operation. In the following few moments of radio silence, he asked, 'Oscar, can you call up Father Will to check whether we really need to move that statue? Is it obstructing the exit route and are there any other objects that should be moved to allow the stretcher team to operate?'

'Yes,' replied Will who had heard Prior Tuck. 'We need to move as much as possible, some of it only to one side to clear a path. The floors of all the passages are littered with debris – rocks, broken tree branches and the like, but if the rescuers have good torches, preferably hands-free, they will cope. We don't need to move everything, but the rescuers will have to be careful where they put their feet.'

'OK. The stretcher bearers will be despatched now. The

stretcher has wheels on, it's really a porter's trolley but has handles at each end. A versatile thing.'

Joe Sampson had been listening. 'That will be fine. We have miners' helmets with lights on them. We'll have him out in no time.'

'Father Mutch and Harvey will go ahead to deal with the fallen tree.'

'We don't want too many people down there ... space will be limited.'

Father Will's voice, echoing slightly, responded. 'We can cope, I think. There's a surprising amount of room in some of the old passages.'

As the rescue party assembled with their equipment, I glanced around at the crowd which had increased considerably since going-home time and noticed some familiar faces among them. One was Sister Mary who was in charge of the infirmary. She had a young girl at her side and they were standing near the ambulance; it had a team of two, the driver and an attendant, both of whom were qualified members of the infirmary staff. They were prepared to follow with one of their own stretchers if necessary.

Prior Tuck addressed two monstables – Fathers Alban and John – and asked, 'Are you prepared to go inside using the stretcher brought by Mr Blaketon? It's dirty and dangerous in there and there are heavy obstructions to be moved first. We have a team ready to deal with whatever is found.'

'We've all got a role to play, Father Prior. We will head for the casualty whilst the other teams deal with blockages and obstructions. I know it will be crowded, but we'll manage.'

'Fair enough.' So Father Prior clarified the precise arrangements with the teams. As Simon's rescue party moved towards the entrance of the labyrinth, another deep silence descended upon spectators, officials and monkstables. Everyone strained to listen to their progress and I noticed Father Prior moving among his posse of monkstables, thanking them for their role so far and updating them on current progress.

He advised them that Simon would be first taken to the abbey's own infirmary with some urgency to determine whether or not he would need hospital treatment. I watched the stretcher team and doctor vanish into the darkness but with such a strong in-house team, I felt the infirmary was perfectly capable of giving the necessary professional care. And there was no hint of another living casualty.

I wandered towards the dog van where Ventress and Blaketon were firmly in command and thanked them on behalf of the abbey and college authorities. I felt sure there would be a more formal gesture of appreciation in due course. Undoubtedly there would be a feast of some kind organized by Father Prior – he could arrange a feast to celebrate almost any occasion and this would deserve a very special one!

'They're doing brilliantly, those monkstables,' smiled Alf Ventress. 'We trained them well, Oscar. To be honest, I would never have expected them to do all this.'

I said my piece. 'They are keen to undertake more realistic police work, something more challenging than booking litter louts or ensuring that visitors don't stray into forbidden areas of the monastery. This has been a steep learning curve but they've coped well. Now it's the turn of the medical experts.'

Elaine maintained contact with Blaketon to provide a running commentary. It would take a while for the teams to reach her, but she and Father Will were caring for Simon, trying to keep him warm and talking to him even though he was unconscious. Many of the bystanders listened to the radio as they waited without much knowledge of what was really happening, and it was then that Prior Tuck clambered on to a safe high point of the ruin to address them.

In a few moments of radio silence he thanked them for their interest and explained exactly what was happening, albeit without giving Simon's full name. He merely referred to him as Simon, a senior pupil of the college and he reassured the crowd that the lad was alive but unconscious, and that his rescue was imminent. I thought it was a good move on the part of the prior.

And as the people milled around, anxious to listen in to further bulletins or observe events, I found myself standing next to the young girl from the infirmary. I was not sure whether she knew me. I had recognized her as one of the village girls in Maddleskirk.

'You're Claire, aren't you? I've seen you at mass in the village. You work in the infirmary?'

'Yes, I'm on work experience. You're Mr Rhea, aren't you?' she responded. 'When I was little you once gave a talk when I was at school when you told us about the work of a village policeman.'

'I'm delighted you remember. What do you think of all this?'

'It's amazing, all these people and how they all want to help, those men from the building site, the monks, ordinary people coming here after work....'

As we spoke, Prior Tuck joined us and smiled a welcome at Claire.

'You know Claire, do you, Father?' I asked. 'She's on work experience at the infirmary at the moment.'

'I've been meaning to have a chat with you, Claire,' smiled Prior Tuck. 'But other things got in the way!'

'Was it important? I'm with the ambulance for this rescue.' She sounded proud to be present. 'I'm pleased I wasn't with Simon when it happened.'

'Did he ask you?' I put to her.

She blushed just a little and smiled. 'He wanted me to go for a walk with him yesterday, up to St Valentine's holy well. He said it was all right because I don't work here as I'm still in sixth form. But I couldn't go because we had a family baptism at my aunt's house and I had to go there.'

'And what better introduction can there be, eh?' beamed Prior Tuck. 'It involves more than sticking plasters on sore places, or bandaging schoolboys who've cut themselves with their first attempt at shaving.'

'I'm really enjoying it all.' We could see she meant what she said, then she added quietly, 'I do hope they get him out.'

'They will,' I assured her.

Then Father Prior surprised me. He smiled at Claire and said, 'So how's the Virgin Mary this afternoon?'

Claire blushed. 'You know?'

'I recognize your face, Claire. Harvey has replaced the third part of his triptych, the pattern he's made until he completes the entire piece in oak. It's got your face on it.'

'He told me not to tell anyone.'

'Then I will not!' smiled Prior Tuck. 'It will be our secret – shared only by my very discreet friend, Mr Rhea.'

'Now I know why Simon liked visiting the triptych! So did other ladies from the infirmary model for it?' I asked.

She nodded. 'I'm Mary when she is nursing the crucified Jesus; the other two scenes are one with Jesus on the cross between the two thieves with Mary watching and another when she sees the Roman soldier plunge the spear into Jesus's side.'

'So you modelled for Harvey?'

'It wasn't really modelling. Most of the carving had been done and it didn't take long for Harvey to put my face onto Mary – there was a nice face there already but he adjusted her a little – changed the eyelids and lips, made me smile, moved her hands a wee bit. I held a doll so he could get her hands looking right … all very small adjustments. But he was so tender, so caring. He's the first sculptor I've sat for but if they're all like him, I'd do it again. He's a lovely man even if he looks a bit fierce.'

'So he never alarmed you? Threatened you?'

'No, not at all, he was so kind. I know he looks big and frightening but he asked me on the spur of the moment once when he saw me walking to work. He passed me on the road then came back to talk to me.'

'Weren't you worried at getting such a request?'

'I was at first, then he said he would ring my parents to explain to them and also he'd ring Sister Mary to ask for time off work for me.'

'So why did Harvey not want you to tell anyone?' asked Prior Tuck.

'He wanted it to be a secret until the final work is unveiled. We sitters will be his special guests.'

'It all sounds very pleasant!'

'It was, and he paid me a fee, Mr Rhea, with half of it – fifty pounds – when I agreed to sit for him and the other half to be paid if I keep the secret until the unveiling ceremony. I haven't kept it secret though, have I?'

'It's our secret, Claire. Now, can I ask you one thing?'

'Yes?' She had a frown on her face.

'Where is Harvey's studio?'

'I don't know, and that is being honest, Mr Rhea. It's somewhere deep in one of the local forests, he drove in circles on twisting roads through trees all looking alike, then said it was an old ice-house that he uses from time to time, but it is not his permanent studio. I could never find it again. Really I couldn't.'

'Does he live there?'

'Not permanently, only camps there when he's working nearby. Once this work is complete, he says he'll move on somewhere else and close the ice-house.'

As I was trying to visualize the whereabouts of the ice-house, my thoughts were interrupted by activity on Blaketon's radio.

'Sierra Two Five to base. Rescue party now at the scene. Simon is alive but still unconscious. We are cutting up and moving the heavy tree before he can be freed – that's being done now. We have lights and a stretcher. Over and out.'

'Thank you Sierra Two Five,' acknowledged Blaketon, and everything went silent again.

Eight or nine minutes later, the radio burst into life again.

'Sierra Two Five to base. Tree removed. Access to patient now available. The men are leaving the scene and the casualty does not appear to have any injuries other than abrasions. No broken bones according to Dr Raymund. But he remains unconscious. He is being placed on the stretcher to be carried out for transfer to the ambulance.'

Once again cheers rose from the assembled spectators, then we heard Elaine's voice once more, this time louder. 'Please keep all exits clear and have the ambulance conveniently positioned for a smooth journey to the infirmary. Over and out.'

Prior Tuck burst into action and called, 'All available constables please prepare to ensure a free and safe transfer of the patient to the ambulance, and then ensure his route to the infirmary is clear.'

His team of monkstables responded immediately and cleared bystanders from any places that might produce an obstruction. The mud-covered tree-shifters, except for Father Mutch Miller, emerged to cheers from the crowd and within quarter of an hour or so, the stretcher-bearing party emerged into the fading light covered in mud and dirt as more cheers rose from the bystanders. The ambulance waited with its engine running. Father Mutch had remained behind to clear debris from the path of the stretcher-bearers and he wanted to do something with the heavy stone statue. The wheels on Joe's trolley had proved ineffective in the deep mud.

'I must go.' Claire ran towards the waiting vehicle as the stretcher-bearers eased their unconscious patient into the ambulance.

As Claire leapt into the rear to be at the side of Simon Houghton, Father Raymund followed, then the doors closed and the ambulance swept away with its blue light flashing. I now realized there really was some kind of relationship between Simon and Claire. I wondered if it was puppy love or something more serious. But it was truly no concern of mine.

As the ambulance sped smoothly across the valley towards the campus, Father Mutch and Harvey emerged carrying between them the mud-covered statue of a handsome youth. They received a mighty cheer too as we all crowded around to look at it.

'Who is it?' I asked. 'It's not St Luke, is it?'

'No, it's St Valentine,' said Prior Tuck. 'See, he is depicted with an invalid child at his feet, one of the many saints called

Valentine. The old chapel near the holy well was dedicated to one of them and the site used to attract young lovers on pilgrimages. Who does he belong to now?'

'Probably the owner of Ashwell Priory,' I smiled. 'But I think the abbey should care for him until the matter is resolved.'

With the drama over, the bystanders drifted away. Elaine and her dogs left the scene after a hearty round of applause. I remained with Prior Tuck as his monkstables assembled to be formally dismissed. He thanked them all for their work and announced they could return to their normal duties, adding that he would organize a celebratory feast once this was all over.

'I'll pencil it in my diary,' he promised us all. 'I'll aim for 26 October which is the feast day of two local saints, Chad and Cedd. Two for the price of one,' he laughed. 'That might mean an extra bottle of wine or two.'

Whilst he was attending to his own tasks, we heard that Claire was paying very close attention to the patient now partially under her care. She remained at his side that evening, not wishing to claim she was working overtime but merely tending a friend. When Simon opened his eyes, they settled upon Claire and she took his hand. He mouthed the word, 'Hello, Claire', and she smiled as she repeated his name with tears in her eyes.

'He's fine. He's a fit, strong young man, well able to cope with all this,' Father Raymund announced, after carrying out a detailed examination. 'He has a lot of bruises and abrasions but nothing broken. It's nothing that some good food, warmth, a relaxed sleep and some loving care and attention won't cure. I'll keep him in here for a few days to recuperate.'

And so the day's excitements drew to a close and I found myself the owner of a statue of St Valentine which, I felt, should rightly stand near the shores of the pond in the woods. Maybe I could rebuild the chapel and encourage pilgrims to return to the holy well? Not knowing of my intentions, Father Mutch and Harvey said they would carry it into the crypt where it could stand until it was cleaned and a decision made about its future. I wondered if the crypt had been reopened yet – I doubted it. Forensic examination of the scene of a crime always took a long time.

As I walked back to my car, I heard a voice behind me. 'Nick.' It was the abbot. 'I've been looking for you. I just wanted to thank you for today's efforts. It's been quite exciting and your monkstables acquitted themselves very well. I think we may also have a budding romance – and you are the proud owner of a statue of St Valentine. How very symbolic!'

'In view of what's happened today, Father Abbot, I think he should stand in the hallway of the infirmary! There's ample room. He'd be better placed there than shut away in the crypt.'

'Now that is a good idea. In art, you know, Valentine is shown with disabled children and is also invoked against various illness and fainting attacks. Not only that, he is the patron saint of young people and engaged couples. So, yes, I will have him cleaned and positioned in the infirmary. We could dedicate the infirmary to him. Unless you want to rebuild the chapel on the hill near the holy well?'

'I can't see that happening in the foreseeable future, Father. The infirmary is the right place.'

'I agree, and I hope Claire and Simon recognize the symbolism in the gesture. And, you know, I wonder what would happen if they remained together as a couple, and he fulfils his destiny? Could she be a future Queen of Poland?'

'That's a question I can't – and daren't – answer, Father. But one thing does strike me: we haven't found the lost statues of St Luke and his winged ox. Who or what are they?'

'I'll tell you one day when we have some free time, perhaps at an assembly of the monkstables. The missing statues might be buried in Ashwell Priory and after all today's excavations and activity, our monkstables might care to look for them. And there is another question, Nick.'

'Which is?'

'Who's going to tell Simon's mother about all this?'

'I think that might be a job for you, Father Abbot, while I visit the murder room to tell the detectives about Simon's rescue and find out what's happening in the murder investigation. Harvey did a good job today. I wonder if he is still in the frame?'

CHAPTER 19

'THERE HAS BEEN an important development, Nick,' DCS Napier told me as I entered the murder room, so busy with detectives and monkstables. 'Our circulars have produced a brilliant response from surrounding police forces. I've just been told by Northumbria that the dead man's fingerprints have produced a result. And guess what – he's got a criminal record and his name's not Thorpe. He has convictions under the Treasure Act for offences relating to buried gold and silver. He was renowned – or infamous is perhaps the word – for locating treasure with his metal detector, and not declaring it. He sold his finds through antique shops or auctions and avoided sharing any proceeds with landowners. He often used false names for his activities. Quite simply he earned himself a tax-free fortune, but we can't trace any of it. Is it buried? We've also learned that he is – or was – detested by other treasure hunters who obeyed the law and who haven't had the good luck he seemed to generate. Certainly he had an uncanny instinct for locating hidden treasure.

'He was fifty-one years of age and recorded his occupation as a freelance archaeologist. The fingerprint check showed a match with those on the glass in his bedroom at the retreat and he's been identified as Leonard John Larkfield with an address in Newcastle-on-Tyne. He owned the camper-van used by Rawdon; they travelled here together with Rawdon driving, probably to get accustomed to the vehicle. Local CID went to the flat and when they showed a photo of his face, taken in the coffin, a neighbour confirmed his identity. We'll need more than that for legal purposes, of course, but it's a great breakthrough.

'Is that why Thorpe attended the course?' I asked. 'Did he expect it to reveal hidden wealth or was he – or the pair of them – really chasing the legendary treasure under the coffin in the crypt.

DI Lindsey joined in. 'I reckon they used both the course and the dig as cover for their intentions. They wanted to find a way of getting their hands on that treasure, if it exists. In other words, their trip was an early recce.'

'Do you think Thorpe found a way in but was killed to prevent him revealing it?' I asked.

'Perhaps killed to prevent him reaching the treasure so that someone else could get their hands on it, that's a more feasible scenario,' said Napier, who added, 'And it also provided us with a motive.'

'Is it really feasible that Rawdon would kill to get his hands on it?' I asked.

'It's possible, people have killed for less,' added DI Lindsey. 'That Thorpe was gifted and clever is not in doubt – the problem was he used his skills in very unpleasant ways. The pair of them were a good match for each other but unlikely allies. I'm sure he would have double-crossed Rawdon given half a chance.'

'Yet Thorpe loaned Rawdon his van?'

Napier continued, 'They weren't friends, according to my contacts in Newcastle. Rawdon was a clever con man; he persuaded Larkfield/Thorpe into lending him the van and in return promised to show him where a massive treasure lay concealed. It doesn't take much imagination to realize both wanted to get their hands on it – to the exclusion of each other and everyone else. Rawdon has done this sort of thing before – pretended to be an archaeologist on a site identified by aerial photo whilst getting another man to hunt treasure nearby – then going for the treasure himself.'

I wanted further clarification and asked, 'I don't understand why Rawdon persuaded Thorpe to get involved in such an unlikely partnership?'

'As Rawdon made his plans, he realized Thorpe's specialist knowledge could help him achieve his objectives – and the van was useful for Rawdon to establish a feasible base on the site.'

'Thanks, you've all been very busy!'

'I've had the benefit of computers and many contacts within the police service,' beamed Napier, 'all of which produced a lot of useful information.'

But I continued my efforts to understand. 'If they visited the treasure's hiding place, surely they realized they'd never be able to retrieve it? The idea was doomed from the start. That coffin and black curtain form the mythical raven that's guarded it for centuries! And still doing a good job.'

'It wasn't impossible in their minds,' said Napier, as if it explained everything. 'But Thorpe alias Larkfield is dead and Rawdon has vanished. The students have all packed up and returned to the university with their equipment. That suggests they're not coming back. I've checked at the university but Rawdon is not with them.

'Were the students in league with him?'

'No; he would never share anything. They were dupes who provided him with a reason for being here; raw recruits learning to be archaeologists. I'm sure he taught them something and I don't believe they were aware of his real activities. Right now, there's a nationwide alert for Rawdon and the vehicle.'

'You really think he is the killer?' I wanted to be sure.

'We're as certain as we can be, Nick. He had the motive and the means to commit the crime. And he was here at the material time. No matter what he does or where he goes, he will be found and I can guess there'll be scientific evidence on him and his belongings, however small, that will be enough to secure his conviction. Some of his clothing might bear traces of his victim's blood and if we find the weapon that killed him, it's handle might bear his prints, even if it's been thrown into a river or pond. Our team are searching every patch of water in the locality.'

'Including the cricket field?'

'Yes, we're looking at George's Field in case Rawdon buried it there. If he has we'll find it with a deep search metal detector. When we do, I'm sure forensics will show that it corresponds to the fatal wound at the back of the victim's head. If we find the mallet, I'd guess the personal belongings of the dead man will also be buried nearby. Now we can understand why Rawdon remained here alone at weekends to carry out his own excavations! A dodge that almost worked.'

'So how did you discover the secret of the hidden treasure?' I asked.

'I'd heard the legend, but the truth came via one of your monkstables, Father Will Redman. He told us and it provided the motive.'

'Do we know where the actual cellar is?'

Prior Tuck explained, 'It's more of a vault than a cellar, Nick. One entrance is immediately beneath the stone coffin. The coffin room's stone floor forms the roof of the vault directly beneath but there are suggestions of a secret entrance at the end of the underground maze, wherever that is! The treasure will remain beneath that old stone coffin, probably for ever – if it really exists!'

'So, in spite of knowing all that,' I put to Napier, 'can it be proved now that Rawdon was the killer?'

'Not unless we find him. You can now understand that a lot has been going on behind the scenes and the tempo builds up as we discover more. It's a bit like building bricks being moved from a carelessly built pile and then being slotted into their correct place when building a house ... after a time it all begins to make sense.'

'What caused you to suspect Rawdon?' I asked Napier.

'He was associated with Thorpe and that put him in the frame almost from the beginning, but it was Brother George and the fake photo that clinched it. We're checking relevant timings to be sure the killer and his victim could have entered the crypt without anyone seeing them. We've not found anyone who saw them there, not even Harvey, but the crypt opens very early and closes late – and neither Harvey nor anyone else is there the whole time. And there are plenty of hiding places.'

'Did Brother George come up with more information?'

'Yes he did. He reckons Thorpe and Rawdon went down to the crypt early on Sunday morning, before the hectic part of the day began for the monks—'

'Sunday morning?'

'The pathologist agrees with Brother George. His opinion is based on the state of the body when it was found, but, of course, he cannot be absolutely sure. That day was probably one time in the week when neither monks nor anyone else would be in the crypt early, apart from the monk who opens it at five. The others would all be occupied, at least for most of the morning, with matins and Sunday masses in the abbey church and at the parishes they serve in the vicinity.'

'Even so, it would be easy and indeed normal for a person on a retreat course to rise early, even venturing into the abbey church or one of the chapels in the crypt for a few moments of prayerful silence,' I reminded them.

Prior Tuck added, 'Who would think anything suspicious about a person in there as early as five o'clock? Especially if he was dressed in a monk's black habit? Rawdon could easily have borrowed one; they hang in unlocked wardrobes on the corridors leading into the church. It has been known for visitors to help themselves to a habit, usually for nothing more than an atmospheric photo! They're not counted. One could be removed temporarily without anyone noticing. Some real monks could have been in there from five but not later than six. They have matins then in the abbey church with a busy day to follow.'

'How would the killer know his victim was in there at that time?'

Napier spoke. 'Because Rawdon had seen Harvey's tools on open display during an earlier recce, then arranged a joint visit away from crowds and witnesses at a time when the monks were at matins. We believe Rawdon convinced Thorpe that he would reveal the secret hiding place, ostensibly to a friend, but in reality to his rival. And in that callous way, he planned the disposal of the man he regarded as a threat to his own future.'

'Then after killing Thorpe, he calmly awaited the discovery of the body?'

'Right. He's clearly a cool customer because he didn't flee the scene of his crime. If he had, that would have indicated his guilt, so he remained calm and collected, and buried the evidence as the enquiry continued around him. He was totally confident his guilt would never be discovered – the trail of false names helped.'

'But he hadn't bargained for Brother George and his cricket field,' I said, adding, 'So who left that note?'

'Harvey, without a doubt,' responded Napier.

'Harvey? Why him?'

'He's dyslexic, Nick; he never writes things down and won't have any truck with written contracts and so forth. He admits being in the crypt very early on Monday morning when he was looking for his missing mallet. Thorpe was lying dead in the coffin at that time. Harvey must have looked into the curtained-off area as he hunted his mallet and he must have noticed the body. He would never admit to finding it because, as a former villain, he would know that the person who reports finding a murder victim is invariably a prime suspect. Remember there was a lot of circumstantial evidence against Harvey – the place of death, the timing, his missing mallet, his own past and the opportunity. He did not want to be questioned so he caused someone else to "find" it. With his mis-spelt note.'

'You'll be interviewing him about it?'

'No,' said Napier. 'I've decided against it. I'm satisfied that Harvey left the note, and I've seen Harvey's handwriting and spelling faults in the past ... this one can remain on the file. Anyway, it is anonymous! We know who the killer is. I'll keep the note just in case there's a need for it in the future, which I doubt.'

'Now it's a case of finding Rawdon.'

'It is.'

'Well, I think I'll go home now, it's been a long day,' I said. 'But interesting.'

'We've more to do here,' Napier reminded me. 'We'll be around for some time.'

I rang Mary on my mobile and told her I was on my way home. She said she would make sure supper was ready. It was almost 10.30 that evening when DCS Napier rang me at home to say that John Wayne Rawdon had been stopped in the camper-van on the A1M in County Durham and arrested on suspicion of murdering Leonard John Larkfield alias Thorpe. He had been returned to the Maddleskirk Murder Room where he had been interviewed by Napier.

When tiny spots of blood were indentified forensically on his shoes, he made a statement in which he admitted killing the man he knew as Larkfield but he claimed they were old friends, saying Larkfield had attacked him without warning to claim the treasure for himself. He insists he hit Larkfield in self-defence. However, the fact the wound was at such a distinct site at the back of the victim's head rendered that defence useless. He was arrested and placed in police cells prior to appearing before a court.

The mallet, wrapped in a monk's habit, was quickly found buried in the excavation area of George's Field – with Larkfield's blood on it along with Rawdon's DNA and finger-prints. There were specks of blood on the habit too. Larkfield's personal belongings from his pockets were also discovered at the other side of the field, six feet beneath a huge slab of stone. Some items bore Rawdon's fingerprints. All well hidden, but not well enough.

Six months later when Rawdon appeared at Crown Court

charged with murder, he was found guilty and sentenced to life imprisonment.

The Ashlea Priory Coffin, often called the Maddleskirk Coffin, remains on its traditional site with the underground maze being secured against unlawful treasure hunters. The coffin, behind its famous black curtain, is now overlooked from the outer wall of the Lady Chapel, not by a raven but by a superb triptych depicting the Crucifixion and the Virgin Mary's sad beautiful face.

And if anyone stands quietly near the stone coffin, or in front of the triptych, they might hear monks in the abbey church above them as they practise their Gregorian chants, perhaps with the *Misereri Mei* among them. Or they might be celebrating Holy Mass before a congregation with yet more singing and chanted prayers. Some prayers will be for the repose of the soul of Leonard John Larkfield and his killer.

Deep below Maddleskirk Abbey Church, the centuries-old treasure remains secure as the monkstables continue their vigilant patrols.

I was told that when DCS Napier shut the doors of the murder room for the last time, DI Brian Lindsey had said, 'Well, boss, the legend of the black raven can now rest in peace.'

'Amen,' quipped Napier in reply.